JENNY GOODNIGHT

Enjoy The
Ride!
Kimberly
Lang

JENNY GOODNIGHT

A NOVEL BY KILLARNEY TRAYNOR

ORIGINAL THIRTEEN
Publishing

This is a work of fiction.

Names, characters, businesses, organizations, places, events, and incidents are either products of the author's imagination, or are used fictiously. Any resemblance to actual events, locales, organizations, or persons (living or dead) is entirely coincidental.

"Truth is the only safe ground to stand on."
— Elizabeth Cady Stanton

"When you come against trouble, it's never half as bad if you face up to it." — John Wayne

PROLOGUE

February 6, 1875

My dearest niece,
News of your father's death has hit all of us very hard. Samuel was a good man, a strong leader, and a great speaker of the Word. He will be sorely missed, not only by his family, but by anyone who knew him well.

I can't imagine how hard it was for you, who loved him best of all, to watch his suffering and death. No suffering goes to waste, but all works for the glory of God and the increase of His kingdom. But I need not tell you this, you who have spent your adult years in the mission field, working alongside your father to bring the savage to Christ. For both this and your weeks spent faithfully nursing your father you will reap rich reward.

You know, of course, that the Society will be recalling you to Dandridge. Years of scolding and lecturing from myself and the admirable Mrs. Brown have not changed the council's mind about allowing unmarried women to serve in the field. (You can take comfort in the fact that the council considers you the most dangerous of creatures, more to be feared than the scorpion or the jackal). You may have already received the summons from the Society Council –if not, it will come shortly. Perhaps this is not such a disappointment for you. Having worked so long with your father, carrying on without him will be difficult. You know you are always welcome here in my home. If you are worried about keeping busy, the Ladies of Salem are building a new school for the immigrants. I've already written to the woman in charge and asked if there might be a position you could fill. If not that, there is always some useful work for a responsible young woman like yourself.

Now I must ask a favor. You may have heard that your Uncle Matthew has settled in California, not too far (comparatively) from where you are now, in a town called Legacy. Last we heard, he had a considerable parcel of land, of which he was very proud, and his own paper which has been an ambition of his for some time. It has been weeks since we've heard from him and the tenor of his last letter was such that it aroused some concern from the aunts. Perhaps the distance and isolation are wearing on him. I have always worried that his high ideals may prove too far to reach and that the inevitable disappointment will prove too much for him; you know what a firebrand crusader your uncle can be. Or perhaps his writing has caused trouble once again. Western politics being what they are, I hope he has not bitten off more than he can chew.

There may be another explanation: he wrote to Aunt Chastity once of settling down and starting a family, as though he had already picked out a wife. He has not spoken of this in some time now and I wonder if his romance had gone awry and he is now suffering for it. If so, it is not good for him to be alone. Even if my fears are unfounded, he will nevertheless be glad to see family and you would be sure of a welcome to his home.

If you could visit him and report on his state, it would be a great relief to the aunts and myself. I have taken the liberty of writing to him and informing him of your coming visit, so you need only telegraph him your arrival time. I've enclosed a map with this letter and will wire funds so that Mr. and Mrs. Whitcomb, your successors at the mission, will not be unduly taxed for your departure.

I hope you have a pleasant journey, my dear. I look forward to seeing you and hold you dear to my heart. Be sure to write when you can and be stout-hearted, as the Good Book tells us. God watches over all who love Him.

Yours always,
Aunt Alice
Dandridge, Massachusetts

ONE

I arrived in Legacy on a day so miserably hot that even the birds forsook the sky and clung to the shade of trees. I was ill, but didn't know it. I'd attributed my weakness to the exhaustion of travel, exaggerated by repressed grief.

It was hot in the stagecoach. We'd drawn the leather curtains to keep the dust out and the humidity in the close interior became overwhelming. The scent of sweating, unwashed bodies and the swaying of the carriage would have induced sickness even in the strongest stomachs.

I spent the better part of the trip slipping in and out of consciousness, clutching at my shawl and making sure I could always feel my carpetbag by my feet. My dreams were violent and frightening, memories blending with nightmares until I couldn't tell what was real and what was imagination. I was nursing my father through yet another of his seemingly endless bouts of chills when the driver's shrill call cut through my dreaming: "Legacy! Legacy! Last call of the day!"

I pulled myself up and shook my head clear. Around me, the other passengers were also recovering from semi-somnolent states. The well-dressed woman across from me had eyes puffy from sleep, but her glare, as she adjusted her hat and her outfit, dared anyone to mention it.

Someone lifted the heavy leather curtain. A shaft of sharp light pierced the gloom of the carriage, dazzling me. I closed my eyes against it, feeling the stage sway and buck as the passengers disembarked. The cloth of my thin, well-worn cotton dress clung damply to my shoulders and my mouth felt as though it had been stuffed with cotton. I wished desperately for water even as I resisted movement.

Sleep... all I need is sleep.

A gruff voice erupted by my ear: "Can't stay here, ma'am. This is the last stop of the day."

The stage hand helped me out of the carriage and left me alone on the boardwalk under the blazing hot sun. Legacy stretched out before me in a long line of dusty, sun-worn buildings that bustled with heat-subdued activity.

The post master, a small, thin man with pinstriped shirtsleeves rolled up above his elbows, talked with the driver while the assistant and a boy unloaded the baggage from the stage. The male passengers crossed the street to the nearest saloon. The quiet young woman who'd gotten on at the last station with her mother was met by a quiet older man, probably her father, and all three disappeared down the street in familial harmony.

I stood alone, blinking against the sun, bag in one hand, my shawl in the other. Strange men hovered around the station and the stage, chatting with the driver or collecting the packages that swamped the boardwalk. No one called out my name or ran out to greet me. No one was looking for me.

Two days ago, when I was reasonably assured that the roads were good and there was nothing in the foreseeable future to delay the stage's arrival into town, I'd sent a telegraph to Uncle Matthew, stating the proposed arrival time. Though I'd given the address of my boarding house to the operator, hoping for a reply, none arrived. I'd assumed that his reply had been too late for me to receive it. That afternoon, standing on that platform, I wondered for the first time if Aunt Alice's concerns hadn't been realized in the worst way possible.

It wasn't until the post master said, "Excuse me, ma'am, are you lost?" that I realized how long I'd been standing there. It came to me, too, how pathetic I must look and a flush of heat washed over me. I turned to him, threw my shoulders back and tried to appear as though I had never expected to be met at all.

"Excuse me," I said, as though I were interrupting him. "Can you tell me where the *Legacy Bi-Weekly* office is?"

His small eyes blinked in surprise. "Sure can, ma'am. It's right down that street. Walk a ways, and it'll be on your left. Want that we should hold on to your trunk and bag for you?"

I'd almost forgotten about my nearly-empty trunk. It sat amidst the others, a faded thing with the gilt initials almost entirely gone. Back when I was fresh from seminary, it had been new and filled to bursting with tracts, Bibles, and clothing. Now, little more than ten years later, it was nearly as worn and empty as I felt.

"You can hold on to the trunk," I said. "But I'll keep the carpetbag with me. Thank you."

His eyes darted to the heavy little carpetbag in my hand and I instinctively drew it closer. If the suitcase was valuable to me in and of itself, this bag contained my most prized possessions, including my father's Bible and a few mementos from my time in the territories. My mother's memento, the most foreign of all, I kept hidden in my pocket.

The postman agreed to hold the trunk until called for and I set off down the street to my uncle's place of work.

Legacy was like any small western town, perhaps better than most. There were signs of new and prodigious growth and the broad streets bustled with activity. Wagons loaded with supplies rumbled past me. Men in dust-cover leather rode by, calling to other men working in doorways or in stalls. Women, tan from the sun and dressed in neat calico or muslin, hurried into stores, followed by children too small for school.

Posters for the upcoming election were plastered everywhere. I'd heard enough local gossip to know that there were two contenders: the incumbent, Honest Joe Turner, and his challenger Ben Evans. Ben Evans was the son of Legacy's legendary founder, John Evans, who'd come west with a partner to find gold and discovered land instead. John was dead now, leaving behind a widow and two sons in charge of the Evans Empire. As they were the de facto rulers of the town, the election was generating a lot of interest. My uncle, ever the defender of the underdog, sided with Honest Joe. There seemed an equal amount of posters for both men. The Evans family might be royalty, but Honest Joe had a fair number of supporters as well.

I passed the sheriff's office. A man sat on a rocking chair out front, whittling and spitting and watching passersby with narrowed eyes. Wanted posters, yellow and smudged, fluttered in the breeze kicked up by passing wagons, but there were no campaign posters. The sheriff was either bipartisan or wise enough to keep politics off his property.

Two shaggy, emaciated dogs ran barking past me, nearly upsetting a man carrying sacks out of the hardware store. He swore viciously at them as he threw his load into the waiting wagon, his small eyes following me. Though it was nothing less than what I had grown used to over the years, I felt small and very exposed. The feeling eased when I saw, at the far end of the street, a church steeple. I was not, after all, alone.

Pray God he's there when I arrive.

I passed three or four more buildings before I found what I was looking for: a small shop with square, curtained windows, on which *Legacy Bi-Weekly and Print Shop - Matthew Goodnight, proprietor* was carefully etched. At the sight of the name, my heart squeezed. His name was a small glimpse of home, a candle lighting a darkened window.

The door opened to the touch and a bell jingled to signal my entry. For a moment, the difference between the dazzling light outside and the relative darkness of the interior blinded me. I stood just inside the door, blinking, when I heard a timid voice call out.

"Can I help you, ma'am?"

It was not my uncle's voice. It had none of the warmth or the ring of the Goodnight tone, as my father and aunts had. It was thinner, as though it had outgrown its strength, and when I spied the owner of the voice, I saw at once why.

Behind the counter was a gangly youth - I reckoned he was still a few years short of twenty - with red hair and a confused expression. He was dressed in a worn white shirt rolled up to his elbows and his hands bore ink stains, as did his face from where he'd rubbed it. Through the thin walls, I could hear the murmur of voices, but they were indistinct and there was no sound of an operating press. There was no sign of Uncle Matthew.

"Can I help you, ma'am?"

The boy's repeated question cut through my momentary disappointment.

"Is Mr. Goodnight here?" I asked, stepping up to the counter.

He looked over his shoulder and hesitated. I looked, too, and saw that the back of the store was divided into a walled-off office and a print room, where a big printing press sat with paper piled on one side of it. The boy was apparently in the middle of printing more copies of the *Bi-Weekly*.

"He is, but he can't be disturbed," the boy said.

I realized that the voices were coming from the direction of the office. *He's in a meeting,* I thought, relief washing over me. *Of course - that's why he forgot. It must have run longer than he expected...*

"Can *I* help you?" the boy asked. He had a lean, sun-burnt look and his ink-stained hands were roughened from more than handling papers. If I were to guess, I would have said he'd spent most of his life outdoors and this job was his first office work. Conversing with customers was probably a recent experience for him and speaking with a woman who was obviously from out of town was likely even more foreign.

"If you could tell him I'm here, that would be very helpful." I smiled. "I'm his niece, Jenny. I believe he's expecting me."

He looked surprised. "He told me he was expecting a missionary lady."

"And so he is. As soon as my uncle is available, would you let him know I'm here?"

The boy stumbled over apologies, promising that Uncle Matthew wouldn't be more than a minute and would I mind having a seat?

"I don't have coffee or nothin' to give you, ma'am, but if you want, you might read one of these papers."

He held out a sheaf of printed paper, warm and limp from the press. I took it and said, "I'm sorry, I didn't catch your name."

He flushed again.

"Danaher, ma'am," he said. "Jeremiah Danaher."

With that, he hurried out of sight. After a few moments, he reappeared with his hat in hand and a heavy bag slung over his shoulder. He slipped out the back door before I could say anything else to him.

I took his advice and went over to collapse on the bench.

I made it.

Now that I knew I was in the right place, exhaustion rolled over me again. I would have given anything for water, but as it was obvious that there was nothing to be had, I could wait. After all, it would only be a little while before Uncle Matthew came out to greet me properly.

The room in which I waited was small, and sparsely furnished with a counter at the end and a bench against one of the walls. A big picture window faced out into the street, almost obscured by the wealth of printed materials on display: newspapers, tracts, notebooks, posters, and other paraphernalia crowded the window and overflowed in the case facing the bench. Ads decorated the walls, offering all manner of print services, including copy writing, art for ads, and posters. A few classic books – clothbound with gold embellishments – were available for sale. I could see Uncle Matthew's touch in the arrangement of the selection of the books: mostly adventure stories, like *Ivanhoe* and *The Last of the Mohicans.* When I closed my eyes, I could hear his rich tones, reading stories about Greek gods and honorable knights when I was a child. It had surprised no one when he announced that he was going to be a correspondent during the war. He'd been as obsessed with stories of derring-do and noble deeds as my father had been about spreading God's Word.

"When I was younger, I thought your father and your uncle were as different as night and day," Aunt Alice had said to me once, when I was upset at Uncle Matthew's going. "Now, I realize that they are similar – different expressions of the same creed."

She'd been right. Uncle Matthew had proven his courage again and again in the war, first by going into dangerous areas to report, then by writing articles that dared to criticize the Union and the Confederacy alike. He was horrified by the field hospitals and the treatment of prisoners of war and then horrified again when he realized how society and government ignored the returning veterans. Articles and commentary flowed from his pen like water, inciting pity and righteous rage. If he was doing for Legacy what he had done for the veterans at the end of the war, he was doing these people a great favor.

I wondered why he hadn't told his assistant that I was his niece.

With the exception of the buzz of street noise from outside and the sound of a clock, marking the time somewhere, the little shop was silent. Having endured a week and a half on jarring stages and rocking boats with chattering passengers, the stillness and quiet felt luxurious. I leaned back against the bench, and closed my eyes.

So quiet. So peaceful.

How long I waited, I can't say. Time stretched out until I lost track of it. My head grew lighter until it seemed ready to float away. My legs were heavy, like blocks of wood, and there was a general fogginess about my ears that blurred what few sounds there were. I was slipping away again – dreams beckoned with dark arms.

Then, just I was on the verge of falling asleep properly, an explosion occurred.

I exaggerate, of course. It was merely the front door bursting open under someone's impatient shove – but it might as well have been an explosion from the way it made my heart skip a beat and shook me out of my reverie.

The door slammed back against the wall, making the windows rattle. A big, bulky man stormed past me. His boots hit the floorboards like weights, and when he slammed his large fist down on the counter, everything on it shook and danced the jig.

"Goodnight!" the man roared. "Goodnight, where are you?"

I caught my breath.

The man's voice was as big as his presence. He was dressed in the usual cowboy gear – blue jeans, a faded button down, boots curiously spur-less, and a hat which he pulled off to reveal a head full of dark hair. He was coated in dust and grime and might have been just any no-account worker, except for his good quality leather vest and the hand-tooled leather belt carrying his six-gun – both too expensive for the ordinary ranch hand.

I jumped when his fist struck the counter again.

"Dammit, Goodnight, don't make me come in there after you!"

He tossed his hat on to the counter, freeing his gun hand. It was then that I saw the newspaper, clutched tight in his fist. The white knuckle grasp on the newspaper, the rigid clench of his jaw, and the tension of his big shoulders radiated not only outrage, but the ability to act on it. This was a very dangerous man.

Slowly, lest he catch sight of me, I bent down towards my carpet bag.

"John Henry!"

The call came, not from my uncle's office, but from the open doorway behind me. A slim man stood there, also dusty and breathing heavily.

The big man at the counter whirled around and pointed at the new figure.

"Stay out of this, Olsen," he threatened. He saw me then and I froze, bent at the waist over my carpetbag. His eyes raked over me, a brief but penetrating evaluation. Then he looked back at Olsen. "I'm just going to have a friendly chat with Mister Newspaperman here." He turned and pounded the counter once more. "Goodnight!"

"This ain't no way to do it," Olsen said. He pushed the hat back from his sun-weathered face and stepped cautiously into the room. "Let Schuyler handle it – that's what you pay him for."

That only seemed to enrage the big man more. He slammed his palm into the counter (I was surprised that the board withstood such punishment) and roared, "This is a family matter and I'm not paying any lawyer to do what I can do myself. Goodnight, are you coming out here or am I coming in there?"

I fumbled with the catch on the carpetbag.

Then the office door opened and Matthew Goodnight emerged.

A decade had passed since I had seen my uncle, but I would have known him anywhere. The fearless smile, the sharp blue eyes, the almost military carriage were all so reminiscent of my father that, under other circumstances, I might have had a misty moment.

But Uncle Matthew was not my father and he had changed with the passage of time. Though his good looks remained, his features had softened and his face showed shades of cream and pink beneath the ever-present tan. There was something disheveled about his person, as though he no longer cared so much for appearances. He and my father shared the same feckless courage in the face of danger and he displayed it now, stepping out of his office as casually as if this were a social call.

"Ah," he said, carefully shutting the office door behind him. "Mr. Evans – to what do I owe the pleasure?"

Evans?

I did a double take. So the big man beating the counter was John Henry Evans, a member of the Evans clan I'd heard so much about. It explained the swagger, Olsen's deferential manner, and Evans's air of outraged dignity. It was his brother, Ben, who was running for office and it was their mother who was running the campaign. His family had founded this town and they weren't accustomed to be being argued with or challenged. They were, in short, precisely the kind of people most likely to provoke my uncle's ire.

"You know what a firebrand crusader your uncle can be..."

Aunt Alice always said that Uncle Matthew had the looks of a politician and the manner of an Irish pugilist with a sense of justice that would have impressed Solomon himself. It looked as though that moral courage was about to be reckoned with.

Matthew Goodnight didn't act like a man afraid. His voice was the same as I remembered from childhood – a blend of formality and superiority – and he smiled up at the big man as though he wasn't concerned in the least. It was not calculated to be conciliatory and it had the expected effect.

The big man slapped the newspaper down on the counter with such force that even Uncle Matthew jumped and Olsen took a half step forward.

Evans pointed at the open page.

"What do you mean by this, Goodnight?" he demanded, through gritted teeth.

Uncle Matthew leaned over to look.

"That," he said, "is an editorial, an opinion piece. It is common in all papers, and it is usually meant to stir thought and to comment on recent events." He flicked some dust from his jacket.

"It's a pack of lies, is what it is," Evans said. "You came just short of calling my father a murderer!"

Olsen took another cautious step forward.

Uncle Matthew grinned.

"I stopped short enough so that you won't have a case if you try to sue this paper for libel. Not that you would or could, anyhow. Neither you nor your mother or your brother or his pretty little wife want to risk any of this going to court, do you?"

He had barely finished when Evans grasped him by the shirtfront and drew him half-way across the counter until they were nose to nose. Olsen squawked, but didn't try to interfere. I gasped and rose before I remembered what I was doing.

"Now, you listen here." Evans' voice was low and dangerous. "You leave my mother and brother alone. If you've got a problem with the Evans family, you go through the court system, when and if you ever get the evidence. Do you understand me, Goodnight?"

Matthew was as helpless as a ragdoll in his grasp, but he eyed the big man with a steely gaze.

"You couldn't be more clear, Evans," he said.

Evans dropped him. Uncle Matthew recovered quickly, straightening his shirt front. Olsen relaxed, until Evans asked, "You'll print a retraction, then?"

Uncle Matthew laughed.

"Retraction? You listen here, Evans, this paper doesn't apologize for its opinions. We apologize for errors in facts, but never for our interpretation of them. No one asked your brother to make this foolish attempt at public office and someone should have warned him that all candidates are subject to scrutiny. If the precious Evans name doesn't hold up under it, that's not my fault. Tell your mother, the grand lady herself, to keep a tighter leash on Ben – better yet, make him drop this whole run."

"Not on your life," Evans said. "The Evans family has nothing to be ashamed of, Benjamin the least of all."

"Oh, he's too young to have done too much harm," Uncle Matthew agreed. "But you might want to warn your mother that all good investigative reporters dig into the backgrounds of candidates and their families. I'm famous for my excavations, you know. The skeletons in your family closet had better be buried pretty deep if you don't want me to find them."

"You're a damned fool, Goodnight," Evans said. His hands were balled into fists, his knuckles white under the pressure.

"I'm just repeating what everyone else is already thinking. Twenty-two years ago, your father, Jacob Evans, and Ezra Jones, his partner, rode into this valley to look for gold. Five months into the search, up in the hills, Jones was bitten by a snake and your father was just a little too slow getting him to the doc – something about his horse stumbling and dying on the way. A month later, he finds ore in those same hills and is suddenly the biggest man this side of the Mississippi. And he doesn't have to share it with anybody. All I'm suggesting here," he laid his hand on the offending paper, "is that it was awful lucky for your old man: that snake bite and that accident with the horse."

Olsen whistled and half turned.

My hand found what it was looking for. Buried under layer of calico, the smooth heft of the pistol grip filled me with reassurance and a trickle of fear. I always kept my revolver loaded, with one empty chamber so it wouldn't go off by accident. Wrapping my hand around it, I pulled myself back into an upright position, careful to keep my hands hidden in my skirts.

Evans put both hands on the counter and leaned in.

"You've got an accusation to make, newspaperman?" he asked. His voice was low, slow, and dangerous, and my pulse jumped. "Why don't you just make it to my face and quit hiding behind that paper of yours?"

"I'm just asking questions, John Henry..."

"You call me Evans, Goodnight. *Mister* Evans."

"...and I'm not the only one who's asking these questions."

Uncle Matthew leaned forward and even from that distance, I could see the dangerous glitter in his eyes. My hands began to sweat, slicking up the grip.

My uncle said, "Now, folks around here have been asking a very logical question: Was it just luck that caused that snake bite and that horse to stumble? Maybe it was. But if *you,* the great John Henry Evans of the Evans Empire, are so sure this is the truth, why would a little thing like this opinion piece bother you, eh? If your father was the man you claim he is, if there isn't a shadow of a doubt that he did all he could to get his partner to the doctor, that he had *no* idea of the ore up in those hills, if this was just one huge lucky break, why would you take time out of your busy day to come down here and threaten me?"

"Goodnight, I'm a patient man..." Evans said warningly, but Uncle Matthew didn't let him finish – he just leaned in further.

"The only reason I can think of, John Henry, is that you yourself aren't all that sure. You have doubts too. Did the horse really die of an accident? Was Jones even bitten in the first place? Or did your father decide that he didn't want to share the ore up in those hills, so he killed his partner to keep it all for himself? Does your mother know–?"

He never finished the sentence.

Evans' fist flashed and Uncle Matthew's head snapped back with a sickening crack. Olsen cried out and jumped forward as the newspaperman dropped behind the counter. Evans was half-way across the counter when I found my feet and made my voice ring out across the room.

"Now, you just hold it right there, Mr. Evans."

I doubt he would have stopped had I not accompanied my words with the ominous sound of the hammer of a Remington New Model Army .44 being drawn back.

Everyone froze. Time slowed. I was keenly, sharply aware of every detail in that room, from the line of sweat curling down my side to the slowly relaxing grip of Evans' hands on the counter. For a moment I had the upper hand, a firm grip on the pistol, and the knowledge that I was a sure shot. That didn't stop my heart from pounding like a native drum in my chest or my hands from shaking. Evans wasn't alone after all. If he and Olsen decided to charge, I might be able to fire off one shot - but I'd never shot a man before and I didn't want to now.

I kept my voice low and steady.

"Now, why don't you two boys just go on and get, before..." I stuttered, trying to remember the name, "Jeremiah gets back with the sheriff."

That was a gamble. They knew the sheriff and I didn't. Most lawmen were little better than hired guns, owing their allegiance to the men who ran the town. It was entirely possible that Legacy's was the same, though I clung to the memory that no campaign posters graced the front of the sheriff's office.

Evans was slowly, carefully turning around - the sound of the hammer had not been lost on him. When he finally faced me, my mouth went dry and my hand gripped the stock tighter. Now I could see his face, deeply tan and villainously handsome. His jaw was tight and his sharp blue eyes sized me up again - his first analysis hadn't done me enough credit and it was plain that his oversight annoyed him. He could have been any age from twenty-five to forty-five. I guessed near the middle of these. He carried himself with the assurance of a man used to getting his own way.

Evans had kept his hands up where I could see them but now, facing me fully, his manner changed. He dropped his hands, folded his arms and leaned against the counter. Olsen, at least, had the good manners to look nervous.

"Isn't that a big pistol for such a little lady?" Evans asked. He smirked as he said it.

"Get out, Evans," I said, relieved that my voice sounded less shaky than I felt. "You aren't wanted."

He looked back over the counter, towards the sounds of a recovering Uncle Matthew. "I was beginning to get that idea."

I tightened my grip.

Sharp-eyed Olsen saw this and gingerly reached out to pluck his boss's sleeve.

"Come on, John Henry," he said, never taking his eyes off of me. "Let's go. We can't do nothing here anyhow."

I could feel sweat snaking down my sides. My head was about ready to float off my shoulders.

Leave, Evans, please, leave...

"That's real good advice," I said, keeping my voice low and even. "It's been a long day. I'm really tired. My finger might slip at any moment and then there'd be a dreadful mess."

Evans fixed me with a look. I could almost hear what he was thinking: a little woman in a worn dress with a pistol too big for her hands threatening what was definitely one of the most powerful men in town. I must have looked ridiculous. But he didn't know how experienced I was and, if he was a thinking man, he was calculating the risk and finding it too much. At my distance, even a green Boston city woman couldn't have missed.

He must have seen that, but I couldn't wait for his thoughts to catch up to reality. I stepped to the side and gestured with the pistol.

"Out. Now," I said.

Now Olsen was tugging at Evans' arm. Behind them, Uncle Matthew pulled himself back to his feet. Blood and shock marred his handsome white face. He stared at me open-mouthed.

The only person who didn't appear convinced was Evans. He just stood there, leaning against the counter, frowning, his eyes sharp points of observation. He wasn't afraid – and that had me worried. But neither did he press forward or challenge me. For reasons I couldn't decipher, he was hesitating.

Leave, Evans, please, just leave...

I stared back at him, hoping that Uncle Matthew would have the good sense to stay quiet. For a long moment, nothing was said. My uncle leaned against the wall, rubbing his jaw and looking thoughtful. Olsen seemed trapped, looking from me to Evans and back again, concern creasing deeper and deeper lines into his face.

Then, just when I was convinced that I was going to have to do something drastic, Evans pushed himself abruptly from the counter and flung away Olsen's hand.

"Come on," he said gruffly.

To my astonishment, he gestured toward the door. Olsen scampered for it gratefully. Evans grabbed his hat and lumbered after him, a granite wall following a wizened gazelle. I held my breath as Evans moved – and then, when he close enough that his shoulder almost brushed the barrel of my gun, he stopped.

My heart jumped into my throat.

No! I wanted to scream. *Just GO!*

Up close, John Henry Evans appeared even more dangerous. He stood head and shoulders taller than me, his bulk casting a shadow over my small frame. I caught the scent of leather and the outdoors. His features were chiseled and darkly handsome as I'd noted before. A lock of thick, brown hair fell across his forehead. Dark stubble stained his face and there was a tiny scar on the left corner of his mouth, another sign of his already apparent rough-and-tumble nature. His most striking feature was his eyes: they were as hard and blue as sapphires and as magnetic as the North Pole. Caught in his gaze, I felt then, not for the last time, that this was a man who could move mountains if he thought they needed to go.

Between his looks and his position, he was probably accustomed to women easily bending to his will. I didn't, I wouldn't, but that was no great sign of self-control on my part: I simply couldn't afford to. He knew this, too, for he didn't even try to talk me down or take the gun. In those magnetic eyes, I saw frustration, anger, and a deep sense of injustice. But there was also something I hadn't expected to see: admiration.

He scanned me up and down, as though trying to analyze me properly this time. I was, after all, the unexpected foe. I thought, *He's trying to intimidate me.* So I squared my shoulders and raised my chin. When my eyes locked with his, I dared him silently.

Finally, Evans spoke.

"This isn't over, Goodnight," he said. He didn't shout or take his eyes off of me, but his deep voice rumbled, filling the room. "We'll be discussing this again."

"Anytime, anywhere, Evans," Uncle Matthew said and I thought, *Of course. Why not anger the beast?*

Evans turned to glare back at my uncle. Then he pinned me with that ice-blue gaze again and, with an old-fashioned courtesy that seemed out of place in the situation, he touched the brim of his hat.

"'Day, ma'am."

Then the door was swinging shut behind him.

I stood there, swaying like a cripple who has suddenly lost her crutch. My knees were weak, my legs like water. Uncle Matthew was crowing but I couldn't properly hear him. I had enough presence of mind to lower the hammer safely before the floor came rushing up to meet me.

Everything went black after that.

ARTICLE

June 13, 1875
Letter from the Editor of the *Legacy Bi-Weekly*

Much has been said about the upcoming election for State Representative this year. Legacy stands at a crossroads: whether to go with the tried and true leadership of Mr. Turner or to venture forth under the new and untested path marked by Benjamin Evans.

This paper has made no secret of its views: we believe this town, this county, and this state would be ill-used to elect a man who has never had to make his own way in life, who has lived under the shadow of his powerful family and is probably much influenced by the same. The youthful Mr. Evans has a college education, this is true, but are we to view four years at an expensive eastern university as a good substitute for life experience? Turner has fought in our wars, plowed his own fields, and made his own way through life. His brand of man, the self-made man, is better suited to represent the people of this city than a school boy from a wealthy family.

And not just any family, either. The Evans family founded this community, this claim stemming back twenty-five years, when Benjamin's father, Jacob Evans, came west in search of gold with his partner, Ezra Jones. They found no gold, but a rich valley, ready for settlement. When Jones passed away, Evans remained the sole owner of the valley.

Questions have been raised regarding the circumstances around Jones' death. The official story is that Jones was bitten in the leg by a venomous snake while out in the hills. Jacob Evans, concerned for his partner, rode his horse to death trying to get him to a doctor in time. They arrived at the doctor's home in a dramatic manner more suited for novels than real-life: Jones slung over Evans' shoulder, wheezing his last breath. When Jones died, the Evans Empire did not exist and so there was no reason to question the manner of his death.

But now we do question it: we have only Evans' word (and since his passing, only the statement of his wife, who was back east when the incident occurred) that Jones was bitten by a snake, and that Evans' horse broke a leg on the ride back, thus delaying their arrival at the doctor's office until it was too late. The doctor has since moved on, Jones and Evans are dead, and the snake will never talk.

Naturally, even if foul play should be found, this need not mark the character of young Mr. Evans, who is himself now married and living what appears to be an upstanding life in the family home with his mother. He is not his father, after all. But there are still others who would argue that blood is thicker than water and that as the father goes, so goes the son.

We would not care to comment on the personal ethics of Benjamin Evans, though it might interest the readers to know that we are investigating what little evidence there is in the Evans/Jones story. We have good reason to think that we will have breaking news on that front soon. But what concerns us most at this moment is the election, and our original argument still stands. The pampered scion of Legacy's wealthiest family is not an ideal representative of the good, hardworking, hard-living people of Legacy.

"Government for the people, by the people" is what built this country. We at the Legacy Bi-Weekly *believe that this would not best be served by electing a man who would, by all accounts, be a member of the privileged aristocracy in Europe.*

Turner for Legacy.

Matthew Goodnight, editor

TWO

For the next few days, I lay in delirium. The illness which I had so long ignored now held me firmly in its grip, convulsing me with fevers one minute and chills the next. Days and nights blended into one another. I drifted through my past in dreams. I stood at my father's deathbed, then sat at my mother's. I was ten years old again, in my cotton shift, watching her slight frame struggle to breathe, begging her not to go, begging her forgiveness - a boon she was too weak to give. All she could do was look at me with eyes too large for her wan face, her dark hair slick with sweat, one hand wrapped in her rosary, and the other grasping mine in a slackening grip.

Then I stood at her graveside, wrapped in my coat as the rain poured down on the funeral gathering. The minister stood under Uncle Franklin's umbrella, intoning the prayers while behind him, at a discreet distance, stood Père Fortier, a dark and silent reminder of my mother's religious betrayal and of my own. I didn't want to look at him, I didn't want to think about what I'd failed to do, but I couldn't look away.

"My Genevieve, you know what I would ask of you. It is a small thing..."

It was too much, Maman. It was too much to ask of me...

Guilt rolled over me like a cloak and then the dreams changed. I was a young woman on a train, heading west to join my father, only

I was gripping my father's carpetbag, which I should not have had. Then I was older, walking alone down the dark streets toward my boarding house. Once again, I felt the chill of terror slip down my back when I heard a stranger's stout boots sounding loud on the boardwalk behind me. Hands gripped me and I fought desperately, shrieking into the dark night until hands, real hands, shook me out of the dream.

"...Still, Jenny, be still..."

I am not Jenny, I am Genevieve... I am not Genevieve, I am Jenny...

Memories entwined with dreams. I was in Dandridge, older and a missionary still, trying to convince my aunt's neighbors to take the worn Bible I offered. I was in the territories again, hearing the wolves outside my tent, wondering whether my father, who'd gone hunting, hadn't already been taken by them. I saw Trailing Rose, her warm smile marred by tears, offering shards of broken pottery, which I rejected. Little Fox, a boy of no more than five, tugged on my skirt as he had been accustomed to do when he was hungry. Real memories of the night we were under siege by drunken railway workers inflated with imagination until the windows they broke became the wall and they burst in among us, staggering with blank faces. I held Little Fox in my arms, his face tucked into my neck, as I tried to convince Trailing Rose to run with me, but she, poor woman, was paralyzed with fear.

There that dream ended, but others followed. I saw the rough-hewn pews of our chapel, and smelled the sweet scent of corn being ground into meal by many hands. I could feel the taut muscles in my mustang's shoulders as I rode him up the hillside. I felt again that drop in my stomach when I first met my father and saw where and how he lived. And I cried anew when the soldiers came and took Trailing Rose and Little Fox away. Standing in the doorway of our too-quiet hut, I watched the as the column rode out of sight, pillars of dust kicked up in their wake. Behind me, my father sat at the table he'd built with his own hands and opened his first bottle of red-eye.

On and on and on the visions went, reality blending with imagination, fading to nothing only to revive again. Voices from the past blended with those in the present. I heard my uncle, talking at a great distance, and another, unfamiliar male voice speaking in soft and deep tones. An arm would lift me and a spoon would force pungent oil between my lips, no matter how I choked and limply protested.

"...Feel better soon..."

I felt a cool hand on my forehead, a wet cloth over my eyes, and in my confusion, I heard my mother's voice.

"Ma peuvre fille. Ma petite Genevieve, je tu prie, dors..."
Maman!

I swear sometimes she was there, holding my hand, reciting on her beads, speaking to me in French or tormented English, always calm, always gentle. But she would never stay long. She would fade away even as I cried out for her to stay.

"Sleep, Jenny," another voice said. It was deep and commanding. "Sleep."

I am Genevieve, not Jenny. I am Jenny, not Genevieve...

I drifted out into the vast nothing that kept me suspended in time and place. I was neither present nor gone, a ghost in a living shell. I distinctly remember wondering whether the Catholics were right about purgatory after all and whether I was in it. But this was mere fancy. I skirted death, closely, it is true, but I avoided it.

One night, the fever broke, the dreams stopped, and I slipped into true sleep. This particular crisis had passed: there were, of course, more to come.

LETTER

June 18, 1875

Letter to the Editor:

Despite rumors to the contrary, I have not decided to suspend my campaign for the position of State Representative. While my esteemed rival may enjoy the confidence of the press, he has run unopposed for too long and I and many others feel that it is time for a change. We, as a nation, stand on the brink of a new and vast future. The old ways were good for their times, but the present demands a different type of candidate.

I do not claim to have the experience or wisdom of age that Mr. Turner purports to have. "Barba tenus sapientes." I can only claim my willingness to serve and my eagerness to take this country and the good, hard working people who live in it to new and greater things.

As to the accusations and rumors regarding the foundation of this town and my father's part in it, I will not dignify them with an answer. My father was well-respected when he was alive and his achievements speak for themselves. The Evans family has nothing to hide and nothing to be ashamed of. Frankly, I would have thought that this sort of reporting was beneath the dignity of a reporter with your reputation. It appears either I was wrong or the esteem with which you are held is greatly exaggerated.

In the coming campaign, I look forward to meeting with Mr. Turner in a public place to discuss our various platforms. I also look forward to the day when I can take my oath to this great state and take the first steps towards the future.

Bona fide,

Benjamin Evans

Candidate for State Representative

THREE

"And if he *wants* to quote from the Latin primer, I've one for him: 'Ne puero gladium'."

A voice rang loud, startling me out of my slumber. I turned my head toward the sound and opened my eyes.

Uncle Matthew was pacing the length of the room with furious energy. Another man, wearing a black coat and gray vest, sat in a rocking chair, watching him. The black bag at his feet and the look of worn humanity on his face proclaimed him a doctor. The afternoon sunlight, worn and ageing, shafted through curtain-less windows. The room was plain, dusty, and sparsely furnished. There was wallpaper on the walls, but the trims were unfinished, as though the workers were expected back any day. My carpet bag sat on the floor by the door. I wondered if my pistol were inside.

The doctor's long, thin fingers drummed nervously on his legs and his black eyes glittered. Neither noticed I was awake yet.

"Ignorant upstart," my uncle fumed.

"Ignorant yet college educated," the other man said. His southern accent was so warm it could melt butter. It sounded familiar, as though I'd heard it once in a dream.

"Ignorant of life," Uncle Matthew spat back. He moved with short, jerky steps, his chin buried deep into his chest. "Backed by dirty money and dirty deeds."

"You're obsessed, Goodnight."

"That's your diagnosis, is it, Doctor?"

"Obsession is dangerous," the doctor said softly. "It can ruin a man."

My uncle stopped and stared at the tall, cadaverous medic.

"There are many ways to ruin a life," he said. "So many ways, so many inconvenient tales that will shatter even the sturdiest of reputations. Don't you find?"

Now it was the doctor's turn to shift with discomfort.

My uncle continued in that same saccharin tone. "I took up fencing while I was in college. Do you know what they teach you, these fencing masters?"

The doctor sighed and looked at his hands. I was still, my eyes slits, keeping my breathing soft and even, afraid to shatter the moment with the slightest sound.

"They taught me," my uncle said, "to use the opponent's thrust against him. You play with your opponent, frustrating him, pushing him, taunting him, until finally he thrusts so far that he cannot recover. That's when you strike." I could hear the smile in his voice, a voice that sounded familiar and yet like no man I could claim to know. "Isn't that interesting? Using a man's own action to bring about his downfall? Have you ever fenced, Lowe?"

After a brief pause, Lowe nodded.

"I did," he said. "Long time ago."

"I thought you'd understand."

Uncle Matthew swung about to continue his pacing and his eyes fell on me. For one long moment, he stood still with his mouth hanging open, as though in dismay. I saw the greenish-blue badge of his disagreement with Evans on his jaw and remembered, again, why I'd come here in the first place.

Doctor Lowe followed his gaze and his concerned expression changed to one of relief.

"Well there now," he said, grabbing his bag and leaving his chair to approach me. "Look who decided to rejoin the living. How are we feeling today, Miss Goodnight?"

"Thirsty," I managed to say, through a painfully dry mouth.

"I shouldn't wonder," Doctor Lowe said, sitting on the bed beside me. "Goodnight, fetch your niece a glass of water, will you?" Without waiting for a reply, he continued: "You had us worried there, Miss Goodnight. Open your mouth, please."

After a moment's hesitation, Uncle Matthew disappeared through the door. The doctor introduced himself as Abraham Lowe and chatted in a friendly, easy way while he examined me. I found myself relaxing in his presence. Dr. Lowe's engaging manner suited his handsome face and dark, glittering eyes. He had reached a healthy middle age, yet still had curly hair, mostly dark. He was the type of man that my perennially single Aunt Chastity would have proclaimed "a real catch".

Lowe was repacking his bag when Uncle Matthew returned with a tin cup.

"You'll be happy know your niece is on the road to recovery," Lowe announced. "She'll need to stay in bed a few days, but a healthy girl like her won't remain there for long."

"Good."

The stark response was startling. I looked up at my uncle in time to see him pass the tin cup to Lowe. Lowe took it and sat on the bed to help me drink. The water was tepid and as soothing as honey on my throat. I drank eagerly until the cup was drained. Even this small effort was exhausting.

"There," Lowe said, when I'd finished. "Rest now."

Lowe lay me back on the pillows and got up. Uncle Matthew moved closer, his hands behind his back. He stared down at me.

"Well, well, well," he said softly. "Little Miss Goodnight. What brings you to town?"

"Aunt Alice," I whispered. "She was worried. Seems she had good reason."

"You mean the other day?" He shrugged. "John Henry Evans, the so-called king of the country didn't like a little opinion piece I wrote in the paper. I can handle him. Though I appreciated the help." He turned. "You heard about that, didn't you, Lowe? How Mr. Evans was driven out of town by a little girl with a big gun?"

Lowe, who was putting on his coat, answered, "I read the column, Matthew. I think the whole town did."

Column?

I shot up, only to be hit by a wall of dizziness and pain. "You wrote a *column* about that?"

Pulling a gun on a member of the leading family in town wasn't something that well-bred ladies did. I couldn't just hear Aunt

Chastity's scolding cackle. Not to mention that John Henry Evans was not likely to take the publically broadcasted humiliation well.

Uncle Matthew grinned. "Of course I did! You're a hero, girl."

"But..."

Lowe was at my side then, pushing me back down.

"Now, then, Miss Goodnight, you aren't to be fussing, now, you hear? You need rest and your uncle can handle himself."

"That's right, girl," Uncle Matthew said. "The Evanses and I may have our differences but we haven't come to blows or gunfights yet." He grinned. "At least, we hadn't until you arrived."

My stomach was starting to slosh dangerously and the room tilted and spun even as I closed my eyes. Whatever the danger Uncle Matthew was in, I was going to be no help to him at present. I heard Lowe get back up and the scratching sound of pencil against paper.

"Don't worry her, Goodnight," he scolded. "She needs rest and nursing. Make sure she drinks, water, broth or tea if she can stomach it, then try some toast."

"I'm not much for nursing," Uncle Matthew said. "Jeremiah will tend to it or maybe Annie Walsh."

"Jeremiah'd be much better served if he were in school."

"Not my call, Doc. The boy wanted a job, I gave him one. What's this?"

"Dosing instructions. I expect you'll have to read it to him. I'll write up a prescription and Sarah will have it ready tonight."

"Sarah?" I asked. I was getting tired of being spoken of as though I wasn't in the room.

"My sister," Lowe said. "She's the schoolmarm, but she also mixes medications for me."

"Skilled lady," Uncle Matthew commented. He was grinning again. "I reckon she's going to do very well for herself."

For some reason, that seemed to rile Lowe. "She already does," he said stiffly and dropped his notebook into his little black bag. "You can send Jeremiah over to my place to pick up the medication."

"Right," Uncle Matthew said.

"I'll be back tomorrow afternoon to check in on her. Got to ride out the Evans place in the morning, check on Helen."

"The wealthy always get preferential treatment," Uncle Matthew growled.

Lowe stopped at the door, peering at my uncle with narrowed eyes. Now he was angry and I, once again, felt the over whelming urge to interfere. I was, after all, supposed to protect my own.

"Doctor Lowe," I called. When he turned to me, I smiled. "Thank you."

Lowe smiled at me, the expression softening his eyes.

"My pleasure, Miss Goodnight," he said, in his soft, deep, rolling tone. "Get better."

"I will."

"Right." He looked at my uncle, hesitated, and then left us alone.

Uncle Matthew stood there, turned towards the door, his eyes on the page in his hand. From down below, we heard the door slam and a cheery cry of "Hello, Doc!" as Lowe left the house. Only then did Uncle Matthew look at me. His eyes were softer now.

"You've had a bad time of it," he said.

I shrugged. Exhaustion rolled on me and I closed my eyes. The world swam. I heard the floorboards creak as he walked back to stand over me again.

"I meant to come," he said. "When I got your telegram, I... Did he suffer?"

He was speaking of my father, his brother. I forced my eyes open to look at him. Uncle Matthew's face, so like my father's especially in that light was contorted with pain. For a moment, I pitied him.

"He died peacefully," I whispered.

It wasn't a total lie. Though my father had been tormented for weeks with nightmares and visions as he slipped in and out of his coma, his last lucid few moments had been painless and comfortable. He'd lost track of time and place, as one does in such instances. Once he woke and, seeing me sitting quietly on the other side of his bed, his eyes had lit up.

"Claire!" he'd breathed.

But I was not my mother and the disappointment when he realized this was so sharp and keen that he closed his eyes and turned away from me in painful memory. I remember a strong feeling of triumph - Trailing Rose had not replaced my mother in his affections after all. Guilt followed hard after.

Uncle Matthew didn't need to know this and I was too tired to explain. I closed my eyes again. After a few moments, I heard him clear his throat. Sleep beckoned me, but I forced my eyes open again and he asked the question.

"The watch," he said. "Do you... still have it?"

I knew this question would come, had dreaded it. My father's pocket watch was an heirloom, brought from England before the Revolution and handed down from father to eldest son until the line stopped with me. It should have been given to Matthew, but my father had lost his respect for such rituals out in the plains. He'd given it to James Little Fox to play with one day, and it had gone with the boy and his mother when the soldiers came.

"It's better with him," my father said when I discovered it was missing a few days after. He'd rubbed his blood-shot eyes with one hand, the other gripping his bottle. "It belongs to him now."

It was a close as my father ever came to speaking the truth out loud. We never spoke of the watch again, but it's loss divided us like an impassable wall.

I didn't explain that either. I merely said, "It was lost."

Uncle Matthew's face was haggard as he nodded.

Then he said, "I wonder if I might have Sam's Bible."

A shock raced through my system. My father's Bible was all I had left of him, aside from a few letters. It had been his one constant companion, his rock through all trying times, and there wasn't a page in it that didn't bear his mark in some way. I'd carried it with me all this way and the thought of parting with it gave me a pang of exquisite pain.

Uncle Matthew sensed my hesitation. He leveled a look at me – a lost, lonely look.

"I don't have anything of his," he said whispered. "Not even a lock of hair."

I didn't want to, I truly didn't. My father would have been the first to tell me to give the Bible to someone in need; after all, I had my own. If I had suggested that I wanted the Bible because it was his, he'd have told me that the words were the same in each and wondering at my Romanish tendency.

"It's in my carpetbag," I finally said.

He fished it out with the eagerness of a child at Christmas. I watched him as he lifted the book and ran his hands over the flaking cover. It might have been the crown jewels for the way he was handling it and I understood. It was a remnant of a past now gone.

"I'll miss your father," he said simply. "He was a good man and a good brother to me."

His voice choked and he covered his eyes with his hand. He remained quiet for a moment, fighting for control of himself. I saw then how thin he was. His day-old stubble failed to hide the hollow of his cheeks or the pallor of his skin. His clothes, well cut and fashionable, hung loosely on his frame, wrinkled as though he'd lost weight and then slept in them.

"Have you been ill, Uncle?" I asked.

"No," he said. "Just trouble sleeping."

He was obviously lying. I could see the dark circles under his eyes. Were they from lack of sleep? Or the remnants of John Henry's displeasure? I couldn't tell in that light and considered the difference to be slight. One way or another, the circles were caused by the Evans family.

With a sigh, my uncle came to himself and turned abruptly. "You need sleep, girl."

He turned down my lamp and was gone before I could say anything else.

LETTER

April 13, 1875

Mr. Schuyler,
I am sure you have read the latest edition of Goodnight's so-called newspaper. I know we have spoken before about libel. You know my feelings on this subject, but I defer to your judgment. I am very concerned about this mention of 'breaking news.' I have been informed that Goodnight has initiated an investigation – there are even rumors that he has Pinkerton men in his employ.
This cannot continue. Enough harm has been done and digging into old matters only brings forth that which is better left buried.
Goodnight must be stopped. I have only my sons left and I will not have their lives ruined. You may call upon me at any time for a consultation. Action must be taken. I prefer it be done by you, but if I must resort to other methods, I shall.
Yours,
Mrs. Thomas Evans

FOUR

At first, I didn't know what awakened me. I lay in my bed, looking at the ceiling, trying to collect myself. It was two days later and my recovery had been rapid. My appetite came back the day after I woke up and I was able to hold conversations with Jeremiah while sitting up in bed, an achievement in his eyes, but I had yet to leave the dusty bedroom. I spent most of my time sleeping, reading, or memorizing every creak and sound in the building. I learned to tell Jeremiah's step from the doctor's buoyant tread on the stairs and I'd learned that Uncle Matthew scarcely came home at all. It was a silent house, a tomb of a building, and yet something had awakened me.

I heard it again; sounds emanating from downstairs. Someone was moving about without a care for the noise, opening and closing small doors, like cabinets. I'd have said the sound was coming from direction of the kitchen, but as I had never actually seen the kitchen, I didn't really know. It didn't sound like anyone I knew.

The clatter continued, firm steps moving across board flooring. I reached for my wrapper and swung my legs out of bed. I didn't know who the intruder was, but I was going to find them before they found me. I was relieved to find my pistol still in my bag. I pulled it out, unlatched the door and stepped out into the landing.

I was immediately overwhelmed with déjà vu. The landing *was* familiar. It was narrow with two doors off it, a railing, ornate and unpainted, and a steep staircase leading downstairs. It had the same unfinished look as the bedroom and the sound from the kitchen was even louder here, thanks to the lack of carpeting or even wallpaper. I automatically looked up and, sure enough, there was a door in the ceiling for the attic.

I knew this landing almost as well as I knew myself. It was an incomplete copy of my Aunt Alice's house, the place both my uncle and I had grown up.

A shiver ran through my spine. This meant something. I was sure of it.

The heavy sound of something wooden hitting floor boards drew me out of my astonishment. I drew my wrapper around my shoulders, shielded the pistol in my skirts, and crept downstairs.

The stairs terminated in a dark and narrow entry way, as I already knew. At the end of the passage was the front door, different from my aunt's in that it was solid, without a window. Painted wainscoting and paper covered these walls. The thick carpet crunching under my feet spoke loudly of neglect and mold. A lacquered stand for umbrellas and hats stood next to a gilt mirror, its glass coated in dust so thick I could have written my name in it. It was an odd room, curiously finished and obviously neglected and I wondered how a house so new could feel so abandoned.

The stairs left off in front of the exterior door and there were three other doors off the hall. Acting on old memory, I took the door immediately in front of me and found myself in the parlor, a dusty, abandoned looking room papered in pink and trimmed with unvarnished wainscoting. A fine fireplace yawned in the corner, an empty frame suspended over the bare mantelpiece. A shrouded love seat lent a ghostly air to the room, but it was the other piece of furniture that made me stop.

Back east, the presence of a piano would have excited no undue attention, but here in the new states, it was rare that you found one in a private home, even one as relatively inexpensive as this. The instrument gleamed golden brown in the dim light. I experienced a moment of intense desire to lift the lid and run my hands over the cool ivory keys. How long had it been since I played? How long since those evenings at my aunt's house, listening to the music of Bach and Beethoven and Mozart, played with varying degrees of skills by friends and performers just passing through? I'd encountered a few musicians out here, but they were a rarity and true skill was even rarer.

I touched the polished wood. It was smooth and velvety beneath my skin. I thought, *it's been so long...* I paused in my caress. *When did Uncle Matthew learn to play?*

"Who are you?"

The words cut through my ruminations and made me jump. I wasn't exactly clutching at my pearls as I turned, hefting the pistol with both hands, but I was no towering figure of strength as I confronted the speaker, the woman I had meant to sneak up on before I'd gotten distracted by the piano.

The woman before me was tall and pale as a ghost. She had a magnificent head of copper-red hair and a face that might have been pretty, had it not been marred by her confrontational expression. She wore the shapeless garb of a working woman, the material bleached by the sun and worn thin with work. She carried a basket, tucked snug into one hip, and her free hand was fisted and pressed into her side. She glared at me as though I were the intruder, her eyes darting between my face and the gun in my hand.

"Ain't no call for that," she said.

"You startled me," I said. It came out more accusatory than I intended. I lowered the pistol guiltily and a movement behind the woman's long tired skirts caught my attention.

A small boy with eyes too big for his face slipped past the woman and into the parlor. He was of compact build, with rough, well-sewn clothes that he was about to outgrow. His black hair was cropped short and his feet were unshod and dirty. He couldn't have been more than seven or eight, but he looked at me with huge solemn brown eyes that appeared ageless.

Where do you belong? I found myself wondering. *To her?*

He held my gaze but could not hear my thoughts.

"You haven't answered me." The woman's sharp voice broke the spell yet again. She stepped forward as I turned my attention to her. "Who are you? What are you doing here?"

They were a contrast, the narrow-eyed woman with the cream-colored skin and the short brown boy with eyes you could lose your soul in. I looked from one to the other and finally I remembered where I was.

"I might ask you the same thing," I said, pulling myself up. "Who are you and what are *you* doing in my uncle's house?"

"Your *uncle?*" The woman looked me up and down. She was young, too, possibly no more than thirty, but she acted as though the years weighed heavily on her shoulders. "He didn't say anything about a niece."

"You haven't answered my question. What are you two doing here?"

I nodded to the boy to include him in my inquiry. He looked to the woman, who adjusted the basket on her hip. She raised her chin and looked me square in the eye.

"Just what it looks like, ma'am," she said. "Bringing back the washing. Put that gun away before you hurt yourself. Jonas." The boy straightened. "Go and fetch the next load."

He ran off and I heard him pounding up the staircase a moment later. The woman was already turning away when I asked, "Where is he going?"

"To fetch the washing and the mending," she returned over her shoulder. By now she was out of the room. I picked up my skirts, wincing at the realization that I was still in my nightgown, and followed her.

The door led into the kitchen, a cavernous place lined with cabinets. A potbellied stove took up one end of the room and there was a generous sized sink along the back wall. The redheaded woman dropped the basket on rough-hewn table that ran along the center of the room and moved towards one of the cabinets.

"If you are his niece," she was saying, "you'll want to know that I leave the bread in here." She opened a door to reveal several towel-wrapped rolls. "I didn't know there'd be two of you, though it doesn't change things. Our agreement is for three loaves a week and that's what he's got." The cabinet door slammed shut and she turned to me, reddened hands on her hips. "You can tell your uncle that the meat's almost cured. I expect I'll be bringing it up next week."

"You cook and clean for my uncle?"

She gave me a look that I couldn't decipher. "I take in his laundry and bring bread," she clarified. "When Danaher's got wood for him, I deliver it. I have my own house to clean."

The woman looked around the kitchen and I followed her gaze. It looked like a bachelor's kitchen: there were dishes piled in a bucket by the door and crumbs at one end of the table. It was obvious that no one really lived here – they only passed through.

I turned to find the woman studying me.

"There's not a lot of living going on here," she observed. "Maybe you'll be changing that. Maybe not. You look like you've only just left death's doorway yourself."

I drew my wrap tighter around my shoulders.

"I've been ill," I said. "I still didn't catch your name."

"Any more than I caught yours," was the quick retort. She softened almost immediately. "I'm Mrs. Washington. I live outside of town."

I caught the accent this time. It was distinctly north-eastern, Pennsylvania if I had my guess. She had the hardness of a coal miner's daughter, the attitude of a hard-knock-life and the skin tone of an Irish immigrant. All of which made the presence of the boy more of a worrying puzzle. What *was* he doing with her?

Mrs. Washington was looking me up and down as though sizing me up and weighing me for purchase. From the expression on her face, I came up short. "You look like your uncle," she declared. "In the eyes."

It did not sound like a compliment.

"Oh..." I awkwardly shifted. "Well...I am a Goodnight. Jenny Goodnight."

"I reckon you're proud of the association."

Jonas returned then, carrying a bundle. She jerked her head for him to go out the back. As she did this, we both heard my uncle's whistle forcefully piercing its way down the street towards the house.

"We'll be off then," she said.

She moved to leave and I stepped in time after her. "Wait, Mrs. Washington! Don't you need to get...?"

I choked on the last word. We didn't keep regular servants at my aunt's house back in Massachusetts, though we did hire the occasional help, pale nervous Irish girls who were as likely to giggle as leave something undone. They were unreliable and frequently clumsy, but they did have a modicum of pride and that pride prevented them or my aunt from ever directly addressing the subject of pay. It was something that was done in silence, as though paying someone a day's wage was an inherently dirty act.

I'd grown so accustomed to western openness that I'd nearly forgotten this nicety. I tripped over my words, trying to come up with the polite way of asking if she needed payment. Mrs. Washington, after a moment of confusion, shook her head.

"We don't work on a cash basis, miss," she said. "Your uncle and I don't like to bother each other if we can help it."

Behind me, we could hear my uncle's whistling cease as the front door opened. Boots, bigger and heavier than those worn by Jonas, beat their way in our direction. The door opened behind and an expression crossed Mrs. Washington's face too fast for me to read. Then her eyes hardened.

"Mrs. Washington."

I turned to face him. Uncle Matthew's tone was jovial, but his face was white beneath the tan and his eyes were blood-shot and wide. His hat sat far back on his head, as though he'd pushed it there to get a better view. He held himself almost as defensively as Mrs. Washington, his shoulders thrown back, his stance wide and his right hand tucked under the left side of his worn yet stylish black jacket. I thought, of course, that he was holding his hand over a holstered gun, but Uncle Matthew wasn't wearing a gun belt and, in any case, what did he have to fear here?

Mrs. Washington's expression coalesced into extreme distaste.

"Goodnight." She jerked her head at the cabinets. "I left you some bread. Just tellin' your niece here that the meat will be cured shortly. We'll bring it by next week."

He nodded and shifted with a sharp intake of breath.

"I'd appreciate it," he said. "I've two mouths to feed, what with Jenny coming here and all." His gaze shifted to me. "You're up."

It was a question as well as a statement and though his gaze was on me, I knew his attention was focused as strongly on Mrs. Washington as it had been on John Henry Evans that first day. For the second time since my arrival in Legacy, I felt like the unfortunate pawn in the middle of dueling kings.

"I'm feeling much better," I said. I wanted nothing more than to be out of that dreadful kitchen and back in my quiet room. "I suppose I ought to change. It was a pleasure meeting you, Mrs. Washington."

She muttered something about it being mutual. I made a move as though to go past my uncle, but he stopped me with a small gesture of his left hand. The right, I noticed, was still tucked under his jacket. It was then that I noticed the sweat beading around his face and the unnatural pallor of his skin.

"Abby," he said.

Mrs. Washington was stepping towards the door when he spoke. She stopped as short as if she'd run into a wall. The familiarity was as surprising to her as it was to me. For a second, I thought, *Is she the...*

But if she was the woman that my uncle had once considered marrying, there was no trace of that affection or any other kind in her stone-cold face when she turned back to him. Uncle Matthew placed a hand on my shoulder and gripped it tightly as he smiled at her.

"How's your husband?" he asked.

Her spine stiffened. "He's in tolerable health," she said with frosty distance. "Thank you."

"I'm glad to hear it. Tell him I'll be sending Jeremiah out with his ad copy as soon as I pull it together."

She opened her mouth, closed it again, looked at me, and then looked at him. "It's renewal time again?"

"Time flies," my uncle said lightly. He took a step towards the table, bringing me along with him. "Of course, if he doesn't want the ad..."

Mrs. Washington was silent in the time that it took my uncle to lower himself on to one of the few simple wooden chairs around the table, watching us with expressionless eyes. My uncle's grip on my shoulder was painful and it was a relief when he released me. When we finished, he wiped his streaming forehead. "Would you get me some water, Jenny?"

His appearance had worsened. It was obvious that he didn't want me to say anything in front of Mrs. Washington. The look in his eye was very much like the one my father would get when we were in a situation that could turn dangerous. I wondered then about that look. Later, I would understand it.

A water barrel sat on the kitchen counter, glistening with fresh condensation. Mrs. Washington or Jonas must have filled it recently. I went over to where the dirty dishes stood waiting to be cleaned and pulled out a mug. The conversation continued behind me.

"If he doesn't want to renew," my uncle said, "I'll understand. The paper will be sorry to lose your family, of course."

"We can consider it," Mrs. Washington declared, "but only for the same rate. Times are hard, Mr. Goodnight."

"They are. And just getting harder all the time."

When I turned back with the full mug, they were staring at each other, volumes being spoken in the dread silence. I was out of place, standing there in my nightgown, awkwardly holding the mug, watching my uncle conduct business with a woman married to another man. Was she the woman Aunt Alice had thought to have stolen my uncle's heart? She was married to another – how recent was that? I looked Mrs. Washington up and down and wondered what she might have looked like had she lived in Massachusetts instead of this waste of a promised land. Would she have been acceptable to my aunts then?

My uncle's eyes glittered. ·

"We'd hate to lose you both," he said softly.

"I reckon it won't come to that, Mr. Goodnight," Mrs. Washington said coolly. She was as remote as an island in the middle of a vast ocean.

Uncle Matthew nodded, his Adam's apple bobbing as he swallowed hard.

"Jeremiah will be around in a few days," he said.

"We'll expect him."

"Good. Jenny, have you that water, please?"

I stepped forward, Mrs. Washington stepped back. My uncle took the mug from me with a shaky hand. He saw my pistol then and an expression of puzzlement crossed his face.

Mrs. Washington said, "Good day, Mr. Goodnight. Miss Goodnight - I'll be seeing you, I suppose."

She withdrew with practiced haste, the door closing hard after her.

I stood staring after her, bewildered, as my uncle drained the glass. Through the thin walls, I heard her harsh voice calling to the team and to Jonas. There was a slap of reins and the sounds of jingling harness. I turned to my uncle, sitting slumped now in the chair, white as a sheet, questions clouding my mind.

Who is she, Uncle? Why didn't you tell me you had someone coming over to do work for you? Who is Mrs. Washington? Who is Jonas? Why do you act like I am an intruder here?

I opened my mouth to ask, but he beat me to the punch.

"Do you pull your gun on every new acquaintance, Jenny?" he asked. Then, before I could respond, he went on: "Are they gone?"

I shrugged. "I expect so."

"Check."

I opened the door and looked. The dried-up little yard was deserted, though clouds of dust remained from their departure. I turned back to my uncle.

"She's gone."

He blew out a deep sigh of relief. "Good."

Uncle Matthew's expression changed from one of careful strength to pain. He pulled his hand slowly out from under his jacket. I gasped. It was covered in blood, fresh blood, his blood, drenching his coat sleeve and dripping on to the table top as he lay his hand carefully down on it.

"I don't suppose," Uncle Matthew said, through labored breath. "That you know anything about bandaging and stitching?"

FIVE

The wound was a gash across the top of his hand, starting from about an inch above the wrist crease and ending in a jagged mess of flesh just above the first knuckle of the index finger. It wasn't deep. I got the impression that Uncle Matthew had managed to pull his hand away before the knife struck bone. It was ugly and brought back uncomfortable memories from some of my father's assignments. However uncomfortable, those memories came with instincts, honed by time and practice. I went through the motions of care almost mechanically, tucking my questions and my reactions away for later.

There wasn't a kettle in the kitchen, but there was a sauce pan. As the stove apparently hadn't been lit in days, it took forever to get the water to boil. Thankful to Mrs. Washington, I tore up some of the clean sheets in her basket and gave some to my uncle to stanch the blood.

"Where's Jeremiah?" I asked as I tore more sheets into long white strips.

My uncle was sweating. We'd taken off the blood-soaked jacket and cast it aside. He loosened his neck-tie and unbuttoned the top of his shirt. I thought I glimpsed bruising there. He'd been in another fight, it seemed, and he was not in the mood to talk about it.

"What'd you need Jeremiah for?" he grunted.

"I don't know where Doctor Lowe lives."

"We aren't sending for Lowe. He'll like as not poison me with his potions and cure-alls. Just patch me up and get me some whiskey. It's only a scratch."

"It is not a scratch – it's deep and there might be infection."

"I've had worse. The whiskey is in the cabinet."

"Doctor Lowe will..."

His good hand slammed down on the table, cutting me off mid-sentence and making the boards rattle. I stared.

Uncle Matthew was wild-eyed and ominous. "No one is to know," he said firmly. "No one but you and me. That's the way I want it."

I stared at him, trying to keep my temper in check. "It's your hand, Uncle Matthew. I don't know how you can hide that. Or why you'd want to, for that matter."

"It's a private affair," he said, stubbornly. "No one's business but my own."

It's mine now.

He must have seen something in my face, for he leaned forward, pointing a finger from his good hand at me. "You mention this to no one, you hear?"

The water was boiling, so I got up and went to the stove.

"Was it Evans?" I asked, keeping my face away from him.

"Doesn't matter," he grumbled. "Private affair."

"If someone's threatening you..."

"Jenny."

I gave up. I found two bottles of cheap whiskey in the cabinet, one half full, which I used to clean his wound. As I cleaned and bound his hand, I determined I was through with being an invalid. It was clear that my uncle needed more help than even he knew.

Men's hands are strong and my uncle's were thick and scarred, but pain comes blindingly and quickly. He could hardly stand to have me touch the wound and writhed in his chair. When the worst was over and the bandaging done, he was panting and sweating as though he'd just run a mile through knee-high mud.

"How much whiskey is in the house?" he gasped as I bundled up the cloth and the coat and put them in the corner for cleaning later.

"You'd know better than I," I said shortly. I was beginning to feel tired again, a headache budding at my temples.

"Send Jeremiah to fetch more when he comes." He rose unsteadily. "I'm laying down. Jeremiah's the only one allowed in this house unless I say so, you hear?"

"It *was* the Evanses, wasn't it?" I asked, angry. I was frightened and tired. The relatively simple acts of climbing down the stairs and cleaning the wound had worn me out - my knees were watery and my head felt light enough to float away. But how could I sleep now? This wasn't the first time I'd lived in a house under siege, but every other time I'd at least known which enemy I was expecting.

He didn't answer. He went to the cabinet and pulled out the last bottle of whiskey with his good hand. Then he left the room, with me standing there, wondering why on earth a newspaperman would be silent about an attack on his life.

SIX

The next time Jeremiah arrived at the house to check on me, I asked him to bring me the last couple of newspapers that Uncle Matthew had printed. He readily agreed and then told me that his mother wanted to invite me to church with them this Sunday morning.

"She says she'd be pleased to have you sit in our pew," he reported, and I gathered from his manner that this was a signal honor not given to just anyone.

I accepted, of course, as any excuse to get out of the house was a welcome one. Besides this, I'd grown to like Jeremiah. He was earnest and sweet and inadvertently had given me something to do while I recovered.

It hadn't taken me long to realize that Jeremiah was a functioning illiterate. It was a common enough story. Life out here was hard and there was often more work than hands to do it. In Jeremiah's case, he lived in his mother's boarding house with his younger brother, Oscar. His father and older brother worked on the struggling family ranch while his uncle Liam ran Uncle Matthew's ranch. Jeremiah was forced to drop out of school when finances grew too tight. Oscar, being more academically inclined, still attended classes and was considered the hope of the family future.

When I offered to teach Jeremiah during our meal breaks, he was initially shy and hesitant and only acquiesced once I promised keep these lessons a secret. We started immediately, tracing letters in the dust that proliferated my room. Jeremiah wasn't quick, but he was determined. He could already write all three of his names – Jeremiah Michael Danaher – and so we worked on the usual simple words, like CAT and DOG and his progress was rapid. I thought he must be one of those who studied better when there was not an audience of peers watching.

Time passed quietly and when Sunday finally arrived, it was oppressively hot. I felt well enough to go to services, but Jeremiah's mother, who met me at my door with her two younger sons, was concerned about my walking so far.

"Jeremiah wouldn't mind fetching the horse," she said. "It can be a long way for someone who's been in bed so long."

Her concern was touching, even more so because she was such a strong-looking woman with an older, more feminine version of her son's face. She gave the impression that she'd been through fire, wind, rain, and drought, and was immoveable through all. Indeed, even if the family stories Jeremiah had told me were exaggerated, she and her family had faced more than their fair share of troubles coming west. As she fussed, I remembered that her husband, Jeremiah's father, had been forced to leave his home town for his health – weak chest, if I recall correctly – and so Mrs. Danaher had long been accustomed to tending the sick.

I wouldn't let her send Jeremiah for the horse. I'd decided that I would recover quicker if I stopped acting like an invalid. My uncle's wound had convinced me that I no longer had the luxury of being sick.

The little clapboard church was set on the edge of town by the creek, not far from my uncle's house. It gleamed in the sun, the whitewashing still fresh on its sides. Jeremiah and his mother didn't say much as they walked beside me. Mrs. Danaher carried a pail, and Jeremiah a basket. Oscar trailed along behind, his nose in a book. Jeremiah had warned me that the neighbors always gather for a picnic after fellowship and everyone brought something to eat. All I had to bring was one of the loaves that Mrs. Washington had left for my uncle. I hoped he wouldn't miss it and I wondered if he or Mrs. Washington would be joining us.

The air in the church hung hot and still, despite all the windows and doors being open. I followed the Danahers into their pew, aware of curious gazes and grateful that I had a sponsor family of sorts. Jeremiah sat next to me, fiddling with his hat, his pale blue eyes scanning the crowd. Oscar sat on the other side of his mother, pretending to read but in reality exchanging glances and smiles with a blonde girl in a blue checked dress sitting three rows ahead of us.

I was arranging my skirts when Jeremiah nudged me.

"Mrs. Evans," he whispered, nodding towards the front.

I followed his gaze. For a moment, I thought I saw John Henry and my pulse jumped. As quickly as I thought it, though, I knew better. John Henry wasn't in church. I'd noticed this upon entering, though I don't remember consciously looking for him.

The man that sat in the second-to-front pew looked like John Henry, only shorter, with lighter hair and smaller shoulders. He bore himself with no less pride for these differences. I could only see his back and the side of his face when he turned and I noted that his jacket had been well cut and carefully fitted to his frame.

Two women sat on either side of him, one a small-boned woman with a chignon of silver hair and the same poise as her son. She wore purple, a good quality though not showy gown and she read from a worn Bible. On the other side of the man was a younger woman, with gold hair and a long, elegant neck. She wore a navy blue dress and looked, for all the world, like a model from a magazine.

"That's Ben Evans?" I whispered. Really, there was no one else it could be.

"Yes," Jeremiah said. "And his wife, Helen, the prettiest girl in town."

His mother nudged him and fixed him with a glare. He looked at me with an expression of horror.

I shrugged, amused. "I'm not really a girl in town," I said and his face relaxed.

I looked around again. Doctor Lowe had arrived, escorting a woman very nearly Helen Evans' match, though a brunette.

I guessed who she was even as Jeremiah whispered: "That's Sarah Lowe, the schoolmarm. John Henry's sparking her."

That caught my attention. I studied her with new interest.

Miss Sarah Lowe was no shrinking, mincing schoolmarm, nor was she a battle-ax old maid. She was tall and graceful and wore her green linen like it was silk trimmed in gold. Mounds of dark, curling hair were pinned neatly on top her head, and her bright-eyed gaze and sure step spoke of confidence, faith in herself and in her appearance. She slid into the pew a row behind Helen, close but not too close. Helen turned to greet Sarah and her husband nodded and smiled. Mrs. Evans resolutely faced the front.

I found *that* to be even more interesting.

Miss Lowe didn't seem to notice her would-be mother-in-law's snub. As she settled in, her gaze swept past the three Evanses and worked its way around the room. Doctor Lowe sat next to her with his arm resting on the top of the pew possessively behind her shoulders. When he surveyed the room, his eyes lit on me. I nodded to him and he nodded back, and then whispered to his sister. She looked at me curiously, then reached to tap Helen on the arm. As Helen turned in my direction, I buried my burning face in my hymnal. Blast my uncle and his report on my first meeting with John Henry Evans!

Luckily services started then. The preacher was a short man with a round face and limp hair. He announced the hymn and we stood to sing it without musical accompaniment. After a verse or two, I saw Jeremiah's interested gaze and tilted my hymnal so he could better see the page. He sang out of memory, his attention focused on the letters my fingers traced and I felt my spirits lift whenever his eyes brightened with recognition.

We sang three hymns all the way through and then settled in for the readings and the sermon. What the preacher lacked in imagination, he made up for in the vim and vigor of his delivery. I think he knew how thin his own arguments were, for he read quite a bit from the scriptures and lingered on pat phrases that I recognized from various concordances and philosophers. Whenever he read from the Bible, I found the scripture and held my book so that Jeremiah could follow along. I could see Jeremiah sounding out the simpler words, his lips moving unconsciously.

Something changed in the room during one of these readings. I sensed it like a temperature drop when a door opens in winter, even before I registered the sound of shuffling along the side aisle. I lifted my head and met John Henry's gaze.

He'd come in late, his hat in his hands, his shirt dusty with travel. He was alone – Olsen wasn't with him – and like the other men, had probably left his gun belt in the foyer. When I spotted him, he was half-way down the side aisle on his way to either his mother's pew or his girl's. He wasn't looking at them, though. He was looking at me.

I wasn't as presentable as the other women in his life. Besides the worn dress, I had been bent over the book with Jeremiah, and my hair, in need of a trim and reacting to the heat besides, had begun to pull out of my bun to curl around my face. I felt at once threadbare, disheveled, and plain, hardly capable of meeting such a threat, yet I would not flinch. I met his gaze as coolly as possible.

He didn't flinch either. He took in my position with the Danahers and his mouth curved into a grin.

The preacher paused then for dramatic emphasis and the sudden silence startled John Henry. He broke eye contact and resumed his quiet shuffling down the aisle until he reached his family's pew. I wasn't the only woman who'd noticed his arrival, but one reaction caught my attention: Sarah Lowe shuffled in her seat to make her presence known and beamed when she caught his eye. She received a smile and a nod for her efforts. As she settled back into her pew, she shot another curious look at me.

I pretended I didn't see it. I kept my gaze on John Henry, waiting until his focus was entirely on the preacher. He settled in, sitting like a true cowboy, hunched over with his hat in his hands, and probably his elbows on his spread knees. Not exactly the most reverent pose, but at least he was no longer trying to stare me down.

I breathed easier and turned back to Jeremiah. He'd been watching this with some concern and I smiled at him to let him know that everything was all right. I spent the rest of the service praying that John Henry's family would leave immediately after the service.

* * *

God partially answered my request. John Henry slipped out of the church before the last note was sung, but neither the remaining Evanses nor the Lowes appeared in any hurry to leave. I should have expected this, really. Churches were, for all the cynicism of the East, still the heart of frontier communities. Ben and his wife would not leave until they'd swung the church-going voters to their side. I thought of my uncle's bloodied hand and seethed.

Ben began to go around, shaking hands with the men while Helen beamed in rosy-cheeked beauty at his side. Now that she was standing, I could see from the way her dress fell, despite the carefully arranged stays, that the Evanses were about to have another generation born on their land.

Mrs. Danaher, to my relief, did not wait around to be solicited by the Evans' poster boy. She hustled her two boys and me down the aisle and out the church doors before the bulk of the crowd had a chance to gather themselves together.

Once outside, she practically dragged me into the shade of the building.

"It's far too hot in there for you," she chided, as though the heat were somehow the pastor's fault. "The boys and I have to bring the food to the tables. You stay here until you feel well enough to come over."

It was cool and breezy in the shade, so naturally I didn't object. She gave my loaf of bread to Oscar, told him to put the book away before he got weak eyes, and bullied him towards the picnic tables. Jeremiah lingered for a moment.

"You were reading, weren't you?" I asked, fanning myself with my hymnal.

He grinned shyly, looking pleased.

"Not much, ma'am," he said in a low voice. "But I got a lot of sounding done!"

"That's the way, Jeremiah. One step at a time."

"Jeremi-ah!" his mother called and the boy hurried away in his own uniquely awkward manner.

I was thinking, *He's a good man, or will be,* when a deep, familiar voice spoke from close by, echoing my thoughts.

"He's a good boy, Jeremiah Danaher."

My chest began to pound. I turned to find John Henry, standing by a black horse with his feet spread wide and his hands toying with the reins.

In the quiet, early days of my recovery, I'd thought back to my first encounter with him and decided that my fevered imagination must have exaggerated his height. Standing in the shadow of the church that morning, I found that my imagination had added nothing. He was as big as I remembered and even if he hadn't been, the darkness of his presence would have loomed large anyway.

The horse whickered. John Henry was watching the picnic grounds, apparently unconcerned at the curiosity of the people streaming out of the church. I barely noticed them myself. I was too busy watching him, digging my fingers into the leather covers of my books, trying to maintain my calm.

What do you want?

I didn't say it out loud. I waited and after a moment, John Henry glanced at me. "I heard you were ill," he said.

"I was."

He looked me over quickly. I felt the wear of my gown and thought briefly of Sarah's magnificent appearance.

"You've recovered," he said.

"So it seems."

"Tougher than you look?"

"You don't know the half of it," I retorted before I could stop myself.

He actually smiled at that. Smiled *and* looked at me straight, if only briefly.

"Glad to hear it," he said.

Laughter, pure and dulcet like bells in a cathedral, rang out over the cheerful din of the vacating churchgoers. Sarah Lowe appeared, her arm looped through her brother's, hair glinting like polished mahogany in the noonday sun. She moved with grace, her green dress draped around a curvy figure that portrait artists would have loved to sketch. It was clear that, with Helen Wright safely an Evans, Sarah was well on her way to being the most desirable girl in town.

That she knew this was obvious. That she'd already made her choice among the pickings was equally apparent. She didn't call John Henry's name or crook her finger at him. She didn't have to. All she needed to do was toss him a laughing glance over her brother's shoulder and both she and the rest of the town were sure that he'd come running.

She tossed him that glance. Her gaze slipped over me as though I were part of the white-washed church siding. The amused passersby either laughed openly or shot badly-concealed looks of interest in John Henry's direction.

John Henry did not move. He stood, jaw clenched tight, looking at the reins in his hands until Sarah Lowe and her brother were nearly under the shade of the trees lining the creek. He might not

57

have moved even then if one of the passersby, a man with a sour expression, hadn't muttered to the woman next to him in a tone loud enough for us to hear: "Where's Goodnight? You'd think he'd want to be here for the follow up story."

My face flamed and what little self-assurance I had flew before the terror of notoriety. I didn't know where to look or what to look at.

John Henry felt it as well. He looked disgusted. He shoved his hat back on his head, muttered a "Day, ma'am," in my general direction, and strode off towards Sarah.

I wanted to run home. I watched John Henry approach Sarah, removing his hat, his horse stepping lively in his wake. I saw faces turning towards me, curious faces, hostile, strange, alien. I felt alone, deserted in the midst of foreign, treacherous territory. But it was *my* uncle who'd been assaulted and *my* uncle who was being physically threatened by the very men these people were sharing lunch with. They were in the wrong – I was in the right. So why wasn't I feeling more sure of myself?

Truth be told, I probably would have retreated that morning. I began making excuses to myself, saying that I was still ill and not up to the prospect of dealing with hostiles. I didn't get a chance to finish, for another familiar voice piped up behind me.

"Miss Goodnight!"

Annie Walsh stood a few yards away, beaming like she'd found an old, lost friend. She was a talkative, cheerful young girl, with freckles and unruly hair tied in braids and more energy than she knew what to do with. I knew her only slightly – she'd delivered my medicine one day and brought a dinner made by her mother on another day. As I hesitated on the edge of the crowd, she ran up to me, grabbing my hand like the child she still was.

"Oh, I'm so glad you've come!" she chirruped. "I was telling Ma that I thought it was you sitting with Jeremiah Danaher. Come, you have to sit with us and meet my sister!"

Thus, through kindness, I was trapped.

SEVEN

Attending the Sunday picnic gathering after services was an interesting experience. My uncle's reputation divided the crowd in their opinion of me. Some were openly hostile, staring me down, avoiding conversation, or making comments outright. Others were friendly and welcoming, whispering to me that they were glad someone had the guts to challenge the status quo.

"The Evanses have thrown their weight all over this town. It's time they relearned democracy."

The Evanses did not stay long. John Henry disappeared shortly after our talk, riding off with Sarah's lingering gaze on his back. Ben shook hands with everyone he could reach, and then took his mother and wife home. Perhaps they took the temperature of the crowd and decided against risking what gains they'd made that morning. Perhaps the sun and heat were too much for the delicate Helen. Maybe Honest Joe Turner was due to arrive and the aristocratic Varina Evans didn't want to risk an open confrontation. I didn't know or care. I was just relieved they were gone.

Some of the tension disappeared with their departure and the crowd went about their normal routine. Mr. Walsh and his sons admired a new pony someone had brought to show off. Oscar abandoned his books in favor of a circle of young ladies, one of whom was the blond girl he'd flirted with before. I sat in a comfortable bubble, surrounded by the quiet Danahers and the talkative Walsh family, both of whom seemed determined to adopt me as one of their own. I didn't mind the protection and I found the conversation pleasant.

Mrs. Danaher and Mrs. Walsh were good friends of long standing and sought to draw me out, asking me questions about this or that before finally lapsing into conversation about the upcoming wedding of Annie's sister. I drank lemonade and watched as Annie, perhaps entrusted with the secret of Jeremiah's new-found knowledge of letters, showed him how to spell her name in the mud of the creek bank.

"In case, you know, you should ever need to write me a letter," she said. Jeremiah blushed scarlet.

"...You'll be there, of course," Mrs. Walsh said aloud.

I realized that both women were looking at me expectantly.

"I'll be where?" I asked.

Mrs. Walsh swatted at a fly. "Why, at Caroline's wedding, of course. The whole town has been invited and you know what that means."

I stopped myself from responding, "It means about half will show up." Instead I shrugged.

"It means all the young men will have a look at you." Mrs. Walsh winked at my astonishment.

"Not that there's much to choose from," Mrs. Danaher noted.

"You only need one good man," Mrs. Walsh said. "*I* think a sensible woman like you would suit the good Doctor Lowe right down to the ground, don't you think so, Ruth?"

"Oh, aye," said Mrs. Danaher.

"I'm not staying long, Mrs. Walsh," I stuttered, flattered and flabbergasted. "I don't really think..."

They waved off my protest as one. Mrs. Walsh placed a hand on my arm.

"It's just been the doctor and his sister since they arrived... has it been a year ago already?"

"It has," Mrs. Danaher nodded. "He and Sarah were passing through when Doctor Brown caught the fever. Lowe took over his practice and Sarah took the school when Millie Tucker went back to New York."

Mrs. Walsh fanned herself, nodding. "Once Sarah pins John Henry down, he'll be on his own."

"So John Henry *is* courting her." I regretted the comment instantly, for the two women exchanged excited, mischievous glances.

"He *is* good looking, isn't he?" Mrs. Walsh said. "I'm afraid you're a few months too late."

I blushed. "I didn't – I wasn't..."

"You wouldn't be the only girl to think it," Mrs. Walsh said. "John Henry's a good enough boy, though he was wild when he was younger. When he lost his wife in childbirth, we didn't think he'd ever settle down again. But Sarah's staked a pretty clear claim and I reckon the engagement will be announced fairly soon."

"Which clears the field for her brother," Mrs. Danaher said.

"But I..." I tried to protest, but Mrs. Walsh interrupted: "You won't be leaving before Saturday, will you?"

When I admitted that, no, I would most likely not be leaving for a few weeks, she decided the matter was settled. I would go to the wedding, I would dance with the young men, flirt with the good doctor, and romance would flourish.

I never handle this sort of thing well. I always feel a mixture of discomfort, flattery, hope, and annoyance. But above these usual feelings was another: why, knowing what they must have known about my uncle and his trouble with the Evanses, were they so sure I'd be welcome to stay here?

As though she could read my thoughts, Mrs. Walsh asked, "So has your uncle heard from them yet?"

"Heard from whom?"

"Why, the Pinkertons, of course." She leaned closer and lowered her voice. "Everyone knows he's been in contact with them. When your uncle wrote about information that he was expecting about the Evanses, well..." she shrugged. "We just all assumed."

"I'm afraid I don't know," I said. "My uncle doesn't confide in me."

"Cynthia, if he had something worth publishing, don't you think he'd have done so by now?" Mrs. Danaher asked sharply. "He's never held anything back, for any reason, not unless there was something to be gained from it. No offense, Jenny, but your uncle isn't a man to keep from writing the truth."

She made it sound like a critique.

"He's not afraid of ruffling feathers, that's for sure," Mrs. Walsh stated cheerfully. "But I like that in a man. Shows courage."

"He seems to have irritated the Evanses," I said and both women laughed.

"You have the gift of understatement," Mrs. Walsh said. "No one was surprised that John Henry picked a fight with your uncle. He has a temper. Everyone knows it."

"You can't poke a bear," Mrs. Danaher noted.

"My husband says they're laying odds on when your uncle and John Henry come to blows again. The sheriff already said he'd have no fighting in the town limits."

"As though an Evans would abide by that!" Mrs. Danaher scoffed.

"So the Evans family really does run the town?" I said.

"I wouldn't put it quite like that," Mrs. Walsh said thoughtfully. "They founded it, or at least Jacob Evans did, Varina's husband. Naturally, as the founding family, their opinion carries a lot of weight. But I wouldn't say they outright run things."

Families like theirs seldom do, publicly.

Mrs. Danaher said, "They live better than most, but that's because they got here first. Everything they have, they worked for. Of course, that doesn't stop some folks from envying."

"Some people," Mrs. Walsh agreed, "would complain about gold raining down from the sky."

"So, by and large, people like the Evanses?" I asked.

The two women exchanged concerned glances. I sensed resistance, so I explained, "I'm worried about my uncle. He's headstrong and if public opinion swings completely against him, he could be in a lot of trouble."

They relaxed. I wasn't trying to get information for a story. I was a niece worried about her uncle, something that they, as mothers, could readily sympathize with. Mrs. Walsh reached out and patted me on the hand.

"I wouldn't worry," she said soothingly. "The Evanses are law-abiding, good people. They wouldn't do anything to hurt your uncle."

Except attack him. What I said out loud was, "Do people think there's more to the Evans story than what they're telling?"

"Some say there's no smoke without fire," Mrs. Walsh said. "That's the newer folk mostly, the ones who came and settled here after the war. Those who came before think differently."

"Why?"

"Because they knew Jacob. He only died ten, fifteen years ago."

"And those that knew Jacob Evans know that he wasn't the kind of man who'd kill his partner?"

"Of course not!" Mrs. Walsh said immediately. "He was good people."

Mrs. Danaher merely tightened her lips and looked at her hands.

Mrs. Walsh was undaunted by my questions or Mrs. Danaher's silent opinion. "It's too bad you don't know about the Pinkerton report, but I knew asking you was a long shot. If something had come in, Fred would have told Danny."

"Fred?" I asked.

"Fred handles the mail," Mrs. Danaher said.

"He says your uncle sends a lot of business to the Pinkertons," Mrs. Walsh said. "Reckon he has some people there he knows very well. Speaking of people in the know, what brings Henry Sage out of his office today?"

She nodded off behind me and I turned. A man stood at the edge of the gathering, hat in his hands, studying the scene. He had a compact, active build and his face was tanned and lined from exposure to the sun. I could tell from the way he stood that, though he wasn't expecting trouble, he could handle whatever was thrown at him. The badge on his chest proved I wasn't the only one who thought so.

I glanced around the picnic grounds. Everything seemed calm and happy. There were no signs of trouble that I could discern, but then again, I was new in town.

I haven't even met Honest Joe, yet.

It occurred to me that I hadn't asked the ladies about Honest Joe Turner. My uncle's defense of the incumbent had confused me. Goodnights generally preferred good actions to good relationships. Yet even though Uncle Matthew all but admitted that Honest Joe wasn't as honest as the posters made him out to be, he insisted on supporting him, rather than picking a dark horse candidate. It was out of character.

When I looked to ask the question, however, the ladies had turned away. Mrs. Walsh called out dire threats to her boys, wrestling in the dust, while Mrs. Danaher had gone off to talk to a short, round woman with a worried expression on her face. Her expression reminded me of Mrs. Washington and I looked around for the tall red head. She wasn't here. Neither was the dark boy.

"Miss Goodnight?"

Sheriff Sage loomed over me, his hat in his hands and his blue eyes squinting in the noon-day sun. Close-up, he appeared even more sun-dried than he had at a distance.

Something about him made me immediately go on the defensive. "I'm Miss Goodnight," I said. "Have we met?"

He didn't extend his hand to me, just shifted his weight to one side. "Henry Sage, ma'am. Sheriff. I was hoping to speak to your uncle."

"Is there a problem?"

"I'd prefer to speak to him, ma'am."

He wasn't impolite, exactly. But he wasn't going to budge.

I gestured around the picnic area. "I'm afraid he's not here."

"Do you know where he is?"

"No."

Sage cocked his head at me, his eyes narrowing, his manner becoming wolfish. "You wouldn't be trying to throw me off, would you, ma'am?"

"Now, why would I want to do that, sheriff?"

Some children came running, giggling, by the blanket I sat on. Their happy noise reminded me how close everyone was and that most were listening in with thinly concealed interest. The sheriff saw this, too, and apparently didn't like it, for he reached out his hand to me.

"A word in private, if you wouldn't mind, Miss Goodnight."

My hand was swallowed up in his large, calloused paw. He pulled me to my feet and released me immediately, keeping a healthy distance between us. If the intent of the move was to attract less attention, we failed. People were staring openly now, among them Doctor Lowe, who was standing in the shade by his sister, munching cake. I was somewhat reassured when I saw that he appeared interested, not alarmed.

The sheriff led me alongside the creek. The gentle, tickling sound of water dashing along the shallow bed mingled with the gentle rushing noise of the trees overhead. Growing up in Massachusetts, it had never occurred to me that one might really have to live without trees or how much you might miss them when they were gone. I doubt the sheriff could have known that he was leading me to the one place in town where I felt the most at home.

When we were out of hearing range, he stopped and turned to me. He put his hat back on and the brim of his hat cast a shadow over his already dark, poker-face.

"Miss Goodnight," he said. "I'd appreciate it if you'd quit prevaricating and tell me where I can find your uncle."

"And I," I replied, folding my arms, "would appreciate it if you'd tell me *why* you're so desperate to talk to my uncle. Writing opinion pieces in the paper isn't a crime, even if he is insulting the Evans family."

Sheriff Sage pushed his hat back and looked at me with annoyance.

"Ma'am, you're new to town and I know that you've been laid up with the fever for the past couple of days. Probably this is the first day you've been out, meeting folks. I also know that Matthew Goodnight's your kin and that your first impression of John Henry wasn't exactly cordial. But I would consider it a personal favor if you hold off on judgment before you go condemning an entire community."

I opened my mouth to protest, but he waved his hand and went right on.

"I don't care what your uncle writes in his paper, providing he isn't calling for lynch parties. A man's entitled to his opinion, however he chooses to form it. What does concern me is members of this community consorting with thieves and gunslingers."

"What do thieves and gunslingers have to do with my uncle?"

"Well, ma'am, that's what I was wondering." When I still looked confused, he continued. "It appears there was a private card game over at Markum's Hotel about three nights ago. Your uncle was there, along with a few others. There was an argument that turned into a fight. When my deputy went in there to break it up, he recognized one of the out-of-towners as Pete Matheson. I trust you've heard of him."

I had. Pete Matheson, also known as Red Eye, was a former Calvary man, a crack shot with expensive tastes in clothes and women. He was wanted in most of the territories for murder and robbery and carried with him the dubious honor of a reward being offered for him dead or alive. Like the James gang, he was always surrounded by two-bit hoodlums, men without his brains, but with brawn and rapacious appetites.

That he was in this area didn't surprise me. That my uncle knew him was ludicrous and I said so.

Sage was unmoved by my declaration.

"I have several witnesses, ma'am," he said. "Including Markum and my deputy."

"If your deputy was there...?"

"He was caught off guard and Matheson got away. We've been out riding two full days now, looking for him, but he's managed to give us the slip."

That explained his worn-out appearance.

"I'm sorry to hear it," I said. "But even if my uncle was there-"

"He was," the sheriff interrupted.

"*If* he was," I continued. "What do you need him for? It's obvious that my uncle isn't in cahoots with him."

"No, ma'am," he said evenly. "He was just gambling and fighting with him."

"It was a card game. Maybe he didn't recognize Matheson."

He gave me a look. "Your uncle is as sharp as they come, Miss Goodnight. Do you really think it's likely he didn't know who he was gambling with?"

He was right and I didn't argue the point. My frustration grew. Uncle Matthew was gambling with a known fugitive? Maybe when he was a young reporter, hungry for a good story, but now, when he was a settled member of a community?

"I don't know where he is, Sheriff," I said finally. "He left early this morning without talking to me. Maybe he went to his ranch, maybe to his office, I don't know. But I do know that he's not a man who'd consort with murderers and robbers."

He grunted and looked off into the distance. "I've got witnesses that would say different. When you see him, tell him I'd like a word, will you?"

With that, the interview was over. He walked me back to the common area and left me at the fringe. Several people called out to him in a friendly way. He waved his hand to them before swinging up on to his horse and riding off. Now that the threat had passed, I could see exhaustion weighing him down like a lead-lined overcoat and how his horse stumbled in its pacing. He hadn't been lying about being gone for a long time.

I'd had enough of the picnic. I went to make my excuses to the women and deflected a few well-meaning inquiries about the sheriff's interest in me and my uncle.

"Reckon it's about that trouble at the hotel," Mrs. Walsh said.

Naturally, the whole town already knows.

I explained about wanting to go home and discovered that another decision had been made in my absence.

"You'll need a new dress for the wedding," Mrs. Walsh told me. "That is, unless missionary women keep back finery for such occasions. I have a good cream and brown dress that will suit you just fine. It just needs some tailoring, seeing as you're just a mere slip of a thing."

"I have no money, Mrs. Walsh."

"You can sew, can't you?" Mrs. Danaher said and when I sputtered that *of course* I could sew, she nodded to Mrs. Walsh. "Cynthia here needs help at the shop, mending and hemming and such. You can work there."

"I'll give a fair wage for a fair day's work," Mrs. Walsh confirmed. "Show up tomorrow after breakfast and I'll get you started."

I was too tired to argue, and as I could use the money, I promised to be there the next day. Only then was I allowed to escape to the empty shell of my uncle's house, where I waited the night in vain for his return.

EIGHT

As promised, on Monday morning, I reported for duty at the general store. Inside, the air was already warm and heavy with the scent of spices, leather, and grains. Glass jars of candy surrounded the counter where Mrs. Walsh worked. She was alone as I walked in, bent over a ledger book on the front counter, and she seemed relieved to be distracted from her work. She wore a pince-nez, which she hastily removed and slipped into her pocket.

"Miss Goodnight," she said, hopping down from her stool. "I am so glad you're here. There is such a pile to do, now that Annie is in school again. Let me just go and get it – make yourself comfortable."

She gestured that I should come behind the counter and slipped into the backroom with the ledger book in hand. I went where indicated, loosening my bonnet. I placed my needle case, a practical necessity on the road, on the counter and looked around.

It was clear that Mrs. Walsh took great pride in her shop, for it was clean and well-stocked. Shelves of canned and bagged grocery goods lined the back wall. On the east wall, farm tools and leather items were arranged in neat piles, all carefully organized. More goods hung from the exposed rafters: polished fishing poles, hoes, and rakes, all waiting to be put to use.

On the west wall were the dress goods. Bolts of calico, cotton, and muslin, and spools of thread, lace, and trims made a colorful background. A pre-made cream and brown dress with a feathered bonnet had place of pride in front. I assumed that this was the dress the ladies had picked out for me and studied it. It was too practical to be a party dress, but it was new and pretty without being showy or too young, so I decided I liked it.

Mrs. Walsh re-entered carrying a large basket overflowing with clothes in faded flower and checked prints and plain, sturdy cotton sheets. She told me that she'd had the idea to take in other women's needlework as a way of bolstering the weekly income, but with the advent of her youngest daughter going to school full time, had fallen behind. She didn't like needle-work herself – I assumed the pince-nez had something to do with this distaste – and, anyway, she was already busy running the store and preparing for her daughter's wedding.

"It shouldn't take a clever girl with nimble fingers any time at all," she said and placed the basket down by a rocking chair, which stood in the corner behind the counter. "And you can keep me company during the day."

From the way she said it, I imagined that this last was possibly the most urgent reason she had for hiring me. As a mother, she'd become accustomed to constant company and now all her daughters and younger sons were in school, while her eldest son worked on their plot of land with her husband. Mrs. Walsh was not of the temperament to welcome this change in her situation.

"This is the dress," she said, indicating the pre-made that I'd been examining. "It's modest and subdued, just right for a woman of your age."

We worked out the details of my employment and I was glad when I realized that there would be enough after two weeks work to pay off the dress and have a little extra in the bargain. These details settled, I went right to work. It felt good to be working after so much time spent in bed and alone, even if it was only hemming someone else's sheets. Being useful was something that I was accustomed to, a drug I hadn't quite quit the habit of yet.

I worked through the morning and turned down Mrs. Walsh's invitation to lunch. Instead, I went to my uncle's print shop, where I found Jeremiah working at the press. He seemed relieved to see me and shut down the machine.

"You're looking better, miss," he said, rubbing his nose and leaving an ink stain on it.

"I am feeling better," I agreed. In truth, I was clearer in the head and feeling sturdier. The needlework was already giving me a crick in the neck, but that was a pain I could live with. I held up the pail I'd brought with me from the house. "Feel like having lunch and another lesson?"

His face brightened.

We soon finished off the pail and filled the slate three times over with new words for Jeremiah's memory. He was starting to understand how to pronounce the letters and knew, though he did not mention how he learned this, how to spell Annie and Walsh.

"Before you know it," he crowed proudly, "I won't need the system anymore!"

"The system?"

"The delivery system. Look."

He hopped up and went around the counter. He brought back four envelopes, each marked with a different stamp.

"These are the ad copies," he said proudly, spreading the envelopes out on the table in front of me. "Each symbol means a different client. Like, this one, for instance." He picked up an envelope with a double circle. "This envelope is for the Washington family. It's the symbol that they use on their horses. This one here, the triangle – that's for the Perkins, because their ranch is on the bend of the river. The key symbol is for Markum's Hotel and this one is for my uncle."

"Uncle Matthew has a lot of advertisers."

"Yes, ma'am," Jeremiah said proudly. "He's always been good to me, your uncle. Why, when he found out I couldn't read, he said a bright young man needed a chance, no matter what his education. He created this whole system and even said that it didn't matter, as these envelopes were personal and confidential and having someone that couldn't read was a blessing in disguise." His face fell suddenly and he looked down at the envelopes with new doubt. "I hope he isn't mad when I can read."

"Of course he won't be mad!" I exclaimed. "He'll be proud of you. You'll be much more useful to him when you can read. You can edit the articles and maybe even write them someday. Now, wouldn't that be fine?"

"Me, writing!" he snorted. But he seemed flattered all the same.

"I'd still rather no one knew yet," he said. "Of course, my mother knows and..." he stopped, blushing.

"Annie Walsh?" I guessed.

He blushed deeper and muttered something about Annie being tight-lipped and very helpful. I took my leave then, so the boy could blush and print and daydream on his own. I spent the rest of the afternoon wondering why my gruff and no-nonsense uncle would spend so much time creating an elaborate labeling system for an illiterate employee when that same employee had a bright bookworm for a brother at home.

NINE

When I arrived home that first night, back sore and eyes as dry as the wind that blew through the town, I was surprised to see Uncle Matthew in the kitchen. It was still bright outside – the sun was only just setting – yet the kitchen was dark and dreary. He hadn't thought to draw the drab sackcloth that served as curtains on the windows.

Uncle Matthew sat at the kitchen table, poring over a mass of papers – newspaper clippings, telegrams, and letters – which littered half the counter space. A worn leather journal lay open by his hand. Mrs. Washington's last loaf of bread, torn and half-eaten, sat on a dish close by. A half-filled label-less bottle of amber liquid stood uncorked next to a tin cup. Uncle Matthew was scowling at a yellowed letter, absently scratching at his wounded hand.

He looked up when I came in and closed the journal, leaving the letter tucked among its pages. "Well, there you are," he said. "I'd been wondering where you'd got to."

His voice was thick, though with drink or exhaustion, I didn't know. He certainly looked tired, his face hollow and his eyes sunk deep into his head, but that may have been a trick of the light.

"I've been at the mercantile," I said, taking my bonnet off. "Mrs. Walsh offered me some work."

"Should you be working in your condition? I wouldn't want a relapse."

It sounded less like concern and more like an imposition that he'd like to avoid.

"It's just needlework, Uncle Matthew." I took the chair next to his and gestured for his wounded hand. He gave it readily and I began to loosen the now filthy bandaging. "I would have told you but you haven't been around. Where have you been?"

"Riding," he said shortly, grimacing as I tugged on the cloth. "Trying to clear my head."

"You really need to take better care of yourself. A wound like this will get infected if you neglect it." I peeled away the last of the dressing and winced when I saw the state of the cut. I rose to fetch supplies. "Better not finish that bottle until I'm done here."

"Why do you think I brought it?"

"I spoke to the sheriff yesterday."

"The sheriff?" He sounded defensive.

"He wanted to talk to you about some trouble at the hotel." I gathered some clean cloth strips, a tin plate, and a cup, which I filled with water from the bucket. "I said I didn't know where you were."

I settled back down next to him and tossed away the dressing. He grunted and twisted in his seat as I cleaned the wound with a rag and water. When I paused to reach for the alcohol, he drew in a ragged breath.

"Sheriff Sage," he said, "likes to stick his nose where it doesn't belong."

"He said that you were involved with the Matheson gang. Is that true?"

As I asked, I poured the alcohol over the jagged, festering wound. He twisted and swore and very nearly pulled me over trying to tug his hand away.

"Damn it, girl!" he cried, but I held firm.

"Quit fighting me or you'll rip the cut open again."

I waited until he settled down and then, as I began to rewrap the wound, I asked him again. "Is it true?"

"No," he said sullenly. "I don't run with the Matheson gang. I've not quite fallen that low."

"You just gamble with them."

"I play cards. I don't ask for the credentials of every man that asks to play."

"You're saying you didn't recognize Mad Eye Matheson?"

Uncle Matthew looked me dead in the eye and lied. "That's what I'm saying."

I returned the stare. "Do you really think the Sheriff's going to believe that?"

An insistent pounding at the back door broke through our silent duel of wills. I jumped, my heart pounding.

It's John Henry, coming to...

I didn't know what he was coming to do, but from the look on Uncle Matthew's death-still face, he was just as worried. He got to his feet and looked about the room, as though seeking an escape.

"See who that is," he ordered.

I went over to the door, aware that Uncle Matthew was moving about behind me. I thought, *He's getting a gun*, and I felt reassured, for mine was all the way upstairs.

The back door was not as well built as the front and it shook when the outsider pounded again. This time, a lazy drawl accompanied the knocking.

"You about, Goodnight?"

The unfamiliar voice held an accent I'd not yet heard in this town, a drawl, Louisiana maybe. I looked to my uncle for direction and experienced another surprise. In the three steps that it had taken me to cross to the door, he'd swept the journal out of sight, leaving only a few scraps of paper on the table with the bottle. He stood beside the table now, his jaw tight and his eyes hard. His good hand went and settled behind him, on the small of his back. I realized then that my uncle was never without a weapon.

"Let him in, Jenny," he said.

I'd hardly cracked the door open when our visitor shoved it the rest of the way, tearing it out of my hand.

The newcomer was a smallish man, with dark glittering eyes, dirty sandy hair, and a once-natty striped vest under his dust-coated jacket. He stopped upon seeing me and grinned, shoving the ubiquitous hat further back on his sun-burnt forehead. His voice hissed like a snake. "Well, now, lookee here. The boss didn't say nothing about you having yourself a fancy woman, Matt."

His wink made the fine hair at the back of my neck stand on end. When he moved closer, I stepped back, but he only meant to get in from the night air. He shut the door and leaned against it, lengthening his torso and showcasing the pistol strapped low on his thigh. The leather of his belt was greasy with use and there were notches on the handle of his gun, irregular notches that weren't meant to increase the grip.

When I lifted my eyes, I saw that he'd been watching my examination. His lips pulled back into a leer.

I had rarely come across a man I wanted so much to slap.

"What are you doing here?" Uncle Matthew's voice sounded harsh.

"Just stopped by to be neighborly." The newcomer gestured. "How's the hand?"

There was menace behind his mischievous grin.

"Jenny," my uncle said. "Leave us."

I looked to my uncle. He remained where he was, pale and gripping the back of the chair he'd vacated. Matthew Goodnight had faced the wrath of the Union army, the disapproval of his family, and had taken on the most dangerous family in Legacy. And yet this little runt of a punk was able to drain the color from his face.

It didn't make sense.

"I can stay," I offered and Uncle Matthew snapped, "Go, Jenny."

"Jenny-girl," the man at the door said. "We've got a little business, your man and me, but if you ever want to come my way..."

His wink filled in the blanks.

I still didn't understand my uncle's reaction, but in the immediate situation, you don't often have the luxury of full and complete answers. You can only act in the present and pray that you've read things correctly. There was an intruder in the house, my uncle was frightened, and my pistol was upstairs.

I, accordingly, lifted my skirts and left the kitchen.

As the door swung shut behind me, I heard Uncle Matthew say in disdainful tones, "Speak your piece, Underwood."

I took the stairs two at a time and reached the top lightheaded. I didn't stop, though. I dug my pistol out from under my pillow, double-checked the rounds, and headed back. My skirts rustled loudly as I raced down the stairs, but I didn't care if Underwood heard me. I ran until I got to the kitchen door, where I stopped, breathing heavily and willing the world to stop spinning.

"...you know how the boss is, Matt," Underwood was saying in a lazy drawl. Even through the wooden door, his oily mannerism was enough to set my teeth on edge. "He's a fair man, in his way."

"I've given you my answer," Uncle Matthew replied. "That's all I have to say." He sounded stronger now, more like the man I remembered, and my heart rose a little.

There was a moment of quiet. I pressed my ear to the door, trying to calm the heavy beating of my heart. I breathed in the comforting scent of gun-oil and adjusted the heavy weight of the pistol in my hands. When I left the mission, I'd thought I'd never use a gun again. Here in relatively tame Legacy, I'd pulled one three times. I wondered how many more times I'd need it before I left.

Underwood said, "He won't be very much pleased."

Uncle Matthew snapped, "I can't help that. If he wants the money, he'll have to wait. I'm not a rich man. I need time. Ten days."

My heart skipped a beat and I almost missed Underwood's sly reply.

"Eight would be more convenient."

There was another long pause then a defeated sigh.

"Eight, then," my uncle said.

I heard the squeak of the floorboards as someone shifted their weight. "I'm glad you see it the boss's way. I'll be around, Goodnight, so don't plan on doing anything stupid like skipping town."

"I don't run," my uncle said sharply. "And I won't have you and your boys coming around here and frightening my niece. You keep your distance, you hear me?"

"I wouldn't dream of upsetting that pretty little thing."

"You do and I'll kill you."

"Easy there, hero. There's no cause for getting worked up. I ain't got no love for this town either, seeing how your sheriff loves long, drawn-out chases. So we gotta compromise, meet someplace we both can be comfortable. Like your ranch. I hear it's a nice spread."

"I've got a man out there."

"Better get him out of there, hero. If we see anyone other than your good self, I can't guarantee the outcome. I've a sweet and understanding nature, but the boss... he's got a temper."

"I *understand*, Underwood." My uncle spoke gritted teeth. "Now get out."

There was another moment of silence. Then I heard the creak of the kitchen door and the beat of heavy boots as they moved across the flooring. The door swung shut and my uncle's boots made a hasty movement. I assumed he was moving towards the door and I opened mine, ready for anything.

My uncle was not at the far door. He was by one of the open cabinets, clutching the paper-filled leather journal to his chest. He was pale and his forehead was slick with sweat. He looked at me, then at the pistol in my hand, and his lips tightened.

"I don't need you to rescue me," he said and slammed the cabinet door. "You'll tell no one about this, you hear?"

This was the second time he'd told me that I wasn't to speak. I was growing tired of it.

"Who is Underwood?" I asked.

"He is none of your concern."

He pushed past me, anger radiating out of him. I almost put up my hand to stop him, but thought better of it. I felt a tightness in my chest and recognized it as the feeling you get just before you're about to fall from a great height.

"You lost money to Mad Eye Matheson," I said.

He stopped in the doorway and for a moment, I suffered the hope that he'd take me into his confidence.

We were not there yet.

He turned and glared at me. "This is nothing to do with you."

"You owe a renegade money," I said and he stepped forward and grabbed my arm in a painful grip.

"You tell the sheriff," he said, "and it won't just be my life at risk, you hear?"

He looked desperate and his good hand tightened on my arm. I squirmed, but he only squeezed tighter. He was beyond reason, so I just nodded and held my pistol close.

Uncle Matthew breathed a sigh of relief and released me. "You're a good girl, Jenny. Sam always said you could be trusted."

I glared at him, resenting the reference to my father. Uncle Matthew wasn't looking at me, though. He'd drifted off, staring into the middle distance as though transfixed by the future he saw there. He looked dreadful... and wistful. The silence stretched until I thought I would need smelling salts to bring him back.

Then he wiped the sweat from his brow and started up the stairs, leaving me alone in the hall, where the silence was louder than any noise I'd ever heard.

TEN

That night, my nightmares returned. I was back in that
crowded little cabin with Trailing Rose and her son,
listening to the crowd that chanted their desire to burn
us out. Then I was running down the street, pursued by
a faceless crowd, my dress torn and tripping me, hands reaching for
me. I awoke with a cry to find myself kicking off the covers, my
nightgown soaked in sweat, my whole body trembling as with ague. I
forced myself to stay in bed, to calm my racing heart, to listen to the
night sounds. Eventually my fears stilled and I thought, *Uncle
Matthew must have heard me screaming.*

If he had, he didn't come to check on me.

I managed to get some sleep before dawn and I awoke with a
clear decision: I would keep working for Mrs. Walsh, but I would
turn over the money to Uncle Matthew. I would help to clear his
debt before I left town.

When I arrived at the store, Mrs. Walsh was in the back,
finishing up breakfast. The scent of frying salt pork and fresh coffee
hung heavily in the air, making my stomach grumble and my mouth
water. Mrs. Walsh offered me coffee and listened when I explained
that I needed the money more than I needed the dress. From the
expression on her face, I could tell she disagreed.

"You know your own business best," was all she said and I
settled into work.

The established routine consisted of sitting in the rocking chair and stitching until my hands stiffened and my eyes grew red. Mrs. Walsh divided her time between her customers in the store and wedding preparations in the back. Every day, tantalizing scents drifted from the kitchen, making my mouth water. I met Caroline, the bride-to-be, who worked in the afternoons after school. She came frequently to help and they would talk for hours, making happy plans and hopeful predictions.

Listening to them from my spot behind the counter was a lonely experience and more and more I found myself reaching for my mother's beads in my pocket. It was a silly thing to do, really. I was a good Protestant girl who didn't believe in Roman superstitions about praying to the dead. Yet I could not keep myself from holding on to that rosary even more closely now that Uncle Matthew had my father's Bible.

My mother, Marie Claire, was my father's first and best known scandal. He'd met her during one of his revival meetings up north, by the factories. By then he was in his thirties, the widower of a sterile wife, and already well-respected for his ability to draw and hold crowds in his thrall. She was a French-speaking, barely literate Catholic factory girl with jet-black hair, dark eyes, and a complexion that my Grandmother always said was too dark to be purely European. As the son of a staunch, progressive, Protestant New England family, Samuel Goodnight could hardly have picked a type more likely to antagonize his kin.

No one considered it a good match, not even when my mother allowed herself to be reborn into my father's faith. My mother struggled both with English and homesickness, which did little to endear her to her new family. For a time, my parents traveled the preaching circuit together, faithfully laboring to bring more souls into the fold. When Mother became pregnant, my father sent her home to live with his sister, my Aunt Alice, a generous soul who treated my mother as a welcomed guest each time she came home pregnant.

There were two miscarriages before me. Grandmother Goodnight declared that Mother was not fit to bear children, but my father wanted a son, so they kept trying, my mother weakening with each effort. I was the third try and Aunt Alice confined my mother to bed for the duration of the pregnancy. My birth was the most difficult in family lore and my mother never really recovered. My father's hopes of a male heir ended on my birthday, when the doctor declared Marie Claire incapable of having another child.

"You aren't built for it," he'd said. "You'll die in the attempt. If your husband truly loves you, he won't ask this of you."

I've wondered if that was why my father spent so much time in the field, leaving my mother alone with his family. Was this an act of sacrificial love? Or a disappointment so deep that he was unable to face the woman he was vowed to?

To the chagrin of the family, I was named Genevieve, a French name, a Roman Catholic name. My father, being away in the mission field, had no hand in choosing it. Grandmother Goodnight, unable to thwart the will of my sickly mother, decided that I would be called Jenny, a more properly anglicized name.

"She is ours," she is reported to have said, when first she held me. What my mother thought of this declaration, I don't know.

Thus my dual existence began. My mother called me Genevieve, taught me the Ave Maria in private, and spoke of her family on the provincial farm, her heavy accent thickening as homesickness overcame her. Everyone else called me Jenny. I was brought up with fire and brimstone, strict Sabbath observances and missionary zeal. I loved my mother, but I adored my oft-absent father and my extended family. Jenny was my publicly avowed name – Genevieve became a secret between my mother and me.

As I grew, my mother declined, withdrawing more and more into her room and, though we did not know it until much later, falling back into her Roman faith. She never traveled with my father again. She remained a guest in my Aunt Alice's back bedroom, a quiet, remote presence who seldom bothered anyone. The robust, healthy Goodnights were a stark contrast to her patient suffering, made all the more pathetic by her reliance on beads and incense for comfort. The association of weakness, illness, and popery has ever been in the back of my mind.

I changed, too. I began to dream of joining my father in the field and I learned to be embarrassed by my mother's dark looks and accent. I longed to distinguish myself by becoming the apt pupil she'd never had the chance to be. I still loved her, you understand, with that deep love of a single child for an abandoned parent. But I was torn. My childhood was a push and pull of sentiment versus ambition, of an old, moldy world view and the stark tidiness of the new. My mother was an alien presence in my homeland. In the end, I aligned with the new.

On a hot and awful June day, my mother called me to her bedside. Wheezing and pallid, she pressed her beads into my hands and stroked my face tenderly.

"*Ma belle fille,*" she whispered. "*Je t'aime, ma petite Genevieve.*"

She'd been ill so long that the possibility of her actually dying seemed remote. The realization that her time had come was one of the most painful experiences of my life.

That visit with my mother was the last time anyone called me Genevieve. Now I am simply Jenny and on one of those mornings, stitching to the sound of Mrs. Walsh and her daughter's conversation, it occurred to me that Jenny would likely be the name on my grave. The sharp pang of remorse that accompanied this revelation took me by surprise.

That week with Mrs. Walsh and Caroline was a bittersweet reminder of my mother's absence. But there is no use in mourning the past. What's done is done and there only remains the road ahead. All else is indulgence.

Nevertheless, the beads were my last physical link to Mother, so I kept them tucked deep in my pocket, where no one else would see.

ELEVEN

If you want to learn something about a town, you could find worse ways than to spend all day in a mercantile. I spent hours bent over my work, listening in on conversations between the chatty Mrs. Walsh and anyone and everyone who cared to talk. I learned to keep my head down and my hand motions slow so that I would not be discovered, for folks tended to be silent when they realized there was a stranger among them. When they spoke freely, they talked about weather, gossiped about their friends, discussed the railroads and the economy, but mostly they talked politics.

As town politics were inseparable from my uncle, this was what I was most interested in, too. The ladies were correct when they said that the town was divided between those who hated the Evanses and those who hated my uncle. For the former, Honest Joe was admittedly not a champion, but he was better than the embedded rich getting their hands deeper into local affairs. For the latter, nothing could save the town save the election of young Ben and the showing up of the gutter press.

On occasion, someone would rail on about one of my uncle's opinion pieces. Mrs. Walsh, when she remembered I was present, would try to defend my uncle by saying something like, "A man's entitled to his opinion, isn't he?"

One man was particularly venomous about my uncle and his interference. After ripping into my uncle's professional qualifications, he started in on the person. "He's a low-crawling, vile rat, a booze-soaked bully who hasn't...!" He stopped when our eyes met.

The man was Irish, small, dark, and furious with eyes so light and blue that they appeared to glow with their own radiance. The red tip of his nose spoke loudly of at least one of his vices. He stared at me until Mrs. Walsh gestured an introduction.

"This is Miss Goodnight, Matthew Goodnight's niece," Mrs. Walsh explained. "She's helping me out now that my girl is in school. This is Liam Danaher," she said, almost as an afterthought. "Jeremiah's uncle, of course."

There was very little in Liam Danaher's manner or look to remind me of his gentle, hard-working nephew, though the crinkle of his eyes and the nervous shift of his feet were familiar. Jeremiah had told me that Liam looked after my uncle's spread. I wondered: if he hated my uncle so much, why did he work for him?

Danaher had come in for a sack of chewing tobacco and some shotgun shells. The shells had already disappeared into his leather bag, but if his white-knuckled grip on the bag of tobacco said anything, it was that he was profoundly moved to see me.

"His niece, is she?" he asked and spat a long stream of tobacco in to the spittoon that Mrs. Walsh kept by the counter. "I'll not retract one word, miss. Not one word."

His eyes were blood shot and it was early morning yet.

"No one asked you to," I said and bit off the thread I'd been working with. "As you say, you're entitled to your opinion."

Danaher looked taken aback. He stepped back, swaying a little, and pointed at me as though I'd said something marvelous and weighty.

"You're right," he said. "And no one has to pay for my opinion neither. I give it for free. You tell your uncle that, you tell him. No one pays *me* for my opinion." There was a moment's pause, then he said, "Ruth tells me you've been helping Jeremiah to read."

"He's a nice young man," I said. "I'm glad to help."

Liam Danaher stared at me as though he couldn't believe what he had heard. Then the confusion passed and, having had his say, he turned and staggered out the door.

Mrs. Walsh turned to me apologetically. "I'm sorry about that, my dear. Danaher is one of *those* Irishmen, a bit on the wild side. Ruth and her husband helped him settle here, but he's still having difficulty."

I assured her that I was fine and we moved on with the business of the day. The encounter, brief though it was, had given me much to think about.

Despite the town's preoccupation with them, Honest Joe Turner and Ben Evans weren't seen much that week. Honest Joe lived on the other side of the county and Ben was working on his ranch and visiting the spreads around the perimeter. His elegant wife, Helen, and his mother, Varina, were spotted shopping and lunching in town with Sarah Lowe and her brother. There was some chatter in the shop about the new fashion that Helen was sporting. Mrs. Walsh commented that she was surprised that Helen hadn't yet been confined, which was the first that I formally heard of her pregnancy.

"Helen is Cole Wright's daughter," Mrs. Walsh's customer responded. "She wasn't raised elegant like Sarah Lowe or Varina. Likely she won't take herself to bed until the day the baby actually comes."

"That could be any day now," Mrs. Walsh mused. "I expect her mother will come and help her. I can ask her about the new drapes in the parlor. I heard Varina sent all the way to Boston for them."

"That's what I heard, too, and why she should do that when we have perfectly fine material in San Francisco, I'll never know."

"When you have money, why not spend it? Anyway, it's the latest thing and I was hoping to make something like it for Caroline..."

I saw John Henry a few times that week. He was polite and distant and I was the same. The only time we spoke was when I encountered him on the road Thursday evening. I was heading home to the empty house with a sore back and tingling fingers. He was alone, riding his mare in the direction of the schoolhouse and I remember thinking, *He isn't dressed for courting.*

To my dismay, he drew up as he came close and tipped his hat. "Evening, Miss Goodnight."

"Evening," I replied, as my insides shivered.

"Fine night."

I looked up at the sky, a bowl of darkening blue, with pink and purple ribbons on the horizon. It was better than fine – it was gorgeous.

"Very," I said.

His horse whickered and kept pace with me as I continued walking. The harness jingled and clinked in the silence. The schoolhouse was a short distance ahead, sitting quietly in the ageing light. Sarah Lowe must have been working late – I saw a flicker of movement through one of the windows and I knew that John Henry was on his way to walk her home. It irritated me that he would ride so slowly next to me.

"You mustn't let me keep you," I said, trying and failing to keep the annoyance out of my tone.

"I won't," he said and continued riding just as before.

In the distance to my left, I saw Doctor Lowe emerge from the schoolhouse, tossing his hat in the air, a curiously boyish motion for a man who looked so like a mortician. He stopped when he spotted us and I heard his rich voice calling to his sister.

By now, John Henry and I had reached the turning point in the road: I was to keep going straight, and he'd have to turn to continue on to the schoolhouse. He reined up his horse at the turn and half turned in his saddle again to tip his hat to me.

"It was pleasant walking with you this little way, ma'am," he said. There was an air of malicious amusement about him. He knew he irritated me and he was enjoying it.

"Reckon we made history tonight," he added.

"What do you mean?"

"We walked a whole half mile without pulling on each other once," he said, his amusement plain. "I think that's worth remarking on."

"If you keep to your side of the road and I keep to mine, I think we can keep things civilized."

His gaze turned thoughtful.

"Yes," he said. "Well, goodnight, Miss Goodnight. You tell your uncle I was asking after him."

"Is that a threat?"

John Henry had the reins high in his hands, ready to ride off toward his girl, when my question brought him up short. He looked down at me and the shade from his hat hid his eyes.

"No, ma'am," he said. "When I threaten a man, there's no mistake about it."

With that, he galloped off towards the schoolhouse.

I stood in the dust kicked up by his horse's hooves, watching as a tall, slender figure with glinting mahogany gold in her hair stepped gracefully out to meet the rider. John Henry swung off his horse, somehow taking his hat off in the same motion, and approached her. Dr. Lowe stood off to the side, his hat gripped tightly in his hand, his posture as rigid as it had been animated before. Apparently, I wasn't the only uncomfortable one in this situation.

I turned my face resolutely toward the house and went on my way.

TWELVE

I hardly saw Uncle Matthew at all that week. He didn't leave messages and I never knew where he was or what he was doing. Nearly every night, I found bandages in the kitchen and ants crowding around the bread crumbs he'd left behind. I would clean the table and leave clean cloth and ointment on the counter where he could find them.

I worried about his wound getting infected. He certainly wasn't favoring it. Jeremiah told me that he was working like a mad man, riding all over town and the environs, and producing lots of ad copy and bills for Jeremiah to deliver. Jeremiah was at his wit's end trying to keep up with all the work.

"Can't imagine what's gotten into him, ma'am," he said.

I knew, but of course, I didn't say.

Like all men who drink, Uncle Matthew was different each of the few times I did see him. Sometimes I'd find him in the kitchen, fixing food and acting like the charming, polished man I'd known as a child. Other times, he was sullen and terse and the distance between us became more and more pronounced.

In my letter to Aunt Alice, I told her I was busy helping Uncle Matthew put his house in order, which was a partial truth. I didn't say that I was beginning to feel that he was beyond my help. But Goodnights are stubborn, and no soul is ever considered beyond aid. I felt that no explanation I could give would justify my feelings, so I kept them to myself.

As the week crawled by, I rediscovered the comfort of routine. I rose early every morning, said my prayers, and sewed at Walsh's mercantile until noon. At noon, I went to the print shop for lunch and my lesson with Jeremiah. The afternoon I spent in the mercantile until it was time to go back to the house.

The house was the uncertainty. If I was alone, I would eat a hasty dinner in the kitchen and then retreat to my room, where I read until I fell asleep. Always I was on the alert, always I was listening and waiting, for what, I really couldn't say.

The *Legacy Bi-Weekly* was my constant companion. Jeremiah gave me a stack of back issues and I read them cover to cover, poring over the news articles, the opinion pieces, the serials, the columns, and the ads. One of the women in town wrote a weekly column on cooking. Some of my uncle's old newspaper cronies from back east, men whose names I recognized, allowed him to reprint their older articles. But it was my uncle's writing that interested me most, and I didn't like what I saw.

Uncle Matthew's reputation had been built on his personal integrity and charm, his objectivity and ruthless pursuit of the facts. What I saw here was not the dispassionate opinion of a professional observer, but the red-hot anger of a man long past caring about particulars. As I worked my way through the material, I watched the quality of his work degrade, becoming more and more sensational until it was borderline hysterical. I began to wonder if this and his gambling and his drinking weren't part of a bigger problem. Perhaps the frontier life was too much for him. He wouldn't be the first, nor the last man to be defeated by the wide open spaces, the feast-or-famine weather patterns, and the overall aching loneliness that every man, woman, and child faces out here.

The more I read, the more my sympathies were aroused. I went out of my way to stop into the print shop just in case he was around. He hardly was and when he was, he was too busy to speak to me.

"Later, later!" he'd call, waving a gloved hand. He'd taken to covering his wound with riding gloves so no one would notice. Why he was so insistent on keeping it from public knowledge, I couldn't fathom. His gambling and drinking habits were open secrets –I had been the only one surprised.

My only real encounter with Uncle Matthew that week was from a distance. On Thursday I forgot my lunch. I waited until the noon hour to go back to the house to get it. I slipped in the back way, expecting to have the house to myself as I always did of late. Yet the moment I stepped through the door, I was stunned to hear sour piano notes, coming from the parlor.

I immediately thought of Underwood and broke out into a cold sweat. My gun was upstairs in my bedroom. I could, of course, slip out the back way and run back to the mercantile, but the minute I thought of that, I rejected the solution. This was *my* house, at least for the duration of my visit, and I would not be driven from it.

There were two doors to the kitchen, one of them leading to the parlor and the other to the hall. I stepped up to the parlor door and lifted the latch. The notes, sour and without any discernible melody, kept sounding with regularity. Reassured, I eased the door open until I could see who it was behind the keyboard.

Uncle Matthew sat slumped on the piano bench, one elbow on the music stand with a bottle of whiskey in hand. The other hand was plucking at the keys, hitting the ivories with hard, meaningless motion. The broken sounds echoed in the empty room, almost covering his hiccupping sobs. Fat tears rolled down his cheeks. As I watched, he lifted the bottle and gulped another mouthful of the amber liquid. Now I recognized the tune: "When This Cruel War is Over."

No man would want to be caught in such a position. I drew back into the kitchen and left the house without a sound.

LETTER

(Undated – circa 1875)

Dear Aunt Alice,
For some time now, I have feared that Uncle Matthew is beyond my aid. He has fallen into some unhappy habits and I confess, I thought it would be best to leave him to his own devices. I have since changed my mind. I believe that you and Aunt Chastity were correct when you suspected that he was suffering from an unhappy love affair. I don't yet know the details – perhaps I shall never know them – but I have witnessed a strong confirmation of this theory. If thwarted love is the source of the problems, then there may yet be a way to help him. I can but try and I will do as I promised you. There is an atmosphere in this town that worries me beyond what I can explain. Pray, but do not worry...

THIRTEEN

The reply from the Pinkerton Detective Agency arrived on Saturday's early stage. The wife of the postmaster, Becky Thornton, delivered it directly to the print shop herself. Hoping to glean some information out of my uncle, she was disappointed when he wasn't in. Jeremiah put the letter in the safe and Mrs. Thornton wasted no time in coming to discuss the matter with Mrs. Walsh.

"What on earth could it be about?" Mrs. Thornton wondered, as she ran her hands through some new lace that she had no intention of buying.

"It's got to be about Jacob Evans. What *else* could it be about?" Mrs. Walsh said.

Both women tossed covert glances in my direction. I kept my eyes on my needlework. When Mrs. Thornton left, disappointed for a second time today, Mrs. Walsh tried her best to get some information out of me. I was forced to admit ignorance. "My uncle just doesn't confide in me, Mrs. Walsh."

She sighed. "I guess we will know soon enough, though what poor Ben and Helen are going to do if your uncle decides Jacob was a crook, I don't know. How is that hem coming along? Is it time for you to model the dress again?"

Annie and her mother had decided that, dress or no dress, I should attend Caroline's wedding. They'd further determined that, since I was going to the wedding, I needed a new dress, and since the brown and cream dress wasn't doing any good just sitting in the window, that was the dress I should have.

"You will wear it," Mrs. Walsh had said when I tried to protest. "You will wear it and maybe either you'll like it so much that you'll want to buy it or some other young lady will, seeing it on you. In any case, the hem will need to be basted, seeing as you're such a little thing and all."

So I spent the morning basting the hem and making the necessary tucks and adjustments so that the dress would fit. Mrs. Walsh divided the morning between the shop and the kitchen out back, where she was preparing the delicacies for the wedding party. That didn't stop her from taking time to chat with her customers, all of whom were invited to Caroline's wedding. In no time at all, the letter was common knowledge and the subject of intense discussion. Everyone was interested and one man reported seeing Uncle Matthew riding out early that morning, heading towards his spread.

"Wonder what he's doing that way," Mrs. Walsh mused. "Liam Danaher came into town last night, preparing for the wedding. The place will be deserted."

Once again, she looked to me and once again, was disappointed. I knew nothing more than they about my uncle's movements. If he was going to the property, perhaps he was preparing for Underwood's visit. Then again, perhaps he merely needed a place to drink in private. That he might have gone there to do some soul-searching was too much to hope for.

The weekend edition of the paper (Uncle Matthew's paper printed faithfully on Wednesday and Saturday and for special occasions) hit the streets by noon. Jeremiah stopped by, harried and red-faced, with a stack for the store and one copy for me. I was too busy with the dress to read it. Mrs. Walsh, after learning from Jeremiah that the Pinkerton letter was still in the safe, set her own aside and concentrated on the wedding.

Caroline spent the day at a friend's house, preparing her dress and hair for the ceremony, which was slated for five o'clock. Mrs. Walsh closed the store early and Annie and I spent the afternoon helping her with the food in the kitchen. The party was to be held in the clearing behind the church, which also acted as the sort of town square. It was a short walking distance from the store, and Mr.

Walsh and his sons spent their day setting up tables and bunting and the like.

At four, Caroline and her friend arrived at the store for Mrs. Walsh to fuss over. Caroline was an older, more filled out version of Annie, with ringlets in her hair and a becoming blush on her cheeks. She didn't really know what to make of all the attention that she was generating and spent the better part of the hour pacing the kitchen floor and being cautioned by her mother not to stand too close to the stove.

"Imagine if you singed that dress!" Mrs. Walsh exclaimed. "Imagine!"

Though the church was a walkable distance, Mrs. Walsh insisted that they drive Caroline over ("Imagine if she should get her dress muddy! Imagine!"). Caroline sat in the front seat between her parents while Annie and I dangled our legs out the back of the wagon. Annie was dressed in blue and we'd taken great pains to do up her hair with a brand new ribbon. She carried herself with a curious mixture of pride and embarrassment, the hallmarks of a young girl realizing her new-found commodities.

"Do I look pretty?" she asked when her parents were too busy fussing over Caroline to overhear.

"You look wonderful," I said and linked my arm through hers. "All the boys won't know what to make of you."

She blushed and muttered something about *that* not being so important, but the idea clearly pleased her. If she hoped to be coy, that was lost the moment she spotted Jeremiah in the church, looking in her direction. Annie immediately turned as red as a cherry and let go of my arm to run down the aisle to where the rest of her family awaited her.

Jeremiah was still staring at Annie as I slid into the pew next to him.

"She's a pretty girl, isn't she?" I asked.

He shrugged and dropped his gaze to the hat he rolled between his hands. His mother sat on the other side of him, stiff as a board, staring straight ahead. Her husband and Oscar sat on the other side of her, heads straight, eyes forward. No one even glanced at me.

I felt the cold touch of dismissal. I had no explanation as to why though and since the ceremony was already starting, I had no chance to ask.

The church was half-filled and I was relieved to see that the Evans' pew remained empty. Doctor Lowe bowed to me before taking his usual place on the opposite side of the church, a gesture that warmed me. He was alone, which was surprising. I wondered where his sister was and whether the ladies were right about Doctor Lowe settling down after his sister secured John Henry. The thought disturbed me and I concentrated on the wedding instead.

The pastor was intoning the vows when Tom turned and muttered to Ruth, "Their majesties didn't show. Reckon Cynthia isn't going to be too pleased."

"They're coming later." Ruth whispered. "At least, that's what she told me."

"Right," he grunted. "Reckon Sage ought to be there, make sure nothing happens."

"Oh, Tom!"

Jeremiah leaned over his mother to tell Tom, "Mr. Walsh told me that the Sheriff is out, chasing down Red Eye Matheson. The sheriff actually told Uncle Liam to keep his gun on him whenever he was out in the fields." His tone implied, "Isn't that exciting?"

Ruth said, "Hush, now, pay attention," in irritation. She knew what I knew: men like Matheson weren't exciting. They were dangerous, wild dogs who knew no restraint. No good ever came out of their appearance. I spent the rest of the short ceremony considering how I could convince Uncle Matthew to confide in the sheriff about his plans to meet Underwood and wondering whether Sage was reliable enough to act on the information.

After the blushing Caleb Jensen finally stuttered "I do" and the glowing Caroline Walsh pulled him into a kiss, we cheered and began to make our way outside. The Jensens, a stout, plain, but smiling family, took charge of escorting the newlyweds to the party awaiting them out back. The Danahers followed, all of them refusing to look at me now.

I tried not to feel snubbed. I volunteered to help the Walshes, who were now using the wagon to transport all of Mrs. Walsh's goodies to the picnic grounds. Annie laughed and joked with her brothers as Mrs. Walsh scolded and worried. Mr. Walsh, quiet yet pleased, wisely stayed with the horses. There was a comradery among them, the ties of family so strong and sure that each was allowed to be themselves. I was envious. I'd had family once and I'd have it again when I went home. But somehow that reassurance didn't stretch very far.

This alienated feeling eased a little when we got to the picnic grounds. The place was bustling with noise and laughter as families arrived from all compass points. A band of four - two fiddles, a guitar, and, remarkably enough, a squeeze box - warmed up on a gazebo that was so new, you could smell the freshly cut wood from across the way. Women in bright cotton and linen dresses clustered around the serving tables, displaying their offerings of chicken, pork, biscuits, cakes, breads, pickles, and other goods. The younger women, in starched skirts and carefully managed hair, mobbed the new bride with congratulations while the men kept their distance and circled the barrels of beer that lined one side of the square. The temperance movement was unknown here.

I stayed with Mrs. Walsh, helping her arrange dishes, shoo flies, slice bread, and whatever else needed doing. Sounds of joyful laughter and conversation pulsed through the small clearing. Only the shrieks of the highest pitched string on the fiddle were able to cut through the noise and call people's attention to the pastor, who wanted to intone a prayer before eating. Hats were removed, heads bowed, and strict attention was paid. I stood next to Mrs. Walsh behind the table, hands clasped in front of my pretty new dress. I saw Doctor Lowe standing in the periphery of the party's circle. His eyes were scanning the crowd, looking for someone, probably Sarah.

I wonder if she was supposed to come with him.

The prayers concluded, the feasting began. I worked at the serving table, dishing out slices of pie and cakes. There was some anonymity there - people were more interested in food than in me. At least they were until Mrs. Jensen, a stout woman, active woman who was frequently out of breath, asked, "Now, who might you be?"

From her easy smile and familiar manner melted away when Mrs. Walsh said, "Oh, this is Jenny Goodnight - she's been helping me in the mercantile."

The last comment was a kindness from Mrs. Walsh, but it didn't stop the look of undisguised discomfort on Mrs. Jensen's face. She said, "Well, how nice!" and slipped away. I saw her talking to a knot of women in a worried manner, glancing nervously in my direction.

Mrs. Walsh was watching, too, her lips pursed in worry. When she saw me staring, she said, "I was just wishing I had time to read your uncle's paper today. I don't mind telling you, he has a way of stirring hornets."

"I hope my being here doesn't make things awkward."

"Nonsense. You're my guest and Annie's friend. Besides, no one blames you for the trouble between your uncle and the Evans family. Like as not, that letter from the Pinkertons will prove exactly what everyone is thinking: that John Evans did all he could to save his partner. What else could it say?"

Doctor Lowe came down the line then, his broadly smiling face a welcome sight in the sea of strangers. I remembered what Mrs. Danaher and Mrs. Walsh had said about him and me and felt foolishly confused when the doctor came up to me.

"How have you been feeling, miss?" he asked, putting on a mock-stern face. "Have you been doing as I told you?"

"Would you believe me if I said I was?"

"With all respect, ma'am, I wouldn't. I know women. The last thing they like to do is follow orders."

"Spoken like a true bachelor," Mrs. Walsh laughed. "Don't you mind him, Jenny. He's more a feminist than you or I will ever be."

"God forbid! Now, more important matters. What have we here?"

When Doctor Lowe bent over to breath in scent of spices and fruit, I saw, for the first time, that his right earlobe was misshapen, as though someone had cut a piece of it away. It was an old wound, judging from the otherwise healthy look of the skin. Had he fought in the war? If he had, it wasn't too hard to guess which side he would have fought on. When I first met him, I'd found his accent charming. Now, seeing that scar, I couldn't help but wonder what he thought of mine.

Doctor Lowe looked back at me with a smile, oblivious to my thoughts. "Better give me two slices of that pie, Miss Jenny. I'll pay for it in the morning, but it'll be worth it."

"Coming right up, Doc," I said.

"Where is your sister tonight?" Mrs. Walsh asked, shooting a knowing smile at me. "I expected her to be the belle of tonight's ball, next to Caroline, of course."

I watched the doctor's face as he replied. The smile remained, but somehow, it stiffened, as though he were speaking through some painful spasm.

"She's riding in with friends," he said evenly. "I expect she's been held up."

There was a general titter and I flushed.

Mrs. Walsh was saying, "Well, she better not be held up too long or all the cake will be..." when there was a shout, like the crack of a whip, and then the whinnying of hardworking horses. Someone shouted, "Well now, here they come!"

Most of the partygoers were sitting at tables, chattering and laughing over full plates, so I could see clearly the barouche that pulled up close to the picnic grounds. It was a grand, gleaming thing, wood polished until it glinted like gold in the fading light of day. Trigger Olsen sat in the driver's seat with a thin, grinning cowboy next to him. Ben Evans rode behind them, resplendent in a city hat and a brown suit cut to show his boyish figure. John Henry rode alongside his brother, dark as a shadow and somehow more real.

The barouche drew to a halt and Mrs. Jensen raced to greet them, her husband on her heels. Ben hopped down from his saddle and pumped Mr. Jensen's hand, his handsome face wreathed with congratulations. As the other Jensens, including Caroline, gathered around, it became clear that only *now* that the Evans were here could the party be considered a success.

No wonder Uncle Matthew can't stand them.

"You better get on over there, Cindy," the small woman said to Mrs. Walsh. "Or Lydia will be stealing all your thunder."

"Right." Mrs. Walsh breathed, breathless and wide-eyed. "Right."

She stepped away from the table, remembered her apron, and fumbled with it helplessly. I helped her out of it and she went hurrying off.

A small woman standing in line grinned at me. "*Now* Lydia Jensen will be happy."

I almost responded, "*Now* I know why she wasn't happy to see me."

Doctor Lowe didn't say anything. He moved off suddenly, with jerky movement, and settled at an empty table. There, he placed a napkin on his knee and began to eat, his back resolutely towards the new arrivals.

Over by the barouche, the women made their appearance. The Evans women had dressed for the part, Mrs. Varina Evans in a well-cut gray blue dress that set off her eyes well and Helen in yellow and black, her pregnancy disguised under clever layers of cloth. Helen looked tired but cheerful and went over to take her husband's arm, an almost protective gesture. I was surprised to see that their outfits, though well-suited and well-cut, were not substantially better than those worn by anyone else in the party.

The same could not be said of Sarah Lowe's dress. Red and black, dripping in detail, and complete with a matching hat and wrap, she looked as though she'd been cut right out of Godey's Lady Book – which was, perhaps, the intention. Trigger Olsen handed her down from the barouche as delicately as though she'd been made of glass.

My gaze shifted and found him. John Henry stood off to the side, his mouth twisted in a sour expression, his rigid posture keeping the crowd from fawning over him as they did over the others. I could appreciate that.

Sarah went right over to Caroline Jensen to congratulate the new bride. Even from a distance, I could see the bright expression on Sarah's face and the jaunty, confident tilt of her head. Standing in her shadow, no one could mistake the manner with which Caroline smoothed her skirt and shifted her feet. She'd been outshone at her own wedding and felt it keenly.

Sarah should know better, I thought. *She's overplaying her hand and the women here won't forget the slight. But maybe she won't have to worry about that when she's an Evans...*

"Sarah Lowe knows how to make an entrance," a small woman said.

"Yes," Ruth Danaher said from close by. "She's caught the fish, but hasn't quite reeled him in yet."

Annie came up beside me, her hands clutching her skirts, her face pinched with defensive anger. She may have been a wild-child of the prairie, but she was more observant than most. After a moment, she went charging through the crowd to her sister's side.

The Evans moved into the crowd and people turned back to the banquet tables. I served, craning my neck to look down the line. I saw Trigger Olsen and the cowboy in the line-up, cheerfully chatting with some of the townsmen. Without wanting to, my gaze shifted and located the Evanses.

They had settled at a table near Doctor Lowe. Ben and Sarah were the center of attention, the former shaking hands and working his salesman smile and the latter helping Helen get comfortable on the hard bench. Varina stood a little apart, talking with Mrs. Jensen, Mrs. Walsh, and the newest Mrs. Jensen. Varina treated Caroline kindly, respectfully, but her sharp gaze was constantly scanning the area, as though on the lookout.

My gaze shifted and I made eye contact with John Henry.

He stood with his hat in his hand, listening with half an ear to Mr. Jensen and a few other men, his expression tense and otherwise unreadable. When he saw that I was watching him, he bobbed his head in recognition, a slow grin stealing over his face.

That small movement was enough to alert the men around him. They glanced at me and I could see their interest spike. They'd all read my uncle's paper and they all knew about our first encounter. They were clearly curious as to whether there would be another scene – if I were a gambler, I'd have laid good odds that some were hoping there would be. The grin on one man's face was confirmation enough.

Then a horrifying thought struck me: I was going to have to serve these people. I was going to have to serve Sarah Lowe.

I won't! I can't and I won't!

Annie came back, shaking her head.

"Some people sure know how to kick up a fuss, don't they?" she asked sourly. She loaded pie on to her plate, dragged her finger through the sticky sweetness and stopped just before putting the finger in her mouth. "Are you all right, Jenny?"

I stirred myself and slapped at a wasp that was trying to get into the pie. "I'm fine."

"You don't look fine." She glanced over her shoulder. "John Henry sure does clean up nice, doesn't he?"

Startled, I looked at Annie and was even more shocked when I saw the grin tugging at her mouth. I should have known – she was her mother's daughter. It was on her account that I was invited to this party and her account that I was wearing a pretty new dress. But

I didn't owe Annie a confession and I wasn't inclined to confide. Especially when I had no clue as to what I was feeling.

"I hadn't noticed," I said stiffly and handed her the pie knife. "I'm feeling faint, standing in all this sun. Would you mind taking over for me?"

Annie took the knife, still grinning. I snatched a glass of lemonade from the drink table and scanned the grounds for a shady place to hide. Then it occurred to me what that would look like.

I'm a Goodnight. We don't hide.

So I straightened my shoulders and boldly made my way to sit next to Doctor Lowe. I didn't hide - but I did turn my back on the Evans family. I might be a Goodnight with too much pride for a proper Christian, but there were still limits.

FOURTEEN

octor Lowe was excellent company and despite a
lingering sense of discomfort that hovered over both of
us, we found plenty to talk about. I learned that he had
been in the war, as a medic. When I asked for details, he just
grinned at me.

"I think I'm going to pass on that question, Miss Jenny," he said.
"Weddings are not the place for war talk."

I didn't press.

The meal passed quickly. When everyone had eaten their full,
the wedding cake was cut and toasts were drunk. Mr. Jensen, pink-
faced and pleased as punch, announced that, once space had been
cleared, there would be dancing. We sprang to work, the women
clearing the dishes and food while the men hauled benches and
tables to the side. I spotted John Henry, sleeves rolled above his
elbows, lifting one side of a heavy table and calling out mock-taunts
to the Jensen and Walsh boys who were helping him. His relaxed
look suited him.

Dusk rolled in and lanterns appeared around the periphery of
the newly-made square. The musicians tuned up. Women gathered
in small bunches, touching their hair and eying prospective partners.
The men joked among themselves, shuffling their feet and trying not
to look at the women. Varina, Helen, and Sarah claimed spaces on
benches set out for the spectators. Ben and Doctor Lowe stood with

them, Ben with his hand on his wife's shoulder, Sarah looking up and laughing at something her brother said. Varina was talking, too, her eyes scanning the area, resting for a moment on John Henry. Her gaze caught mine and she gave me such an icy stare that I actually felt my spine freeze up. I had to turn away.

The band struck up a tune at last. The newlyweds were shoved out into the clearing and cheered as they attempted to dance. Eventually, Caleb gestured for others to join them and the floor filled quickly.

It was a picturesque scene. The music was simple but sweet, swelling into the soft night air. The sunset was a masterpiece of color, a glowing backdrop to the whirling skirts and stomping boots. There was more happiness present than one would expect in a town so plagued by unrest, and I was grateful for it.

The song ended and a lively new tune began. Judging from the roar of approval, it was a favorite. The boys surged forth to claim new partners, a few brushing by me in their quest. I was surprised at how many faces I knew already. Mrs. Thornton, the postmistress, had dragged Doctor Lowe onto the dance floor while her husband whirled about with Mrs. Walsh. Ben Evans danced energetically with Mrs. Jensen, his handsome face alight with childish pleasure.

Uncle Matthew is right – he is very young.

I didn't realize that I was looking for Sarah until I found her. She was standing a little away from Varina's bench, surrounded by a group of men, laughing prettily and a little too loudly at their jokes. She was showing off, but where was John Henry?

I found him quickly enough. He stood by the drinks table, leaning on a barrel, talking earnestly with a small balding man in a checked vest. He held a mug of beer in one hand and seemed absorbed in the conversation.

He may have been oblivious to his woman's displeasure, but Helen, Ben's wife, was not. She sat on the bench next to her mother-in-law, unconsciously stroking her stomach as she studied the schoolmarm. Her spun-gold hair glinted in the gloaming and I found myself wondering if she'd been so radiantly lovely before she married Ben or if this was an effect of the pregnancy.

Helen's worried gaze switched from Sarah to John Henry and then she caught sight of me, watching her. She smiled and tilted her head in a nod, as one might to a friendly new acquaintance.

I dropped my gaze. The music leader called a new song and partners switched again. Annie appeared at my side, holding a cup of lemonade, all nerves and excitement.

"Why aren't you dancing?" I asked.

She scoffed. "Who would I dance with? Why aren't you dancing?"

"I hardly know anyone."

"That's just the thing," she responded. "You're the mysterious woman who's just come into our lives. You're going to attract all kinds of attention, just you wait and see."

She took a drink of her lemonade and the music swelled up around us. Despite my doubts, a shiver of excitement that ran through my spine. It'd been a very long time since I'd been an object of interest to anyone and longer still since I'd been to a dance. The idea of being whirled about the floor made me feel girlish again, despite the haughty presence of Sarah Lowe and her escort across the way.

The music changed again. Sarah bade farewell to her admirers and tripped lightly, laughingly across the way to John Henry. He didn't require much pleading to be led out into the floor. Ben was now leading his mother out. Doctor Lowe had been seized by a woman I didn't know, but whose reddish hair reminded me of Mrs. Washington. I wondered where they were.

"Who needs to dance?" Annie said again. The manner with which she tossed her head and smoothed down her dress gave her away.

"It's good exercise," I said.

"Who needs that?"

She was scanning the crowd and her gaze stopped on Jeremiah. He was sitting on a bench, a little apart from the others, looking forlorn. His mother stood at the cake table, talking with a group of women while his father rested in the shadows by one of the beer barrels. Oscar was nowhere to be seen.

A glance at Annie's face revealed mingled emotions – relief, disappointment, and frustration.

Poor girl, I thought. *First crush.*

Sarah crossed my field of vision then, laughing up into John Henry's face, her body sinuously moving in time with his. They looked a picture, the pair of them, the tall cowboy and the lovely school mistress, and I could hardly stand it.

What difference does it make to you, Goodnight? You're not involved.

Just as I was about to conquer myself with reason, Sarah Lowe lifted her head and looked over his shoulder directly at me. A satisfied, triumphant smile lit her face.

That did it. I turned on Annie and declared, "Well, I'm not waiting around to be asked!" I stalked off around the periphery of the square, towards the bench where Jeremiah sat in misery.

He jumped when I tapped him on the shoulder.

"Mr. Danaher." I held out a hand. "Let's dance."

"*You* dance, ma'am?" He sounded almost scandalized.

"I'm a missionary, not a nun. Will you dance with me?"

He looked at his feet and blushed scarlet. "I'm not sure how."

"Then let me show you," I said.

He hesitated, but I had sudden, furious energy to burn. I dragged him off the bench and on to the edge of the dance square. Taking him by the shoulders, I led him in a simple step. Gradually, he relaxed and began to pick up on the timing.

"Why, Jeremiah!" I exclaimed. "You've been holding out on us!"

He grinned with the compliment, keeping his eyes on our feet. We swept past poor, thunderstruck Annie. The mere act of dancing was like a tonic. I found myself laughing with Jeremiah as our awkward steps led us again and again perilously close to other couples. All too soon, the tune ended and we paused, breathless, to clap for the musicians.

Jeremiah was beaming. "Dancing's fun," he declared. "Once you know how."

The musicians struck up a chord. All around us, couples came back together, eager for the next dance. Jeremiah turned to me to have another go, but I had a better idea. I pulled him across the earth floor until we were standing right in front of Annie.

"I'm winded," I announced. "Annie, would you cut in?"

The pair stared at each other for a long, shocked moment. Jeremiah turned an impossible shade of red and I started to think I'd made a dreadful mistake.

Then Annie said, "Yes!" and thrust her cup of lemonade into my hand. She took Jeremiah's arm and the change that swept over the boy's face was remarkable. He looked like he'd just run the gauntlet and emerged victorious. With a sweep of his arm, he pulled Annie onto the floor and then they were lost among the swirling skirts and stomping boots.

Excellent, I thought. *At least one of us doesn't have to be a wall-flower tonight.*

I was giddy from the exercise and the success of my efforts. The music welled up around me, caressing my shoulders as I stepped back into the crowd. I distinctly remember thinking, *I hope someone dances with me,* with the idea that, of course, I'd be asked. It was the kind of assurance that you have when you're very young or very foolish. For the briefest of moments, I forgot where I was and who I was. I was young again and the world stretched open before me like an unmarked scroll.

The song finished and a new one began. Partners pulled apart and reassembled. I stepped closer to the dance floor, but though I caught a few looks my way, no one approached me. I thought, *Look friendly, that's all,* and I smiled like a simpleton as the dancers whirled by. Sarah's laugh danced across the cheerful din. I saw that John Henry had led her back to the bench where Helen sat while he spoke with Ben. Sarah spoke cheerily to Varina, but her smile was forced and she fanned herself too vigorously.

You're so desperate to be an Evans that you're overplaying your hand.

The thought startled me with its clarity, but from the stiff way Varina Evans was responding to her, I guessed that Sarah's would-be-mother-in-law thought the same.

John Henry was looking in my direction again. I turned back to the dance floor and saw Jeremiah and Annie, merrily moving to their own beat. I was smiling when the tune ended, when the musician demanded that every man find himself a new girl, when the tide of men and women swept past me, chattering and careful to keep a good distance. And I *still* didn't get it, not even when I saw one young man glance at me, then at the Evanses, and turn away. The new tune sounded and the dancers returned to the floor. I stood on the edge of the square, like a child at an adult's party, and then I heard it.

"...some brass." A gruff voice spoke loudly over the merry tune. "But what would you expect from his niece?"

The words cut through my fairy-tale silliness like a knife through skin to bone. I turned and found the speaker, one of a pair of older women sitting a few yards away from me. They were ostensibly watching the dancing but they were old and bold and didn't even try to hide their interest in me.

Her companion agreed, saying, "You'd think she'd have the sense enough to know..."

I could easily have finished the sentence. They each gave me a satisfied glance before turning away. Their work was done - I stood there, stripped and gasping through the invisible wound that gaped open in my chest.

Don't let them get to you. Don't let them get to you, you were invited...

But it was too late. The illusion of inclusion was shattered and I once again stood on the outside looking in, the stranger, the interloper, and worse. I was a Goodnight in an Evans town and that couldn't be forgiven.

I felt a proper fool. I turned on my heel and made my way through the watching crowds, holding Annie's cup in my hand like a talisman, fighting back tears of embarrassment. I'd forgotten myself and my place in a public manner. I might as well have served Sarah Lowe. At least that would have preserved a modicum of my dignity.

The beverage table sat further back from the other tables and, unlit by lanterns, was in dark shadows. I was alone. I set the cup down and pressed my fists into my eyes, willing myself to hold it together. I could leave early, but I couldn't fall apart. I listened to the cheerful music and the sound lashed at my soul.

How could I be so blind, so stupid? Thinking even for a moment that you could be a part of something when you know you're just passing through? Why would you think anyone would...?

"Ma'am, would you like to dance?"

John Henry Evans had come up silently behind me, startling me with his deep rumble. He now stood over me, a barrel-chested statue, dressed in fine cambric and leather boots. His hair was already starting to rebel against the civilizing brush that had been applied to it earlier. His eyes, dark blue and glittering, offered no interpretation as he waited for my reply.

"I'm sorry?" I asked, trying to calm my suddenly thudding heart.

"It's a pretty easy question." He leaned forward until his face was uncomfortably close to mine. "I asked if you'd like to dance." His warm breath touched my face.

Was he mocking me? Had Sarah put him up to it? Yet, that was stupid: Sarah wouldn't waste the time. So what *did* this mean?

I didn't know, so I asked him: "Why would *you* want to dance with *me*?"

You hate my uncle, you should hate me, was what I didn't say.

"Well, ma'am, I don't know what they do back east, but here, there's a tradition of asking pretty girls to dance." He glanced around the floor and looked back at me. "'Sides, seems to me the locals are being a little skittish tonight. Thought I might ease their minds."

So. He'd noticed the shunning. It had nothing to do with being a *pretty girl*. He was asking out of a sense of charity, taking pity on the poor little missionary from out of town. I should have known that from the start. I had known it, actually. I just hadn't realized how lonely I was, how much I *wanted* to dance and be a real part of things until it became obvious that I couldn't. The last thing I wanted to do was be asked out of *pity*, least of all by Sarah Lowe's beau.

"Thank you, Mr. Evans," I said stiffly. "But I'd rather sit this one out."

I moved to go and his hand shot out to stop me.

"Why, Miss Goodnight, are you *afraid* to dance with me?"

My temper flared white hot. I whipped back around on him. "What a perfectly ridiculous suggestion!"

"Well, then?"

He extended his hand to me.

Heads turned to look in our direction. We were drawing attention. If I turned John Henry down, it'd be in front of an audience, an act I could never sponge away. Nevertheless, it would be the wise course of action. After all, he'd attacked my uncle and I had at least enough sense to keep my dignity and my distance. Moreover, I didn't need anyone's charity, especially that of an Evans.

Yet as I drew breath to refuse him, he said in a low tone that only I could hear, "Of course, if you're so afraid that you can't..."

That did it.

As soon as my hand touched his, John Henry grasped it, pulling me forward. Suddenly we were on the dance floor, his hand on my waist, the other firmly gripping my hand, his eyes fixed on mine as though he were trying to pin me in place, to keep me from running.

We went whirling about the square. John Henry set a lively pace and I was too shaken to do more than follow. I stumbled into the steps of the jig, much too occupied with trying not to trip to worry about anything else. It was confusing, awkward, strange, *wrong,* and I longed for the music to end so I could escape and cry by myself.

Finally the jig came to an end and the band, rather than take a breath, began a waltz. I started to pull away - the waltz is for lovers, not truced enemies - but John Henry's arm slipped further around my waist and held me firm.

"We only just got here," he declared.

I looked up and saw that he was grinning.

"Everyone's expecting fireworks between you and me," he said. "Well, let's really give them something to talk about. What do you say, Miss Goodnight?"

Unexpected warmth washed over me. His arm was holding me like he *wanted* me there, and his grin... Oh, his grin. It was boyish, mischievous, hard to resist. So I didn't.

"All right," I whispered.

The couples around us shifted, drifting apart and together again into different configurations, while the fiddles, adequate at the jig, sung the tune with surprising sweetness. John Henry was a good dancer, with firm, sure movements, and I now found myself falling into step without any trouble at all. My grip on his shoulder relaxed as I found less need to balance and we sailed about the floor with a natural ease.

As I grew comfortable, I became aware of other things. John Henry's hand, resting lightly on my waist, the callouses on the hand that held mine, the glint of the silver buttons on his shirt, the scent of cologne and leather, the warmth and proximity of his body. I had to quell a moment of panic and in doing so, I could practically hear Aunt Chastity scolding: *Any other day of the week, you'd have been thrilled to be dancing in the arms of a handsome man.*

I flushed when I realized that I'd referred to John Henry as 'handsome'.

We danced on and I could see the faces of those on the floor around us: curiosity and shock melted away to a new understanding. John Henry had broken the silent shunning by asking me on to the floor. I was now socially acceptable and eligible to dance with any man. Not that I wanted to... not just then, anyway.

Sarah Lowe's white face stood out among the crowd. Her expression was stony, yet calm, her tiny hands clenched into fists. Behind her was Varina Evans, silent, spectral, the very picture of disapproval. John Henry's influence only went so far and there were certain realities no one could change. My heart dropped into my stomach.

Nothing to worry about here, Sarah Lowe, I thought sourly.

John Henry must have noticed something for his arms tensed. When I looked up, there was a question in his eyes. Rather than answer it, I said, "You didn't have to do that, you know."

"Do what?"

"Ask me to dance." He looked at me sharply and I hastened to say, "You needn't take pity on me. I don't need it. I'm a missionary, a preacher's daughter. I'm accustomed to being the outsider, to being..."

Unwanted.

The thought struck without warning, making me stumble.

Unwanted is such a dreadful word and so dreadfully appropriate. I'd been useful once, helping my father, reaching out to souls, and educating the ignorant. Now I was dead weight. The committee didn't need a dried-up, leaderless missionary woman and there was no place for me here in Legacy. Even back in Dandridge, Aunt Alice had said she *might* have a job for me in the new school. A possibility, not a definite. Jenny Goodnight, once the fearless Servant of God with stars in her eyes, was awash, adrift, lost, and in the arms of an enemy on a dance floor in the middle of nowhere, with nowhere to go and no one to serve.

I might as well have said unwanted.

Not that I would have, of course. I still had that much pride.

John Henry hadn't replied. He just looked at me, his blue eyes pensive. I had to drop my gaze, embarrassed that I'd said so much, worrying that he could read my thoughts on my face.

Stupid, stupid...

Then he spoke.

"Miss Goodnight, I don't know what ideas you have in your head about me or Legacy in general. I can't say I've ever understood women. The plain truth of the matter is this: I saw a pretty young woman across the way, helping a shy young kid not only to read but to get out of his own way. I also saw that no man had the intelligence to ask that pretty young woman to dance."

Then he leaned in and whispered in my ear. "I thought, 'John Henry, you better go and do something about that.'" His grip on my hand tightened ever so slightly. "So I did."

He had no idea the effect of his closeness. It was all I could do to keep dancing, to keep my grip from tightening. I wanted to run away and hide and I never wanted to leave the circle of his arms.

John Henry didn't appear to notice my distress. "Miss Goodnight," he murmured in a low rumble, his breath touching my ear. "Why don't you stop worrying about what others might be thinking and just dance with me?"

I couldn't have answered even if I wanted to. John Henry drew me closer, and the dance went on. The music filled the night air and everything else drifted away on it, until there was only the two of us, dancing in time to the music, my hand in his and his shoulder under my grasp, and the moon overhead. I wanted nothing more than to lay my head on his chest and close my eyes and remain there forever.

Just when I was about to slip completely under the spell, whether it was his or the music's or something else altogether, a man's shout, like a crack of a whip, ripped us rudely back into the present.

"Damn you, Goodnight!"

FIFTEEN

The cry came from the other side of the floor. I didn't recognize the voice. Then a second sound, like something heavy and wooden hitting the ground and shattering, rang out, followed by another shout. John Henry was gone then, pulling away from me, and striding towards the fight. I felt stripped, as though something essential had been ripped away. I picked up my skirts and hastened after him though the gradually awakening dancers.

A knot of men had gathered in front of the beer barrels, where all evening the party-goers had been back and forth, refilling their tankards. John Henry elbowed his way through them. I followed in his wake.

Two of the beer barrels lay on the ground in the small clearing. One had burst open and the odor of yeast mingled unpleasantly with the smell of ageing food and sweating bodies.

Trigger Olsen was picking himself off the ground, a thin trickle of blood dripping from his mouth. Ben Evans stood in front of him, defensive, nervous. He was jacketless and rumpled, and he looked ready to fight or run. Judging from the tiny, gold-tinted pistol in his trembling hand, he'd decided to fight. The man he was aiming it at was Matthew Goodnight.

I really ought to have been used to transformations by then, but I still gasped at the sight of my uncle. He stood – or rather swayed –

in the dim twilight, facing Ben with the thuggish sort of courage that drink provides. His face was twisted in a sneer, his good hand reddened from the encounter with Trigger. In the other hand, he held an envelope, dirtied and worn.

"...a pretty gun for a pretty boy," he was saying as he took a lurching step forward. "Are you sure you know how to handle that, sonny?"

"What's going on here?" John Henry's voice was a low, dangerous rumble. When I glanced at him, I saw that the relaxed man I'd been dancing with was gone. Here, instead, was the angry rich rancher I'd met in the print shop only two weeks ago, dark and furious with clenched fists.

Uncle Matthew started at the sound, almost falling over.

"Ah! John Henry," he said, leaning on the drinks cart for support. "I was wondering when you'd get here."

"Stay out of this, John Henry," Ben said. "This has nothing to do with you." The tremor in his gun hand worsened.

Uncle Matthew put his finger to his lips.

"Little children," he said, slowly, "should be seen and not..."

I moved before my uncle could finish the hazardous thought, putting myself between them, my back to Ben, covering my uncle. I put my hand on Uncle Matthew's arm, intending to push him back, yet staggering though he was, he was unyielding.

"Uncle Matthew!" My voice was unnaturally high. "I wasn't expecting you to come tonight."

My father's old saying ran through my head: *"Blessed are the peacemakers, indeed, for they are usually the first martyred..."*

I tried to lace my arm through his, but he shrugged me off.

"Aw, I never miss a good party, Jenny-girl! Besides..." he beamed triumphantly here. "I wanted to see the Evans boys and here they are..."

"Uncle..."

Now he pushed me. "Not now, girl. I have business."

"Uncle Matthew, please..."

He pulled me forward, until all I could see were his eyes, ablaze with anger toward me. "I *saw* you," he hissed. "You, you..."

"Goodnight," John Henry broke through my shock and Uncle Matthew's ramblings. "You're drunk."

Uncle Matthew released me and drew himself upright. "That might be true, Evans. But I'm here on business. *Pinkerton* business."

He held up the letter and a general gasp filled the air. He was pleased and kept his arm extended. Only I saw the trickle of blood, working its way down his arm. At some point in tonight's altercation, the Matheson wound had re-opened.

"That's right!" Uncle Matthew slurred, oblivious to blood and danger. "I have it here, the evidence that I've been waiting for." He pointed to Ben, then to John Henry. "It is over, Evans. All done, finite, caput. You're through. What I have here," and he waved the envelope as he stumbled towards John Henry, his face bright in sickening triumph, "is the end of the Evans legacy. I'm going to ruin you, John Henry Evans. Better still, I'm going to let you ruin yourself."

John Henry glared at him. "Not here, Goodnight. Not here."

"Why not here? Don't the people have a right to know what kind of people they are putting their trust in? Or is there some other reason? Did I, perhaps," and here he turned and sneered at me, "*interrupt* something?"

I blushed up to the roots of my hair and averted my gaze. I saw Doctor Lowe, standing on the outskirts of the crowd. He looked horrified and disgusted, biting his nails in tension, and shame displaced my horror.

I said, "Uncle Matthew, please..." but he made a motion as though to dismiss me.

"Evans," he announced. "You're through. Better get used to it."

"What are you talking about, Goodnight?" Trigger Olsen stood leaning on the table, his long, lean physique poised close enough to interfere if necessary.

"Find yourself a new job, Olsen," Uncle Matthew crowed. "The Evanses won't be able to support a chicken, let alone a stable hand."

"Goodnight, I'm warning you," John Henry said, but someone else shouted, "That's a lot of talk, Goodnight! Why don't you back it up with some evidence?"

There was a general roar of approval. As much as people wanted to support the Evans family, their curiosity overcame loyalties. If there was dirt, they wanted to revel in it.

The sound was hungry and fearsome and it was just what Uncle Matthew had been hoping for. He nodded, swaggering forward with the envelope in his hand. "It's coming, folks, its coming..."

John Henry stood his ground. "You haven't got anything, Goodnight, except a bellyful of liquor and a mouthful of hogwash. Go home."

"That's mighty bold talk for a man standing in quicksand."

"You're drunk."

"Drunk or sober, doesn't change what's written on this here paper, now does it, John Henry Evans, king of the county?"

"Goodnight," Ben said. In the exchange, we'd almost forgotten about him. "You go home, you hear? Just shut up and go home."

The gun glinted in his shaking hands. I saw the pallor in his face, the frightened look melting into resolution and I found myself moving forward, hand extended. John Henry stepped in my way, but he wasn't squaring off to Uncle Matthew – he was facing his own brother.

"Put it down, Ben," he said.

"That's right, Ben," Uncle Matthew said, his voice booming in my ear. "Listen to your big brother. Don't want to start something you can't rightly finish, now, do you?"

John Henry swung about, his face black with anger.

"Goodnight, I've had about all I'm going to take from you," he boomed, glaring over my head to the man behind me. "Be quiet or someone is going to carry you home. Ben, put it away – he just isn't worth it."

But Ben's grip had tightened with his resolve. "You didn't hear what he said, John Henry. You don't know..."

"He's drunk," I pleaded. "He doesn't know what..."

Ben cut me off. "I *know* what he said. I *know* what he means. And he isn't going to get away with it."

He wasn't kidding and he wasn't just making a stand: he intended to kill a man today, no matter how his hands shook. If the sneer on my Uncle Matthew's face said anything, it was that he welcomed the bullet. John Henry and I were all that stopped them, our hands up, our bodies blocking theirs.

There was a breathless anticipation in the crowd around us and the stillness was suffocating. All that could be heard was Ben's ragged breath and my own thudding heart. No one dared speak, lest the slightest sound set off something no one could stop.

John Henry shifted and my eyes locked on him. He was in the middle as I was, trying to keep the balance of danger from shifting. I felt at once alienated from him and united, wishing that I could thrust him out of the way even while praying that he'd be strong enough to hold his position. We were in no-man's land, in as much danger as I'd ever been, and there was nowhere for us to go.

Ben Evans licked his lips, his eyes darting between the three of us.

"I don't care what he said," John Henry said slowly, his eyes never leaving his brother. "It isn't worth it, Ben. You know that it isn't worth it."

"John Henry," Ben spoke low. "Step out of the way or I'll..."

There was a whisper in the crowd, a rustling sound, and suddenly Helen appeared like a heroine in a yellow-back novel, eyes wide and luminous in the moonlight. She stopped, hands clutching her skirt, her eyes jumping from Ben to Uncle Matthew. When she saw my uncle, she looked as though she were about to be sick.

I glanced at Uncle Matthew. Naked pain and anguish stained his face. He looked like he'd just been gutted.

"Helen," he said and there was a world of history in the intonation.

She looked away from him to Ben and the moment was lost. My uncle's face hardened to stone and I turned when I heard Sarah Lowe say, "What in the world...?"

She and Varina had appeared behind Helen. Doctor Lowe moved swiftly, putting himself between Sarah and the men. He looked grim and disgusted. Helen made as though to go to Ben, but Varina caught her arm. She held on to the young wife, her face deadly cold as she surveyed the scene, her two sons squaring off as I shielded my drunk, suicidal relative.

Helen's presence seemed to throw Ben off balance. His eyes flickered from her to John Henry to me to Uncle Matthew and then back to Helen. His grip on the pistol slackened. He licked his lips again, a sign, I hoped, of uncertainty.

Then Uncle Matthew snorted.

"He won't pull that trigger," he said, pulling himself upright. "He's just like his old man – hasn't the guts to kill a man in the open. He's got to do it on the sly, don't you, boy?"

Ben made an inarticulate cry. The pistol came up. My uncle's eyes gleamed in terrible satisfaction. He moved forward. I moved to intercept him. John Henry and Trigger Olsen jumped for Ben, Helen screamed, and in the middle of all of that, the gun went off.

I slammed into Uncle Matthew and fell, bringing him part of the way down with me. In the tangled confusion of arms, legs, and skirts, I couldn't tell whether someone had been shot or not. Uncle Matthew was shouting incoherently and shoved me hard away from him as he staggered back up on his feet. I swallowed dirt and scratched my face. Something warm and wet spread out over my leg and I panicked, thinking Uncle Matthew had been shot and he was bleeding on me. I squirmed and twisted around, looking for him.

It wasn't blood – it was beer, leaking out through the new bullet hole and splashing onto the ground. Trigger Olsen had Ben's gun, rapidly pulling the cartridges out as John Henry shoved back a few eager would-be brawlers. Helen pulled away from Varina to get to Ben.

Uncle Matthew was staggering over to where Ben, defeated and shaken, leaned against the cart. As I watched, my uncle leaned in to say something.

Whatever he whispered sent Ben into a frenzy. Both men went down, fists flying, grunts echoing through the clearing. The crowd roared and Helen cried out, a piteous mew, as Varina caught her. Trigger and John Henry dove into the fray.

The fight lasted forever and ended in a moment, as John Henry and Olsen imposed their will on the others. I was on my feet when they pulled Ben off my uncle. Both men were bloodied and enraged. John Henry had to practically body-slam his brother out of my uncle's reach.

Trigger and another man pinned Ben's arms, restraining the young man while John Henry turned and shoved Uncle Matthew back.

"Now you just cut that out!" Trigger shouted. "This is no way to celebrate a wedding!"

"Always need to have one of your hands to get you out of a scrape, haven't you, Benjie?" Matthew snarled, regaining his footing. "Never can finish a thing yourself, can you?"

"Goodnight!" John Henry's voice boomed ominously over all the other noise, cutting off all smattering of conversations. "You can just shut up."

He towered over everyone and everything and in a split second, I saw what my uncle was saying: it didn't matter who wore the badge or who was elected to which post in this town. When an Evans spoke, the world ground to a halt.

Uncle Matthew was swaying on his feet, the sneer still curling his lips. John Henry, temper completely lost, grabbed my uncle by the shirt collar, and threw him backwards into the dust. Uncle Matthew landed hard, right next to where I stood. His head slapped against the hardened earth, and I saw his face twist in pain. He coughed and spat blood. He looked dazed and turned gray, an expression I knew well - he was about to black out.

John Henry either didn't realize this or he didn't care. He strode forward menacingly, his hands flexing in anticipation. I jumped between him and the fallen man. My hands flew up, landing on his chest.

"Stop!" I cried out. "Just stop it! He's had *enough!*"

John Henry stopped, towering over me, his eyes looking ready to kill someone. But he did stop.

For another long moment, stillness held. I stood where I was, arms extended, eyes on John Henry, wishing he'd look at me. He was coiled as tight as a rattler ready to strike and his eyes blazed with a furious light. I *knew* that if he decided to kill my uncle, I couldn't - and the others wouldn't - stop him.

Look at me, look at me...

He wouldn't look at me. We'd gone back to the beginning, as if the dance had never happened. We were enemies and the only thing keeping him in line was the fragile hold of civilized convention. Men simply didn't beat men to death at a wedding party. As bad as it got out here, it was never quite that barbaric.

John Henry knew this and conformed. When he stepped back, I knew there would be no further bloodshed that night. But he still wouldn't look at me.

"Take him home, Jenny Goodnight," John Henry said, in a hoarse, empty voice. "You get him out of here before he has a chance to say anything else, you hear?"

With that, he turned, grabbed his brother by the arm, and pulled him into the crowd and out of my sight.

SIXTEEN

After the stony-faced Doctor Lowe determined that my uncle would not die of his head wound, Mr. Walsh and his son helped me haul him home.

Uncle Matthew was more drunk than I had ever seen him before. He raved incoherently and fought us at every step. We loaded him into the wagon and drove the short distance through town. I sat in the back, cradling his head from the jolts and jars of the ride, ignoring his wild insults and half-formed accusations. He'd seen me dancing with John Henry and had taken it as a personal betrayal. The Evanses, Lowes, and Walshes were also targets of his fury, along with Ben's supporters. The only exception seemed to be Helen: his rant ended in a strangled cry when he mentioned her.

Humiliation washed over me. I wished he'd come to at the house rather than have the Walshes hear this. "It'll be all right, Uncle Matthew. Just lie still."

"...looking like a hussy and stealing my employees from me..."

I looked down at him, surprised. "Stealing your employees? What are you talking about?"

He didn't hear me. He'd lapsed into unconsciousness again.

We pulled up to the still house and the two silent Walsh men hauled him out of the wagon and on to his feet. He feebly tried to fight them off, accusing them of being 'bought men' and the like. They pinned his arms to his side and half dragged, half carried him into the house and up the stairs. I followed, carrying his hat and the Pinkerton envelope, which he had dropped in the excitement.

Over Uncle Matthew's protests, they dumped him on the bed. Mr. Walsh, his weathered face creased with concern, turned to me, standing in the doorway.

"Are you going to be all right?" he asked.

Behind him, Uncle Matthew attempted to raise himself up, but his head was too heavy and he fell back. His rantings had subsided into mutterings and his movements became less and less violent. I'd dealt with drunks before and knew the patterns. He was about to fall asleep and once he did, memories of tonight would be patchy at best. Like as not, he'd forget everything he said to me. He might even forget about the dance. I hoped he would.

"Thank you," I said. "I can take it from here."

Mr. Walsh looked at his son, who shrugged. Somewhere in the distance, merry fiddles could be heard. The wedding party was carrying on as before.

"You go," I said. "Your daughter got married today. You should be with her, not playing nurse-maid to my uncle. Go on. I'm fine."

Mr. Walsh glanced over his shoulder. Uncle Matthew was flat on his back now, eyes closed, mouth working silently. Reassured, the Walshes departed.

I went downstairs to get some water and a cloth. When I came back, Uncle Matthew was so still that I thought he was asleep. He startled the moment I touched his face with the wet cloth and grabbed my wrist in a tight grip.

"You..." he gasped, his eyes wild. "You came here to ruin me."

I yanked my arm away. "Don't be absurd."

I tried again to clean his face and he slapped at my hand.

"Don't touch me!" he snapped.

"Uncle, please..."

"...acting like you're all sweetness and light..."

His flailing leg sent the night-stand spinning, books and papers scattering in the whirlwind. I ignored my uncle's ramblings and mechanically moved to pick up the mess. I was exhausted, the night's drama weighing heavily on my shoulders. I felt as though I'd run through mud all day and my head was starting to throb with pain. I collected the papers, noting, off-handedly, that they were letters, some of them with Pinkerton's logo. I added his new one to the collection, too tired to even feign interest in them.

Behind me, Uncle Matthew had pulled a bottle from under his pillow. He removed the cork with his teeth, eying me in defiance. *Take it. Try and take it.*

I didn't. I was tired and I thought, *Drink yourself into oblivion.*

"What are we going to do about Matheson?" I asked.

"What do *you* know about Matheson?" he slurred.

"I know you have to pay him in a few days. Have you gotten the money?"

He pulled the bottle from his mouth, smacking his lips. "That's none of your business. And don't touch my things."

"I'm just tidying. Do you have enough to pay him? I earned some this week and I can give you..."

"I won't need *your* money. Don't need the help of any woman, least of all *you.*"

He spat the words out with disdain.

I ignored him. I stacked the papers and the books carefully and reached for the nightstand to straighten it. That's when I spotted the false bottom of the lower shelf. It had popped open when my uncle kicked it and there lay the leather journal that I'd seen my uncle so jealously guarding early on. Newspaper clippings, yellowed and smudged, were spilling out of it.

I glanced over my shoulder, but my uncle had fallen back against the mattress, suckling the bottle like an infant, his eyes closed. He looked as though he might go to sleep. I waited to see if his eyes would flutter open. When they didn't, I reached for the book.

It was water-stained and loosely bound with leather straps that had given way in the tumble. The cream colored pages were lined and most covered in my uncle's cramped handwriting, both in pen and pencil. But it was the clippings that really caught my attention.

They were a disparate bunch, some from newspapers, and others from magazines, some quite old and others very new. I thought at first that they must be about the Evans family – my uncle's research, perhaps, - but there was only one: a short notice regarding the wedding of Ben and Helen Evans. It had been crinkled in anger and smoothed out again dozen times or more.

None were written by my uncle and they were all small articles about small crimes, not the sort of thing he was normally interested in. One was about an immigrant who repeatedly deserted the Union army during the war in order to reenlist as a hired draftsman, another was a notice from a family who was offering a reward for the return of their daughter and the black man who'd kidnapped her. One was about a husband and wife con-team suspected of murder, another about a man who deserted his family back east so he could run off with a dance-hall girl. There were at least a half-dozen of these notices, none of which were local, none of which appeared to have any bearing on anything that was happening in the town.

Why would he keep these hidden? I wondered as I turned the pages of the heavily used journal. *Why have these at all?*

When I lifted my eyes, I saw again the new envelope from the Pinkerton Detective Agency, marked personal and confidential. My curiosity overcame any concerns about privacy and confidentiality. I reached for the envelope and pulled out the letter. Only it wasn't a letter at all: it was a blank sheet of paper whose color did not match the stationery envelope.

Shock and sudden realization washed over me. Uncle Matthew had gone to the wedding to start a fight on purpose. He'd brought the envelope to make his point, but hadn't wanted to risk the real letter being damaged or stolen, so he'd hidden it somewhere else. Which meant that the contents were just as explosive as he'd hinted.

The Evanses are right to be afraid...

I don't know which I was aware of first: Uncle Matthew's roar or the powerful box on the ears that sent me flying across the floor. One minute I was kneeling, poring through my uncle's journal, the next I was on my back, hands empty and flung out protectively in front of my face against the specter of my uncle, looming furious and unsteadily in front of me.

"...private property!" he was screaming over the ringing in my ears. "Getting into *everything*, ruining *everything*! What were you looking for, you snooping little bitch?"

His face was purple with rage. Fear made me choke on my words. In the half-second that it took for me to realize what was happening, he'd grabbed me by the hair, pulling me up to my knees. I cried out in pain and reached for his hand. He shook me, my hair tearing in his grasp.

"What were you looking for?" His whiskey infused breath nearly choked me. "Trying to get in good with the Evanses, were you? Trying to ruin *me*, weren't you? *Weren't* you?!?"

"I wasn't – I'm sorry – "

He shook me again and released me abruptly. But this was only to give him space for the backhand that sent me spinning towards the door. I caught the floor with my hands. My mouth was full of blood – it dripped down my chin, onto the dress, the dress Mrs. Walsh had given me. For a panicked moment, I thought my teeth had been jarred loose. I heard my uncle's step behind me and I rolled over to face him.

He stood over me, black and terrible, the bottle in one hand, the other clenched in a fist. His eyes were crazed, murderous, and the strength leached out of my limbs before his terrible wrath.

"You won't ruin this for me, Jenny Goodnight," he hissed. He swayed and his lack of sobriety was another source of terror for me. "I'll kill you before I let you interfere, do you hear me?"

He's drunk. He doesn't mean it...

I must have said this out loud, for he roared with fury and grabbed my hair again.

"I have the Evanses right where I want them, girl," he screamed at me. "I have them in my grasp and no one can save them, especially not a sanctimonious, dried up little old church mouse like you. No one will stop me, do you hear me? I will ruin them as they ruined me and *nothing* can save them."

He released my hair and took his boot to shove me back towards the door.

"As for you," he said. "You're taking the next stage out of here, do you hear me? You're leaving. Now *get out!*"

I didn't stop to argue. I didn't try to reason. Blind, unthinking panic had me in its cold grip. I crawled out of that room, slipping on the skirt, tearing it as I tried to flee. I was barely out the door when he slammed it shut behind me.

I didn't stop until I was in my own room, with the door shut and latched, the bed against it to bar his entry. I crawled into the furthest corner of the room, and huddled there like an animal, shaking and pressing one fist against my mouth, the other hand wrapped around my father's gun. I didn't realize I was crying until tears fell on my clenched hands. Through the door, I could hear my uncle's rage, venting itself by throwing furniture and roaring into the night.

It seemed that hours passed before finally his rage went still and the house quiet. I cried soundlessly, praying in the corner until at last exhaustion got the better of me. I crawled into bed and shivered there until sleep came to claim me.

SEVENTEEN

I awoke aching all over and more exhausted than when I'd gone to bed. The welt on my mouth had swollen into a bruise, making it painful to move my jaw. I lay there, sweltering in the early morning heat for a long time, memories of last night's fight playing in my head over and over again.

This wasn't the first time I'd had to deal with a drunken family member nor was it the first time I'd been hit, but it had been a while and I was out of practice. Uncle Matthew had frightened me, making me feel as I did when I was a young woman, alone on the prairie with a drunken father who was enraged at the government and still unable to tell me the truth about his relationship with a strange woman. I felt exposed and raw. Whereas before, with my father, my nursing instincts had kicked in, drawing on an inner conviction that all could yet be made right, I had no such feeling that morning.

What exactly had provoked him to attack *me* like that? What could possibly be in that Pinkerton letter? The Ezra Jones scandal was old news, not the sort of thing to provoke the blind panic that I saw in Ben Evans' ashen face or the pain in Helen's.

Uncle Matthew, what have you done?

My head began to throb with the familiar signs of an oncoming headache. I reached up to rub my temples and winced when my fingers found the bruise. I'd hit my head harder than I remembered, which probably accounted for my stiff neck.

I must look a mess.

Worse than that, I looked like a walking inspiration for gossip.

Had it been Monday, I would never have left my room. News of last night's debacle would be everywhere by now and the welt on my lip would only inspire more and worse trouble besides. But it wasn't Monday – it was Sunday and never in my life had I let a Sabbath go by without attending services. Rain or shine, good health or poor, I obeyed that commandment, feeling that, as a minister's daughter, I had a special responsibility to set a good example.

That morning I hesitated. My presence was likely to cause trouble and scandal, which was a good reason not to go. Then I realized that I didn't want to stay here, in this house, under my uncle's roof, within his hearing. I wanted to run away as far as possible. I couldn't leave town, not without breaking my promise to my aunt, but I didn't have to be here when Uncle Matthew woke up.

So I rose, gingerly cleaned my face, and pulled on my old brown dress. The dress that Mrs. Walsh had so generously loaned me was spattered with dust and stained with dried beer and droplets of blood. It would be difficult, if not impossible to clean, another loss from last night's fiasco.

Not likely I'll be invited to another dance in this town anyway.

I didn't allow myself to think about the waltz or of John Henry. The impression of his arm around my waist and his eyes on my face had haunted my dreams and embarrassed me in the light of day. John Henry was either being kind, which was humiliating, or cruel, which was somehow easier to deal with. I decided that either way, the matter was best never thought of.

Physical fear is difficult to overcome, especially when you have once been accustomed to it. I had to force myself to go leave the room and slip silently down the stairs. The air outside was refreshing, yet being outdoors made me feel more exposed. I found myself wishing that I were Catholic, for the veils that my mother used to wear when she slipped out of my aunt's house in the early mornings to join the foreigners in their Mass. I decided I could sit in the back of the church without causing all that much comment, especially if I waited until after the first song began. If I slipped out before the last song ended, no one would even notice me.

I hadn't considered Jeremiah Danaher. He waved me over to his pew the moment I walked in. I couldn't ignore him and the bonnet I wore didn't keep him from seeing the bruise. His face tightened.

"You all right?" he asked.

That drew Mrs. Danaher's attention. Her severe expression melted when she saw my face.

I cursed the weakness that made me sit with a friend rather than in the back as I originally intended. I whispered that I was quite all right and held the hymnal high on my face, blocking the curious stares as much as possible. I spotted the Evanses right away: Varina sitting like a queen, Helen's golden hair glinting, and Ben's pale face nervously scanning the room. Sarah was there, too, back ram-rod straight, her eyes straight ahead. Doctor Lowe looked uncomfortable and more mortician-like than ever.

I avoided looking at John Henry's broad back. When we finished the opening hymn, I focused on my Bible and kept my head low. It was the beginning of another miserably hot day and the church, properly packed with worshipers, was almost unbearable. When the service finally came to an end and the last song began, I left the pew with a nod towards Jeremiah.

The relative coolness of the open air was a relief after the stuffy interior, though I didn't have much time to enjoy it. People were beginning to slip out already. I kept my head down and moved to the side yard, where the horses and buggies were waiting. I thought I'd made it unnoticed, but luck was against me.

"Miss Goodnight."

John Henry was standing not five yards away, his hand on his bridle, and his gaze on me.

In the second it took me grasp his presence, he crossed the distance between us. Putting one gloved hand on my shoulder and the other under my chin, he lifted my face until I was looking into his hard blue eyes.

"Where did you get that?" he demanded.

If he knows, he'll kill Uncle Matthew.

Struck dumb, I hesitated, touching the offending spot. Before I could formulate a reply, chatter drew John Henry's attention. He looked up and I used the opportunity to escape his grasp. I ran, heart pounding, face aflame.

I didn't stop running until I gained the relative security of my uncle's house and slammed the door shut behind me. There in the shadowed hallway, I leaned against the door, struggling to calm my breath and my mind.

I was trapped. I couldn't go out with my face like this and staying in meant that, sooner or later, I would be running into my uncle again. I didn't want to stay, but I couldn't bear to leave, either.

Pull yourself together, girl!

My indecision disgusted me. This wasn't the first time I'd been forced to take shelter, nor the first time I'd had to share a roof with a violent man. And I knew, deep down, that my uncle was not really a threat to me.

At least, that's what I told myself as I absently rubbed at the swelling on my mouth.

Some things must be faced. And the sooner they are, the better.

I forced myself back upstairs.

Uncle Matthew was already gone. His bed was disheveled, some of his clothes were missing. The books that I had so carefully lined up on his shelves were scattered across the floor. The journal, of course, was gone. I stood in the doorway of his abandoned room, rubbing my arms and trying not to admit to myself that I was relieved. I wouldn't be hit again until he returned.

Reprieve, I thought. I could only hope that he wasn't getting into trouble somewhere else.

Unable to stand any more inactivity, I ran into my room. I grabbed my Bible, my mother's rosary, and my stained dress. Hands full, I hesitated nonetheless at the doorway. After a moment, I went back to my bed.

My father's pistol was still under my pillow, loaded and ready. I took it and went downstairs to wait for my uncle's return.

EIGHTEEN

Sunday never passed so slowly. I grew weary of listening for footsteps that never came, and broke the Sabbath to clean. I scrubbed the dress and left it soaking in a solution while I dusted, swept, and scrubbed. I cleaned windows and floors and polished the piano keys until they shone. I went into my uncle's room to tidy it, aware as I was of the possible consequences. Curiosity overrode my natural caution: I even rooted through the ticking in search of the missing scrapbook. It wasn't there, though – all I got were scratches on my arms and a panicked moment when something crawled up my sleeve.

I cleaned until sweat poured down my back. I was exhausted, yet still there was day left. Afternoon crawled into evening, sunlight became twilight. I began to worry. Uncle Matthew had been in such a foul, reckless mood and he had to be worried about Matheson's money. If he was leaning on the wrong people to get it...

I waited until dark to go out in search of him. I pulled a shawl over my head and tucked the edges around my face to disguise the bruising. It did a better job than my bonnet had. I put my father's gun in a satchel and left, only to find myself hesitating on the back step.

A cool breeze sliced through the yard, touching my face and making me feel more exposed than before.

Come on, girl.

Moonlight poured onto the streets. Legacy by night is no different than any other small town. There were lights in the windows, a few people passing silently on foot or horse back. Hardly anyone looked at me as I passed along the street and for this I was glad. I moved quickly and soon found myself in front of the print shop.

It was closed, the shades down and no light coming from any crack. Jeremiah had shown me where the hidden keys were, so I let myself in. There was no sign of my uncle, not in the print shop, nor his office, nor in the attic storage area. I locked the door before I left to continue my search.

Markum's Hotel was in the middle of town, right in the center of the hubbub. Light and raucous laughter poured through the windows out into the street. Legacy, like my uncle, had not quite outgrown its rough and tumble roots.

The hotel was like any one of the dozens of hotels that sprung up like weeds on the frontier, half boarding house, and half-drinking establishment. Inside, it was furnished with a mixture of luxury imported items, furniture from local craftsmen and leftovers from other failed hotels. The front desk was finely made, the polished wood gleaming in stark contrast with the peeling wall paper behind it. Markum had big dreams and was taking the path of least resistance to get there.

There was no one behind the front desk. I rang the bell and looked around. The noise from the bar was loud and friendly. I peeked in to see if Markum was behind the bar or, better still, my uncle was in front of it. I was disappointed on both counts. Traveling salesmen and local yokels in varying states of poverty and dishevelment watched as a youngish woman with a generous figure poured liquor out of a dark bottle. Liam Danaher was among them, a dark and sour specter, drinking his liquor like it was a solemn and painful ritual.

One of the other men spotted me and raised his glass.

"Lookee here!" he said. "It's Jenny Goodnight, the fastest lady draw in town!"

His laughter set off a chain reaction of levity and curious stares from down the bar. As heads turned in my direction, I saw another that I recognized. Trigger Olsen was at the bar with a shot glass in one hand and a bottle in the other. When he saw me, he started and began to rise out of his seat.

"Can I help you?"

A tall young woman now stood behind the front desk. She wore thick makeup and a dress that drew attention to every curve, and her eyes were tired and haughty. She looked me up and down and her estimation was plain on her face: I was no threat, though I was most certainly an annoyance. I saw that she wasn't quite as young as her make-up implied and for a moment, I pitied her, trapped in such a life.

Perhaps the pity showed on my face, for she drew herself up and looked at me with distaste.

"If you're collecting for something, Miss Goodnight, I think you'll find that we gave on Sunday," she drawled.

I ignored this and stepped forward. "I'm looking for my uncle. I thought he might be here."

As I moved, the shawl slipped from my head. She saw my bruise and winced, but she was not inclined to be helpful.

"This hotel operates on strict confidentiality," she said. "I couldn't say if he was or wasn't here, if you know what I mean."

She said it to make me uncomfortable, perhaps even to shock me. She didn't know her audience. I'd seen degradation before, with and without the trimmings of would-be luxury. Suddenly I was weary. I didn't want to play games. I had a hard enough chore to do without descending into a battle of words with a woman whose only means of support was supping off of men's depravities.

"In that case, you may fetch me Mr. Markum, your boss." I arranged the shawl around my shoulders, dismissing her with the chore, a trick I learned from Grandmother Goodnight.

"Why would I do that?" she sneered.

"Because I'm Matthew Goodnight's niece. And he'll want to see me."

Truth be told, this approach was a gamble. Matthew Goodnight had influence, but I didn't know if it extended here.

A hardened, hate-filled expression crossed the other woman's face. When she spoke, her tone was no longer playful. "I'll get him," she said and she fairly stalked around the corner and down the hallway in the back.

I hardly had time to register my success when the front door burst open and heavy boots thundered across the floor. John Henry Evans strode in, ready for war. He didn't see me. He was charging towards the staircase, when I, thinking that he was also looking for my uncle, spoke up.

"I'm starting to think you only have one method of entering a room, Mr. Evans," I called. "As if you had a battle to fight single-handed."

My voice brought him up short. He turned, a frown creasing his expression. He took in the bruising on my face and his lips tightened. He ambled over toward me, hands on his hips, close to the thick leather belt that held his holster. He didn't stop until he was towering over me.

"And you, Miss Goodnight," he said, in his low rumble, "have the habit of showing up in the most unusual places." He gestured towards my face. "Who gave that to you?"

"It was an accident, that's all."

A moment of intense silence. We stood like pieces on a chess board, cool and calculating. Then he stepped closer and said in a low and dangerous voice: "I don't know that it was an accident, Miss Goodnight. But I do know that it was a mistake. And I have a pretty good idea who made it, too."

Oh my God, he'll kill him.

My mouth was dry, but I managed to say, "I can handle myself. Besides," and I smiled, a weak effort. "You should see the other fellow."

He didn't respond. His blue eyes searched my face, as though willing me to tell him the truth. I stared back, wondering why he was so insistent. Perhaps it was some sense of honor or chivalric code. More likely he, who was already looking for reasons to destroy my uncle, was hoping to use my face to do it. After all, the first time I'd met him was when he'd come to my uncle's office to do just that.

"You can't use me to hurt him, John Henry Evans," I whispered. "I won't let you."

He blinked, surprise washing over him, and then Markum came out of the back office. The moment, if it was a moment, was gone.

Charlie Markum was a short man with a red face and a nervous tic of dry-washing his hands. He'd come out in only his shirtsleeves and vest, a telling sign, seeing as he knew he was coming out to see a woman. But then, my summons had been framed as a threat and he probably thought the usual courtesies didn't apply. He certainly took advantage of John Henry's presence to ignore me.

"Evans!" He sounded relieved. "Jane didn't tell me you were here."

John Henry kept his gaze on my face. "Well," he drawled, "I reckon that's because she didn't know I was." He leaned on the counter and nodded to me. "The lady was here first."

"Of course." Markum turned to me, his hands moving at a furious pace. "How can I help, Miss Goodnight?"

Both men were watching me now and I felt uncomfortable and more than a little pathetic. The bruise seemed to stand out like a beacon.

"I'm looking for my uncle," I said. "He's been gone all day. I was wondering if he'd come here." When Markum hesitated, his eyes darting towards John Henry, I hastened to add, "I know you don't like to give out the names of your guests, but he isn't well and I'm worried about him."

Markum licked his thin lips and gestured with his hands.

"Well, I, uh..." he began.

"Come on, Charlie," John Henry spoke low and slow. He toyed with the black hat in his hands. "The girl has the right to check on her uncle. She's hardly a threat."

"Of course, I wouldn't – it's just that..."

"Is he here?" I pressed.

Markum hesitated, then, when John Henry Evans began to stare at him, the words came tumbling out. "He came this morning, with a bag of things. Said he needed a room for a few days, said he didn't want to see you. He did," he added, as though by way of an apology, "look rather ill."

I became alert. "What room is he in?"

"He doesn't want to be disturbed."

"He needs help. Which room?"

When Markum still hesitated, I turned and started towards the staircase. He lurched after me, catching my arm just as I made the first step.

"You can't go up there now," he insisted. "He's got company – he left strict orders not to be disturbed."

The last thing I wanted to do was break in on something intimate, but Markum had gotten my back up with his prevarications. I glared at him and pulled my arm out of his grasp.

"If he's ill, he's in no condition to make demands," I said. "Which room?"

"It's a private meeting," Markum pleaded. "No one is to know, not even you."

"I'll beat on every door until I find him," I warned.

Markum paled. Over his shoulder, I saw John Henry grin.

"You wouldn't," Markum said.

I turned towards the stairs and he squeaked.

"All right, all right, it's... 207 – but..."

Suddenly, upstairs, a door slammed, so hard and so forcefully that the walls shook. Boots pounded on the floor – someone was running towards us. We looked up.

Ben Evans appeared, looking as though he were fleeing the hounds of hell. I barely had time to take in his white face, red-and-black stained hands, and terrified expression before he flung himself down the staircase, shoving me aside as he made his escape.

I fell against the wall with a gasp. Markum jumped out of his way and Ben ran for the door, blood dripping from his hands, the droplets marring the patterned rugs.

"Ben!" John Henry shouted and then he was running after him.

For a moment, I stood braced against the wall, my heart pounding in my chest, my head ringing. I looked to Markum, who was standing in the middle of the foyer like he'd been turned into a pillar of salt.

Blood, I thought. *His hands were covered in blood.*

I flew up the stairs, ending up in a narrow carpeted hallway. A row of doors, all marked with tin numbers, terminated in a door to the outside staircase, open now to allow the night air to circulate in the stuffy hall. There were noises here, too: muffled sounds from the bar, clearer though distant shouts from the men outside, and voices murmuring from behind some of the closed doors.

I raced down the hall, my skirts in my hands, my heart in my throat, until I came to the last door on the left, number 207.

It was swinging slowly back open, creaking in the breeze created by the open outside door. I stood, frozen, watching as it opened, revealing the room beyond.

I saw the larger details first: the oversized bed, the chair, the battered desk, all looking as though they'd had a hard life before coming to furnish Markum Hotel. The curtains were drawn and the bed was unmade. Clothes, blankets, and bottles were littered about and there were papers and playing cards scattered on the desk. An inkwell had overturned, the ink spreading across the desktop and dripping on to the worn carpet below.

My uncle, Matthew Goodnight, lay on the desk. He had slumped forward on his chair, his hands in the ink, his hair spread and tangling with the playing cards and the paper. His eyes were open and glassy like the marbles. His hands gripped the wood of the desk as if he were trying to hold on. But when you're dead, there's nothing to grip.

For I knew he was dead. His throat had been slit like an animal's and the blood on Ben Evans' hands was his.

NINETEEN

I stood in a daze, staring at the blood and ink that dripped from the desk to the floor. I might have taken my uncle by the shoulder and shaken him. I may have tried to tidy the mess of papers that lay scattered about the floor. I don't honestly know what I did. Somehow blood and ink got on my hands and skirt.

Markum was there, trying to convince me to come out of the room. I caught a glimpse of the girl, Jane, leaving the doorway, her face white. Markum took my shoulders and I shrugged him off.

"I can't leave him," I said.

"He's already left you," Markum said. "Jane's gone for the sheriff. You need air."

He looked green and I thought, *He's going to be sick.* I went with him then, for it was unseemly that my uncle's death room should be marred by someone else's sickness.

There was a crowd in the lobby. I hardly noticed who was among them. Markum seated me on one of the plush chairs. Someone pressed a drink into my hand, and then left me alone. Interested chatter pulsed in the air above me and my name was said a few times. I sat with the drink in my hand and ignored everything. I was, I realize now, in shock.

This wasn't the first time I'd seen death, nor even a violent one. In those cases, death was always the logical outcome of a particular set of circumstances: an accident in a field, a fight that went too far, illness claiming victory over a weakened constitution. There was a reason, sometimes stupid, oft-times tragic, but always understandable.

My uncle's death caught me off guard. Despite the danger I'd sensed towards him in this town, I hadn't really expected this. Men broke noses and ribs for a political seat. In New York City, it was worse, but this wasn't New York and people here didn't care as much. The land was still big enough that, if you didn't like the governing party, you simply ignored it. All I could coherently think was, *This came too soon. It happened too soon.*

I heard big boots and turned my head in time to catch Sheriff Sage's black eyes upon me. His weathered face looked as tired and as impassive as it had at the picnic. Markum plucked at his sleeve while the others looked on, nervous now that the law was present. Jane shouldered her way past them into the saloon.

Sage went upstairs with Markum. Once on the stairs, he turned and looked at me. In the space of that glance, I felt the stickiness on my hands and the bruise upon my face. I was too weary and cold to do anything about them.

The lobby was quieter when the sheriff left. Half the crowd went into the saloon and the other half spoke in hushed tones, as though in a funeral parlor. I sat in my corner, studying the amber liquid in my glass and wondering what I could possibly write to Aunt Alice now.

Dear Aunt Alice,
We were too late...

Whiskey slopped over my hand, adding a watery gold stain to the blood on my dress. I was trembling, both with fear and anger.

The front door opened. I turned, expecting John Henry, but it was only another man, dusty and wearing the battered tin star of a deputy. I watched as his worried expression smoothed at the sight of Trigger Olsen, who stepped up to greet him. They spoke in quiet undertones, glances darting in my direction. I went back to gazing into my glass.

All conversation ceased when the sheriff reappeared at the top of the stairs. His hat was in his hands and his expression was stony.

Unhappiness radiated out of him like heat from a furnace. Markum was behind him again, looking even sicker than before.

The deputy slipped through the crowd and joined his boss on the stairs. The room was so still that we all heard Sage say quietly, "Go to room 207. No one goes in or out."

The deputy, a much-younger man than the sheriff, took the stairs two steps at a time and disappeared down the hall. Sage turned to Markum and said, "Get the doc."

That caused some confusion among the crowd. I heard someone whisper, "Then he *isn't* dead?" in a disappointed way and I only just barely refrained from throwing my glass at him.

Markum looked relieved to have an excuse to get out of the hotel and practically ran through the crowd.

Sage surveyed us from the staircase. His hair was rumpled and his manner easy, a wolf relaxed but ready.

"Anyone care to tell me what happened here?" he asked.

Silence. Feet shuffled and throats cleared. Fingers pulled at too-tight collars. Everyone avoided looking at me. I sat there, feeling as though someone had poured cement down my throat.

Sage's gaze went around the room until his eyes landed on me. His walnut brown eyes bore into me like an awl in soft wood. My voice was still choked up. I realized that I was the only woman present and every man in that room was waiting on me.

I forced myself to stand.

"I came to bring my uncle home," I said, fighting to keep my voice steady. "Before I could get upstairs, I heard a door slam and... Ben Evans appeared, covered in my uncle's blood. He ran away before I could stop him."

Saying the story out loud was like reliving it. I felt weak all over. Even my mouth was loose and trembling. I looked down at my glass and focused so hard on keeping myself together that I initially missed what my words had done to the crowd.

"Is that true?"

Is it true?!?!

My head shot back up at Sage's question, but he hadn't directed it to me. He was asking the crowd. They were shuffling their feet, running hands through their hair, and looking everywhere but at me. No one spoke a word. No one looked at me. And no one confirmed the story.

A dark, ill feeling of dread began to pool in my stomach, a feeling that was almost lost in a sudden wash of anger.

"It *is* true!" I insisted. "Ben Evans was covered in blood – he didn't even try to hide it. He killed my uncle and then he ran away and *one of you must have seen it!*"

Hysteria bubbled at the back of my throat. I'd seen what I'd seen, but this was Evans territory and I was the enemy. Who cared what truth was when survival belonged to the fittest? It was *us* versus *them* and I was *them.*

"Anyone care to corroborate?" Sheriff Sage's voice was non-committal.

I'd never actually seen wagons circle in a defensive action, but I witnessed it that night. In the silence that followed the sheriff's question, a tacit agreement had been reached, a defensive wall was erected, and I, the stranger, the dangerous woman, was left on the outside, beating my fists against the brick surface, screaming into the deafening silence.

Us versus them.

Fury overrode my common sense. I took a step forward and glared at all of them. "John Henry was there," I said. "He ran after Ben. And Markum will tell you what he saw. Ben Evans killed my uncle and I will see him hang for it."

Sage's glittering eyes narrowed.

"Well, now, ma'am," he said slowly. "That ain't exactly up to you."

Before I could argue, he turned to Trigger Olsen. "Olsen – your boss in town tonight?"

Olsen nodded, careful to keep his gaze away from mine. "Yes, sir."

"Tell him I'd be obliged if he'd come and speak to me at the office."

"Yes, sir." Olsen was white beneath the tan.

"Sheriff," I said, but I was cut off when the front door swung open again.

John Henry stood in the door, shoulders back, eyes hooded and dark, his whole demeanor one of defensive defiance. His gaze worked around the room and fell on Sage.

"Sheriff," he said. "Ben..."

He hesitated then and for the first time since I'd known the bullish man, he looked unsure. He looked at me for a long moment, and then stepped to the side. Ben stood behind him, covered in drying blood and ink, his face an expressionless mask.

My heart jumped at the sight. I realized that I had neither my satchel nor my pistol and the intensity of my desire for the weapon frightened me.

A startled noise went around the room as the men recognized Ben and the significance of the blood. No one moved towards him, though, and no hue and cry went up. No one acknowledged that I'd spoken the truth. Instead, they went silent and looked to Sage to fix it.

Sage's sharp gaze took in what we all saw and possibly more. He ambled heavily across the room towards the doorway, his spurs jingling, his hand resting easily on his holstered weapon. He stopped in front of Ben and looked at him for a moment before speaking.

"Matthew Goodnight is dead," Sage announced. The words rang like funeral bells in the stillness of that congested, hot room. "Attacked from behind, throat slit as he sat at his desk. The lady here," he jerked his head towards me, "claims you did it, Ben."

John Henry looked at me, frowning darkly. Ben stood swaying as though he hadn't heard.

After a moment, the sheriff said: "What do you say to that, Evans?"

When Ben didn't answer, John Henry did.

"That's ridiculous," he stated. "Ben would never kill a man with his back turned. Tell him, Ben."

Ben Evans dropped his gaze to his feet and said nothing.

Sage rubbed his chin. "Lady says he came running out of here, looking as he does now. Got an explanation for that?"

John Henry glared. "I can think of a few."

"Mind giving me one?"

John Henry looked at his brother and I caught the tiniest hint of pleading in that sharp gaze. It was desperation and, in my fragile, shattered state of mind, I mistook the look for something more than what it was.

"Reckon he shouldn't have to," someone said from behind Sage. "Reckon his word would be good enough."

Olsen jumped on that. "You know Ben Evans, sheriff. You know he ain't capable of something like this. It ain't in his character. Not a knifing."

Fury and rage pounded in my veins. They were *covering* for him. Actually covering for him *in front* of me! I'd known it would be difficult to convict an Evans – it hadn't occurred to me that he might never even get arrested in the first place.

"Judge Parker likes evidence, boys," Sage said slowly. "The way I see it, I have two suspects covered in the victim's blood. I reckon that each of you has a fair reason for doing what has been done." His gaze, fixed firmly on my facial bruise, stopped me from protesting. "John Henry, the lady says she was in the lobby here with you when your brother ran down the stairs and out the door. She claims that he was covered in blood and, I'm guessing, that she wasn't at the time."

I sputtered, "Of course I wasn't!"

He looked to John Henry. "Care to confirm her story?"

All eyes turned to the eldest Evans son. John Henry glanced at his brother, still sunk in sullen silence, and something rippled through him, like a steel curtain being drawn across a window. I thought, for a very long moment, that he was going to deny my story. He had to know that Markum and the whole room would back him. He also knew where my bruise had come from. So when he turned Sheriff Sage, my spine was rigid and my heart was pounding.

John Henry said, "Miss Goodnight is correct. We did see my brother at the top of the stairs. He was covered in blood as you see him now – as though he'd been trying to stop a dying man from bleeding, as no doubt Miss Goodnight here tried to do."

It was an excellent parry. From the twitch of the sheriff's lips, I could tell he thought so too.

Sage said, "Might be. I'd appreciate Ben's weighing in on the matter."

Ben shook his head. He kept his eyes on the floor, away from his brother's face, away from mine, and I thought, *Coward! You low, miserable coward!*

Sage sighed and rubbed his face. "All right then. Reckon you won't mind if we search you, Ben?"

John Henry protested, "I have his gun here, Sheriff."

"It isn't a gun I'm looking for, though I do appreciate you handing it over, Evans." Sage took the proffered pistol and stuck it into his own belt.

"What are you looking for?" someone asked.

"A knife," Sage replied, but instantly, I knew he was lying. The Evans brothers would have been too smart to return with the murder weapon and, anyway, knives of the sort that killed my uncle could hardly have fit in Ben's fine leather wallet that Sage was opening. It was only last night that my uncle threatened Ben and the entire Evans family with a blank paper tucked inside a Pinkerton envelope. Ben had taken the threat so seriously that he pulled a gun in front of the entire town. If he'd killed my uncle, it had to be for that letter.

I thought of my uncle's livid face and the sound of the backhand reverberated through my head, making me shudder. I remembered how he'd snatched the envelope from my hands. The envelope with the *blank* sheet of paper.

Would Ben have actually grabbed the letter? More likely, in his panic, he would have taken the envelope with the blank sheet in it. In any case, he wouldn't have been fool enough to bring it back with him. He either would have stashed it or given it to John Henry, who stood watching Sage search with tension radiating out his big shoulders. There was a chance that the real letter was still in my uncle's room, possibly tucked into the leather-bound journal.

If it were found, the contents might prove a motive and there was a chance that Ben would actually go to trial. But I had to get in there *before* anyone could search that room. I could trust no one but myself.

And, anyway, there was the matter of my satchel.

No one was looking at me now. They were watching Sage and the Evans boys and talking amongst themselves. No one noticed when I slipped back and ran up the staircase towards the second floor.

The hallway was dimmer than I remembered. It took a moment before I spotted the deputy's lanky figure profiled in the open doorway leading to the outside staircase. His back was towards me, his hat pushed back on his head and his thumbs jammed into his heavy belt. I heard a low whistling. Despite the danger and intrigue swirling just down the stairs, the deputy was at peace. He didn't hear me as I slipped down the hallway.

The door to 207 opened soundlessly at my touch. I experienced a moment of panicked reconsideration, like when you'd just finished climbing a wall and realize that you have to look back down at the ground far below. I didn't want to go inside, to see the body - that distorted and too familiar face - and taste the scent of death. Someone had killed tonight and torn the fragile fabric of civility and order. My stomach clenched and my mind whirled, flashing me back to the weakness of when I'd first arrived in town.

But I needed that letter and I needed that satchel, so I took a breath and pushed the door open.

The smell of death was thick in the air, at once familiar and peculiar. I shrank back against the door and took a moment to orient myself. It was impossible not to look at the body – he lay slumped on the desk, his face pale and shocked, his eyes locked in that awful stare. The blood was still thickening and drying around his mouth and wound, and I thought: *Fresh kill. If I'd been a few moments sooner...*

There was no good to come out of following that thought. I tore my eyes away and found my satchel, flopped over on the floor a few feet from me. I must have dropped it in my initial shock. I clasped it to my chest and was immediately reassured when I felt the weight of the heavy pistol inside. Now I felt strong enough to look around.

It was a typical hotel room, square and small with one window on the outside wall and furnished with a bed, chair, and the desk. My uncle's carpet bag sat open on the floor, clothes spilling out of its mouth. A cloudy mirror hung next to a set of clothing pegs on the wall, one of the pegs bearing my uncle's coat. There was another door in the room and a pair of unlit lamps hung on opposite walls. The lamp on my uncle's desk sputtered over a too-short wick.

I had to lean over my uncle's body to get at that lamp. I adjusted the wick and used the increased light to look over the desk. I studied the pages scattered around under his head. I was loathe to touch them and what little I could read proved to be nothing more than drafts of another opinion piece. None of these pieces bore the mark of the Pinkerton Agency. The journal was nowhere to be seen. Ben Evans might well have gotten the Pinkerton letter out of the hotel, but he could not have secreted the bulky book on his person.

The desk drawers proved to be empty, so I moved on to the carpet bag. That contained only my uncle's clothes and, tellingly, the regulation pistol that he'd carried with him on the battlefield.

The hallway floorboards creaked suddenly. I froze with my hands full of my uncle's clothing. The deputy was pacing just outside the door. Now I was trapped and was sure to be discovered when Dr. Lowe arrived.

Figure that out later. Focus now!

I shoved the clothing and the pistol back into the bag and considered. The journal was Uncle Matthew's information Bible and, judging from his manner when he discovered me going through it, he would never have left it at the house where I was. He certainly wouldn't have left it in the office. If so, where was it?

My gaze fell upon the second door. I thought it was a closet, yet when I opened it, I was looking into another hotel room. I shut the door so fast, I didn't even have time to see if the room was occupied.

As I stepped back, I glanced up at the mirror. Over my shoulder, you could see the back of my uncle's head and his broad shoulders slumped over the wood. From behind, if you ignored the blood, he was the spitting image of my father.

For the first time, tears pricked at my eyes. I thought of my father, his last wheezing breath, the peaceful expression on his still face, the way the ticking scratched my arms as I reached under his mattress for the letter he'd asked me to mail on his death...

The mattress!

I threw myself on my knees by the bed, reaching past the sheets into the mattress before I stopped to consider. The ticking pierced through the thin cloth of my sleeves and my fingers brushed more than one squirming thing as I worked my way down the far side of the bed. I heard voices in the hall, Sage's calm tenor against Lowe's soothing bass. Feverishly, heart pounding, I worked my way down one side the mattress, around the foot of the bed, and up the other side towards my uncle's body. The deputy greeted the sheriff, the voices came nearer, their steps were right outside the door... and I found it.

The journal was scratched and worn and held shut with a woven strap, so stuffed with clippings that it appeared ready to bust open.

Steps approached the door. Voices echoed off the hallway walls. Doctor Lowe's low voice was saying, "My sister and I were just about to call it a night..."

"I sure appreciate it, doc," Sage replied.

I shoved the journal into my satchel and managed, with shaking fingers, to close it again. I looked about the room wildly. If Sage was willing to search Ben Evans for the letter, he wasn't about to let me leave the scene of the crime with a book full of my uncle's research. But how could I avoid giving it to him?

The voices had paused just outside the door. The deputy was saying, "...that girl isn't as fragile as she seems..." and the sheriff cut him off: "Evidence. Judge Parker needs evidence..."

Any moment they'd be in here. I spotted the window and raced to it. I grasped the sill and pulled, praying. It slid up smooth and silently.

Thank you, God!

I looked out – no one was below.

A hand rattled the door knob.

I shoved the bag through the window and pulled the pane down, my heart hammering through my chest. As the door swung open, I dove for the floor and my uncle's carpet bag. I need some reason to be in here.

"...not real shook up about it..." Sage was saying as he stepped in. He broke off immediately upon seeing me, his expression hardening. The door swung open further, revealing a slightly disheveled Doctor Lowe and the wide-eyed deputy.

"How did she...?" the deputy started, but Sage cut him off: "What are you doing here, Miss Goodnight?"

I rose, my uncle's carpet bag in my hands. I nodded towards my uncle's body. "I wanted to say goodbye."

Sage's outraged gaze went from my face to the bag in my arms. I tightened my grip instinctively.

"Boyd," he said. "I thought I told you not to let anyone in here."

"I didn't!" The deputy sounded wounded. "I was here the whole time, I don't know how she..."

"Is there any reason why I shouldn't be in here?" I demanded. "You already have the murderer custody."

"You make a bold claim, Miss Goodnight," the sheriff said. "I'd be checking my facts before I started preaching. Lowe." He turned the doctor. "You know what to do here. Boyd – stay on this door and this time, no one comes in, regardless of their relationship to the deceased, do I make myself clear?"

"Sheriff, I..."

"Boyd."

The deputy sighed in resignation and Sage turned back to me. "Miss Goodnight, I'd be obliged if you'd follow me into the hall. What the doc has to do is a mite unpleasant." When I took a step forward, he nodded towards the bag. "Leave it."

"But..." I protested and his gaze hardened.

"I said leave it, Miss Goodnight."

Slowly, with a show of reluctance, I lowered the bag to the floor. I smoothed my skirt, raised my head, and stepped around the bag. As I brushed past Lowe, he caught my hand and gave it a sympathetic squeeze.

"My condolences, Miss Jenny," he whispered.

His hand was warm and his eyes soft. I squeezed his hand back, grateful. I would have said something, had the sheriff not cleared his throat. Sage was watching us, of course, and irritation was written all over him. I released the doctor's hand with an embarrassed movement.

"I'm indebted to you, Doctor," I said.

If the sheriff was irritated, then the doctor was thoroughly annoyed. He shot Sage a look.

"You go home and get some rest, Miss Jenny," he said in his professional tone. "When I'm finished here, I'll send for the mortician. You don't have to worry about a thing."

I'd hardly stepped into the hall when Sage pulled the hotel door firmly shut firmly. When he reached for my elbow, I pulled away and glared at him.

"What were you looking for, Miss Goodnight?" he asked.

"Who says I was searching for something?" I demanded. Exhaustion and fear was making me reckless. "I am my uncle's kin, Sheriff. It's my responsibility to tend to his affairs."

Emotion rippled across his face, something akin to disappointment. I was too irritated and anxious to think what this might mean.

"Just picking up where he left off?" he asked and then went on before I could respond. "I suppose there's no reason to allow sentiment or grief hold up business."

I glared at him. "Did you find the letter?"

He raised an eyebrow.

"Letter?" he repeated.

"The Pinkerton letter," I said. "That *was* what you were searching Evans for, wasn't it?"

"No, ma'am," he said easily. "I was searching for a knife."

"More the fool you. Evans may be panicking, but he isn't fool enough to keep either the knife or the letter on him."

Sage's mouth tightened. He gestured towards the outside door. I lifted my skirts and stepped outside onto the tiny balcony and the warm, sultry night air. Sage stepped out after me, the moonlight drenching his dingy clothes in a silvery coating.

"Still determined that Ben's a murderer, ma'am?" he asked.

"He's a hot head, like his brother."

"No, ma'am," he said firmly. "Ben is not his brother and neither of those men are knifers."

"Someone killed my uncle. His hands were bloody."

"So were yours. Some might say you had a better motive."

I laughed. "What motive would I have?" He gave me a look and suddenly I was offended. "You don't think I would kill my uncle for his *newspaper?*"

"It wouldn't just be his newspaper. There's that fine house and the spread outside of town. I hear the Evanses offered a pretty penny for the property, but your uncle turned them down flat. I don't think you'd be quite so sentimental." His eyes went to my bruise. "And then there's the fact that Matthew Goodnight wasn't exactly a pleasure to live with."

Fury blossomed in my chest, choking me so that it was hard to speak. "This is ridiculous. Ben Evans ran out of here, covered in my uncle's blood!"

"From where I was standing, there were two people covered in blood. Only one was cool enough to keep her head." He went on over my sputtering, "I know Ben. Played cards with him a few times. He can't bluff. His face betrays him. If there's a problem, he faces it head on. If he was going to kill a man, he'd do it like he intended to last night: out in the open for anyone to see and judge. He wouldn't slip up behind a drunken, helpless man and slit his throat. Just ain't his style, you might say. If it wasn't for the fact that he was covered in blood and unwilling to defend himself, I'd have said there was someone else in this town with a much better motive and a character much more inclined to this kind of work."

"Me, you mean."

He rubbed his face again. "I can't claim to know what went on in your house, ma'am. The way I see it, a man who hits a woman isn't doing society any good living. Your uncle hit you and then went and fired the young man you'd been mentoring. I'm not saying that there's no room for sympathy here, but any deed worth doing is worth admitting to."

Rage was roaring in my ears like a steam engine and my heart was punching against the walls of my chest. I felt trapped, torn between wanting to run and a strong desire to slap his face. "Are you saying that, if Ben Evans hadn't been here tonight, you would have arrested me?"

He stared down at me and his face went hard.

"I know Ben Evans, ma'am," he said. "I've known him in all kinds of circumstances that speak to man's character. I don't know *you*, except the fact that you have your problems, both with the Evans family and with your uncle. And you have a temper. Whole town knows that."

"The whole town knows I have a gun," I responded.

"The whole town also knows about your uncle's letter and your bruise. I'm not the only one willing to lay money – and more – that Ben Evans is innocent."

"Even if he isn't?"

His face turned dark.

"I'd be careful who I said such things to, ma'am. You're a stranger here. Folks are already thinking that someone set Ben up. If they decide to take matters into their own hands... People will defend their own, ma'am." He gestured out into the dark night. "That there is just some good neighborly advice."

He was serious, deadly serious, and suddenly I realized that he was right. My uncle's work notwithstanding, Legacy was still very much under Evans control. Ben Evans might go to trial, but he'd never hang. It was in the interest of everyone, especially Sheriff Sage, to see to that, even if they had to find another scapegoat. And since I had a convenient motive, I was a strong candidate. Sage wasn't overemphasizing the danger I was in. If anything, he was underplaying it.

Fear washed over me, then anger. Anger and outrage for, politics aside, I'd just been accused of murder. I swung at the sheriff, though not with my hands.

"I don't think I'm the one who should be worried, Sheriff. I'm not the one who's going to have to face the wrath of Varina Evans when she learns that one of her paid minions is responsible for her pride and joy ending up behind bars."

That got him and he shifted his stance, but I wasn't done yet.

"I don't take too kindly to being accused of murder and I don't like strong men who think that justice is whatever suits their purpose. It was *my uncle* who was killed. *I* didn't kill him and if you won't see that justice is served, I will. *That* is a promise you can take to the bank."

I turned on my heel and strode off, hardly able to keep from stomping my feet. I could feel his gaze on my back. I don't think I breathed until I turned a corner and the darkness swallowed me. I found my bag and, under the cover of darkness, ran the whole way back to my uncle's house.

LETTER

Dakota Territory
October 23, 1874

Mr. Goodnight,
I am responding to your letter of the 24ᵗʰ of June, regarding
Doctor Johnson's records from his time spent in, California. I regret
to inform you that Doctor Johnson is not able to reply himself to
this letter. My predecessor passed away several years ago and left me
his practice and his records.
As to your inquiry into the treatment and subsequent death of
Ezra Jones, all of Doctor Johnson's records from his early practice,
specifically the years between 1847 and 1860 were lost in a fire. I
myself had never heard of Mr. Jones, but I did find, among my
predecessor's papers, a letter from one Mrs. Varina Evans in which
she makes the same inquiry. I know, from notations on the letter in
Dr. Johnson's hand, that he responded to her questions, but I do
not have record of the contents of that response. Mrs. Evans'
address also being Legacy, perhaps she would be willing to share her
information with you.
I regret that I am unable to be of more aid. I wish you luck in
your research.
Yours,
Sincerely,
Doctor Albert P. Livingston

TWENTY

The borrowed rifle was rusting and too heavy, but I didn't dare let it go. It was a dark, oppressive night in the territories and I was in the earthen hut I shared with my father, looking out the window. Armed men on horseback raced back and forth, shouting obscenities and threats, brandishing their weapons and torches. They'd killed Uncle Matthew already. Now they were coming for everyone else.

My father was sick in bed, too weak to even speak. My mother was there, too, though I dimly knew this to be impossible. She bent over her beads, a small, soft figure with dark hair, calmly praying. She didn't understand when I tried to tell her that we were in danger, that there were greater things than my father's illness. She didn't seem to hear anything. She just kept praying, wrapping herself in that foreign Roman mantle of ritual.

I should have been praying, too, but someone had to stand guard. I stood at the windows, trying to convince the men to leave us alone.

"Haven't you had enough?" I screamed at them. "You took my uncle. Isn't that enough?"

They just kept circling the house, the metal of their spurs, belts, and guns glinting in the moon light. With their heavy beards and shiny teeth and the wild cries that came from deep in their throats, they looked more like monsters than men. They were drunk and wanted to destroy things, to rip and tear and mutilate.

Once they began, I knew I wouldn't be able to stop them. I wouldn't be able to save my parents. I was all alone and too small for my rifle and I'd run out of prayers to say.

"Help me, Mother!" I cried. "Help me stop them!"

But Maman didn't hear me. She prayed and she sat and now the men were pounding on the door, shouting, breaking it down...

* * *

I sat up with a gasp. The sun was streaming through the kitchen window. I'd fallen asleep slumped over the kitchen table, my head surrounded by messy piles of newsprint and hand written notes. My uncle's journal was under my arm, where my cheek had been pillowed, and the worn pages were beginning to warp under my body heat.

I wasn't in the territories anymore. I was in Legacy and I'd been dreaming.

All the same, I had lost my mother and father, Uncle Matthew was now dead, and if it was proved that Ben Evans didn't kill my uncle, men on horseback would come for me, too...

I fell back against the chair, pressing my head into my shaking hands. *I can do all things through Christ who strengthens me. I can do all things through...*

The pounding came again, interrupting my recitation. This also wasn't a dream – there was someone at my back door, calling out my name.

"Miss Goodnight!"

I recognized Mrs. Danaher's voice and I opened the door. She stood before me with a basket tucked into her arm, looking alarmed.

"Are you all right?" she demanded. "You cried out."

"Did I?"

I stumbled back into the kitchen, letting Mrs. Danaher follow me.

My Aunt Chastity would have first fainted, then scolded me until next Sunday at least, about the state of my kitchen that morning. The contents of my uncle's journal lay spread all over the table, some pieces having fallen to the floor. Though still early in the morning, the air was stuffy and warm and flies as big as dimes, sluggishly attended to the dishes we'd left neglected on the counter.

Mrs. Danaher barely gave it a second glance. As I dropped back into my chair, she deposited the heavy basket on the table and began to unpack it.

"I brought some fresh bread, a little jam, and a pot of coffee. I hope you like it black and strong. I don't know any other way to make it."

"You brought me food?" I couldn't keep the amazement from my voice.

She shrugged. "Doctor Lowe was called out to the Findlay place," she said. "Helen Evans went into labor last night. Since he couldn't come, I thought I'd check on you."

"The Findlay place?"

"They have a spread near here. The Findlay boy said she was out riding and the labor pains came on sudden-like. It happens. She was too far out to get home, so she rode to the Findlays'."

"Is Helen alright?"

"She's strong, but it's her first child and it's very early." She gave me a sly look. "Anyway, I except Doc Lowe would have been here to check on you himself if he wasn't there. Boyd said he was pretty upset last night."

He wasn't the only one.

The scent of coffee made my mouth water, but I was still shaken from last night's dream. I rolled my head and cried out loud when the crick in my neck screamed with pain.

Mrs. Danaher gave me look. "Shouldn't be at all surprised. A table's not for sleeping on."

Rubbing the crick, I stared down at the journal spread open before me, the pages marked in my uncle's clean hand and then my gaze dropped to my blood-stained skirt. I hopped up from the chair, appalled. Last night, I was so consumed with anger towards Sage and the shock and horror of my uncle's death that I hadn't thought to change. I felt filthy, like a leper whose very touch is infectious. Yet when I looked at Mrs. Danaher in apology, I didn't see condemnation in her eyes. I saw something approaching sympathy – and pity.

"The coffee will wait," she said softly.

I hesitated. The research was spread out all over the table and, though little of it was what I sought to find, I didn't feel right about leaving my uncle's intimate notes uncovered.

Mrs. Danaher's gaze followed mine towards the table and her expression shifted. She said softly, "Jeremiah tells me you're a fine one for teachin'. Even so, I reckon I'm too old to learn now."

The delicacy of the confession caught me off guard. It never occurred to me to disbelieve her, but there were reasons why my uncle wanted these things hidden and until I discovered why, I couldn't risk anything.

"Can't leave a guest in a messy kitchen," I said numbly. The satchel with my father's pistol lay on the chair where I'd dropped it the night before. I swept the clippings and the journal into it and snapped the clasp shut, hugging the bag to my chest as I hefted it up. The weight was like a comfortable old friend.

Mrs. Danaher turned towards the counter, waving for me to go on. "The coffee will keep, girl. Go and clean up."

It was a firm, motherly command and I was relieved to follow it. I slipped upstairs with the satchel and locked it in my old trunk. Then I changed into my oldest blouse, a navy blue that was so washed out it looked periwinkle, and my divided skirt, which I usually only wore for riding. I could hardly stop my hands from shaking. It had been a long night, the longest I'd had in a quite some time.

Sheriff Sage's warning to me had been useful, in that it made me determined to find the Pinkerton letter and prove... whatever it was that my uncle had to prove. But tearing through the journal in feverish haste last night, I'd discovered nothing – not the letter, not the envelope; in fact, nothing I didn't already know about Ezra Jones' death besides a letter from a doctor in Nebraska territory, telling my uncle that all the records of Jones' death had disappeared in a fire.

The leather journal contained the same articles I'd seen the night of the wedding; little notices of little importance, gossipy articles about runaway women, conmen, petty thieves, the occasional suspicious death. Nothing of substance. Nothing to help me decipher any of the events that had recently taken place. All they did was cloud the issue, for why would my uncle hang on to such tittle-tattle as this?

Drunk with grief, anger, and frustration, I'd gone into my uncle's room and torn the place apart, but I couldn't find anything in there. Even my father's Bible had gone missing. I went back to the journal and it was in the middle of trying to decipher my uncle's notes that I must have passed out. Now I reflected on what all this meant.

Ben must have taken the letter.

He could have passed it on to John Henry to dispose of. Barring that, it was either still on him or Sage had it. If Sage had it, it was as good as destroyed – taking with it a crucial piece of evidence proving Ben's motive. Everyone in town had known about the letter, but no one had seen it or read it. We only had my uncle's word that it was about Ezra Jones' death, and any lawyer could dismiss our knowledge of it as hearsay. The sheriff was looking for an opportunity to dismiss the charges against Ben so he could bring them against me. Once Ben lawyered up and got his story straight, I reckoned he'd be released... and once he was, chances of his ever going behind bars were very slim indeed.

Which left me on the cusp of a murder accusation.

Bother it!

I finished dressing and went out to the landing. The door to my uncle's room stood open, as I had left it last night. The room - the entire house for that matter - was an untidy, unfinished place, much like his life. I remembered the piano, my uncle sobbing on the bench, the flat, choked sound the strings made and I thought, *He'll never finish it now. Not the house. Not the story. Not even the tune. It is finished and unfinished.*

Melancholy had me fast. I went downstairs and into what would be the parlor in a finished home. The piano stood in neglected splendor, the bench askew to it. When I sat on the bench, memories of my Aunt Alice's house flooded me. I lifted the cover of the bench to see if it, like the piano bench at home, stored sheet music.

It didn't. The compartment contained letters, some loose, some neatly stacked and tied with a blue ribbon. The envelopes showed varying stages of wear and tear – some had obviously traveled further than others. All the loose envelopes were addressed to my uncle in the same, delicate feminine hand. That same hand wrote the note that rested on top of the ribboned stack of envelopes:

Matthew,

I return your letters with a full heart. I regret the pain I caused you, but I trust that with time, we will become friends again. I ask that, if you are unwilling to return my letters to me, you would do me the courtesy of burning them and letting me know you have done so.

I remain,

Your affectionate friend,

Helen Wright

I sank to the floor, my hands shaking, the love letters fluttering like feathers in the wind.

Helen Wright! Helen Wright Evans...

Suddenly my uncle's unrelenting attack on the Evans family made sense: the manic style of his writing, the pained expression on his face when Helen appeared to break up the fight Saturday night, the way he'd lashed out at me when he saw me with John Henry, another of his family being stolen by an Evans... Uncle Matthew had been in love with Helen Wright. And she'd married Ben. It had been over these letters that my uncle was weeping when I found him that night at the piano. He hadn't simply been drunk.

Aunt Alice, you were right...

It took a moment to collect myself. When I did, I realized that really nothing had changed: in fact, this strengthened the case against Ben.

Mrs. Danaher was clattering away in the kitchen.

I wonder what she'll think of this.

I took the stack of letters and went into the kitchen.

Mrs. Danaher had set up the kitchen table for my breakfast, leaving a cup out for herself, and was hard at work, organizing the dishes for cleaning.

"The coffee's still warm," she said. "I reckon you'll feel better once you've something in you." Her sharp gaze went to the letters in my hand.

I dropped them on the table. "Mrs. Danaher," I said. "Would it surprise you to learn that my uncle and Helen Evans were once...?"

What? Courting? Lovers? Engaged?

Mrs. Danaher folded her wiry arms and her eyes looked deep as wells.

"Well, now, he did build this house for her," she said.

Another piece of the puzzle clicked into place. This unfinished house, the piano... these weren't intended for a bachelor – they were a wedding gift. Of course Mrs. Danaher knew: in a small town like this, everyone must have known. Only I, the relative and the stranger, had been in the dark.

"Oh," I said. I felt foolish.

Mrs. Danaher came over to the table.

"Reckon he wouldn't have told you much," she said gently. "He wouldn't want his niece to know that he'd gone silly for a girl not much younger than yourself. Helen had lots of beaus, but everyone knew that she was Ben's intended. Your uncle came here about the time Ben went off to school. He didn't know how things were. He saw Helen and..." She shrugged. "Once your uncle got marriage into his head, no one could talk him out of it. We tried to warn him. He wouldn't listen. Started building this place. Bought the piano. Made a fool of himself... and then Ben came home."

I looked down at the packet of letters. I could see my uncle's clear, strong handwriting on the envelopes. I thought of my uncle, crying at the piano, the pregnancy that not even clever dress work could hide. Helen had thrown my uncle over to become an Evans. I considered what it must have been to live in a town when the youngest son of town father got married. I wondered how my uncle could have stood it, living in the monument to his own foolish, unfulfilled dreams. How does a man, a Goodnight, handle losing the woman he loved?

I already knew the answer. A Goodnight man drinks, and the whiskey narrows his field of vision until he is deaf to the pleadings of others, blind to anyone else's pain. A man in mourning is the most selfish of beings. When liquor becomes too tame, he gambles or takes foolish risks, like riding untamed horses into the ground or challenging the biggest bully to fight. His future ruined, he becomes hell-bent on destroying his mind and his body until one day, both give out on him. He dies, a ruined shell of the man he might have been.

I know what I speak of. I'd already seen my father pass away and, had the merciful knife not ended Uncle Matthew's life, I would have watched the same happen to him. I wasn't enough to help my father. I wouldn't have been enough for Uncle Matthew either.

I failed, Aunt Alice, like I had already failed. Why did you send me when you know I can't stop them from killing themselves?

Mrs. Danaher was watching me with motherly concern. I pushed the letters away and lowered myself into the chair.

"I reckon a girl like Helen was smart enough to know where the money was." My tone was bitter.

Mrs. Danaher's lean face turned harder. "It had been her and Ben ever since they were children. Everyone knew it. We aren't to blame when a man has decided not to listen."

She was right, of course. My father refused to listen to me when I suggested that he go home, that he give up the missionary life that was killing him, that he forget the squaw he'd made a home with, that he stop mourning the son he hadn't cared to give his name to. My father didn't listen and my uncle was cut from the same familial cloth. Would I be any better? Or was I too closed off from the world to even be challenged - too cold and too old to love anyone enough to sin for them?

It was a chilling thought and I had to dismiss it.

"I'm sorry," I said.

Mrs. Danaher, with that brutal western pragmatic attitude, was already shaking her head and pouring coffee.

"You eat," she commanded.

With everything that had happened, I wasn't in the mood to eat. Once I had forced a few bites, however, my stomach opened up and I was ravenous. It had been almost a full twenty-four hours since I'd eaten. Mrs. Danaher's bread was better than Mrs. Washington's and the coffee was strong and warm.

Mrs. Washington...

I wondered what she'd make of the news of my uncle's passing.

Mrs. Danaher delicately sipped her coffee as she watched me gobble down her bread and jam. When I had taken the edge off my hunger and was drinking my second cup, I saw the drawn expression on her face and noted the way her finger traced the rim of her cup. She'd not come solely out of Christian charity. She wanted something and was waiting for the right moment.

"Was there something you wanted to ask me, Mrs. Danaher?"

She appeared startled. She put her cup on the table and looked me in the eye.

"I *was* wondering if you'd be wanting Jeremiah to come back to work for you, now that you've got the print shop to yourself?" she said.

I didn't know what to make of this. "Why, of course. I'll need him more than ever. Unless he'd rather not come and work for me now that...?"

How do you finish that sentence? *"Now that I'm practically accused of murder?"*

Mrs. Danaher cocked her head. "You didn't know that your uncle fired Jeremiah Saturday?"

I stared open mouthed. Suddenly, Sage's words came back to me like a slap to the face: *"Your uncle hit you and then went and fired the young man you'd been mentoring."*

Uncle Matthew fired *Jeremiah?*

That couldn't be right. It didn't make sense, but then nothing made sense this morning.

"Why would he do a thing like that?" I asked.

She leveled a steady look at me. "I'm sure *I* don't know, Miss Goodnight."

I'd put my foot in it again. Amends had to be made, but apologies would only make me look weak and I was tired of that persona.

"Mrs. Danaher... I'd be much obliged if Jeremiah would overlook what happened Saturday and come to lend me a hand."

"Will you be in the office today?"

"I - yes, I will."

Mrs. Danaher rose. "Then I'll send him along. He was helping his uncle at the stables before he goes back to the ranch. I'll let Jeremiah know he's still wanted."

"Mrs. Danaher," I said. "You tell Jeremiah that he is *needed.*"

Up to this point, I don't think Ruth Danaher had really known what to make of me. She hadn't liked my uncle much, though she was obligated to him for Jeremiah's job, and because I was a transient, no one really had to think much about me at all. But in that long moment's contemplation, I think she made a decision.

Not that she was going to let me know what that decision was.

"I'll tell him," she said. "You want more jam?"

I didn't, but I accepted some anyway. It was a small measure of peace in a world gone mad.

TWENTY-ONE

The more I thought about the print shop, the more it felt important to get there before anyone else, even Jeremiah. Not only was the Pinkerton letter still missing, but I hadn't been able to find even the envelope. There was a small chance, the slightest particle of a chance, that he'd left the letter in the office after opening it. It the letter had been as important as Uncle Matthew wanted us all to believe, he could have left it in his office safe. It was worth a look, in any case.

When Mrs. Danaher left, I draped my head in a shawl, grabbed the bag with Uncle Matthew's journal, and hastened to the office, running around to the back where I usually entered.

I was too late.

The back door hung loose, creaking in the breeze that chased dust along the alleyway. The wood was freshly scarred from where someone had pried it open. Old habits had me scanning the ground for footprints before I dared tread closer, but the earth was dry and hard packed. A Cherokee scout might have been able to pick up a track, but I was no Cherokee.

I pulled my father's pistol out of my satchel and drew back the hammer. It was such a big gun that I needed two hands for the job. There was comfort in the weight and size of the weapon, and by its strength I braved the darkened doorway.

There was no need to call out a warning – the door creaked loud enough to alert anyone still inside. I stepped in swiftly and immediately moved to the side, out of the beam of light pouring in through the back door. It was dark. The front window blinds were drawn and if anyone hid inside, they weren't using a lantern. The breeze blew past me into the quiet room, scattering papers like leaves in a dry forest.

I listened. There was no sound but the breeze and no smell of candle smoke or cigarettes – just the scent of ink and metal and dust. The shaft of light from the doorway revealed little beyond the still and silent print machine and the pages that littered the floor around it. I was too busy trying to spot an invisible enemy to attach any significance to the papers.

There was another shrouded window close by. I stepped toward it and put my foot in something wet and sticky. Memories of my uncle's room washed over me and I squealed as I drew back in an awkward dance. I reached the windows and drew the sacking that made do for curtains. Morning light poured in. I ducked backward again, out of the light, and saw the room for the first time.

It was awash in paper. Blank and printed, torn, whole, or crumbled, they were scattered everywhere, on the floors, on the print machine, on the chairs. A poster advertising various print services sagged on the wall – someone had slashed it through with a large knife blade, possibly the same that had forced open the door. A jar of ink lay shattered in the black puddle that I'd just danced across, pages half-submerged in the drying black liquid. It must have been the last thing the invaders had done, for mine were the only inky footprints on the floor.

Across the room, Uncle Matthew's office door stood open. There were deep gouges on the door and the door jamb where the lock had been forced. A trail of pages, ink, and office wares threaded through the door opening.

I heard heavy boots clomping on dry earth outside. Someone was approaching the back door - two judging from the treads and one was wearing spurs. I hardly had time to turn my gun towards the doorway when the first of the two men appeared.

Jeremiah stopped in the doorway, his mouth a perfect 'o' in shock. His uncle, Liam Danaher, appeared behind him and whistled through the gap in his teeth when he saw what had

Jeremiah spellbound. They started when I emerged from the shadows and both their gazes dropped to the pistol in my hand. I lowered it and gently eased the hammer back down.

"Miss Goodnight!" Jeremiah gasped. "What happened?"

My eyes were on Liam. Satisfaction rippled across his face before he schooled his expression. He pushed his hat further back on his head and whistled again.

"Someone didn't like what your uncle had to say," he said.

His satisfaction repulsed me. I dropped the pistol in my satchel and pulled the shawl from my head.

"Jeremiah," I said. "Please go and get the sheriff."

Jeremiah gaped first at me, then at Liam. Then he seemed to recollect himself and ran off. I lowered the satchel to the ground, being sure to keep it away from the spilled ink, and then began to pick my way across the room toward the drawn blinds.

Liam spoke up. "I reckon someone isn't too happy," he remarked.

The Danahers, I was discovering, had a habit of talking around a subject rather than address it right out.

"If you're talking about me," I said, drawing the blind and letting in the early sunlight. "You'd be correct." I pulled the other blind, too.

"Well, ma'am," he said slowly, the way a man chews on a particularly fine cut of beef. "I don't think you'd go about wrecking your own place."

I turned and folded my arms. "And who do you think *would* do this?"

He was watching me with narrow, amused eyes, eyes that were so like Jeremiah's, but cruel. His eyes lingered on the bruise on my face. I was beginning to grow accustomed to being watched so closely. After all, I'd been watched from the moment I came into town. Where I come from, to be unmarried at a certain age is to become invisible. In Legacy, I was enjoying the benefit of both notoriety and curiosity.

"I'm sure I couldn't say, ma'am," he said and then pushed himself from the doorjamb. "I'm riding out to the ranch. I'll look in on your uncle's place while I'm at it, if that suits you."

The change in subject and manner threw me a little. I murmured something about being grateful for his help, at least until I got my uncle's business matters straightened out.

"You'll be taking over," he stated flatly.

I was studying the pile of mess and nodded. "For the moment, yes."

"Business as usual, then?"

This question was edged with ice. When I looked at him, Liam Danaher was standing, not with insolent ease, as he had been before, but warily.

"Yes," I said, because I didn't know what else to say. "Business as usual."

Ice turned to hatred. He glared at me, his hands clenching into fists on his hat brim. If I'd been standing any closer, I would have felt myself in physical danger.

"Well," he said, with plain disdain. "I guess what they say is true, then. The acorn doesn't fall far from the tree."

Before I could respond to that, he turned on his heel and stormed out.

His departure left me feeling both relieved and confused. My nerves were jangled. I crouched down and began to pick up pages. It was an old instinct – whenever I was trapped someplace with an irreconcilable problem, cleaning and tidying were my ways of handling the discomfort. I had to stop myself this time, for I wanted the sheriff to see the extent of the destruction.

As I drew back, I saw one of Jeremiah's coded delivery envelopes, tucked among pages of newsprint. I didn't recognize the symbol. I plucked it out and realized that it had been torn in half. I found the other piece a few inches away, under a Godey's Lady's Book. I took the pieces and went to the window to examine them.

The envelopes were of cheap rag paper and the only marking on it was Jeremiah's code for delivery, written in my uncle's hand. The envelope was sealed and never opened – when the envelope had been torn, the destroyer had ripped the contents as well. I slipped the two torn pieces out of the remains of the envelope. They themselves were thin receipt paper and the note was so hastily written that I could barely make out the notation:

The reward has gone up.

$25, Room 207, Monday night
MG

So my uncle was still collecting for his ads. But what did he mean by reward? Was this what he was relying on to pay Matheson? Who was this meant for and why was it torn?

"Miss Goodnight?"

Sage stood in the doorway, his long lanky figure blocking the incoming light. His hands were on his hips and he was scanning the room with his narrow-eyed gaze. His gun was strapped low and he hadn't removed his hat.

"Sheriff Sage," I stood and gestured about the room. "I thought you might like to see this. It appears someone came here last night, looking for something."

That they might have found it filled me with poisonous frustration. I thought of John Henry's face when his brother wouldn't speak last night, of Ben's mad desire to run out of the hotel, and Varina's cold fury the night of the wedding party. The Evans were every bit as dangerous as my uncle had said.

Sage's gaze took in the room and he rubbed his face in frustration. Behind him, I saw Jeremiah, his white face testifying to his distress.

"Well, now, ma'am," he said. "I reckon you're right. Any idea who that might have been?"

"Come on, Sheriff," I snapped. I took a long step over a pile of papers to get closer to him. "We both know who my uncle was threatening. You know who wanted his stories silenced. Are you seriously asking me who might have wanted to trash his office and steal his research?"

"*Is* something stolen?" he asked.

There was no way I could know. Uncle Matthew had never let me into his office, let alone his confidence. I wasn't about to tell Sage that, though.

"Look around you!" I threw an arm up to gesture around the whole room. "Someone was looking for something. They broke into the back door to get in here, then again into my uncle's office. And they didn't even have the decency to try to hide the fact. It had to be the Evanses, Sheriff. They're the only ones with the motive and the brass to-"

"Now, just hold on a minute, Miss Goodnight," the sheriff interrupted. "Ben Evans was in my jail last night. There is no way he could have done this."

"I wasn't thinking of Ben."

"If you were thinking John Henry," Sage said calmly, "he was in my office at the time of the break-in."

"Of course he wouldn't do this," I snapped. "The Evanses have men. Any one of them could have slipped in on orders from Ben or his mother, or even on their own, if they thought they could serve their masters."

"You seem mighty determined to blame this on the Evans family."

"Who *else* had reason to break into my uncle's office, Sheriff? Who else would want my uncle dead?"

He pulled off his hat and took a step into the room, being careful to avoid the puddle of ink. "Well, ma'am," he said in a tone of mock respect. "I was thinking maybe that was something you could tell me."

Dead silence settled in on us. I glared and he stared and Jeremiah bit his nails in the back, his worried eyes shifted from one to the other of us. As we stood, practically toe-to-toe in the silent stand-off, something he said came back to me.

I folded my arms and broke the silence. "You said that John Henry was with you at the time of the break-in."

"He was. I'd testify to it."

"How convenient."

His lips tightened. "My word is generally considered good around here, ma'am."

"I don't doubt it. But how can you say that he was there at the time of the break-in? Unless John Henry stayed all night or you knew exactly when the break-in happened, you can't possibly know for sure that..."

"I do know," he interrupted.

"All right. How?"

"I sent my deputy out to make the rounds at midnight. When he passed by this office, he saw something."

This was new information and I struggled to keep my temper in check. "What did he see?"

The sheriff's tone was even, calm, just a friend conveying something of minor interest to an acquaintance. "Thought he saw a light moving around in here. He knew you were home, so he investigated, but the doors were locked."

"So he just... what, went home?"

"He thought his eyes were playing tricks on him. Happens at night sometimes. He didn't think it was worth breaking down your door to check."

"Sheriff," I said, gesturing behind him. "Look at the back door. If your man really did check all the doors, don't you think he would have noticed that back door just hanging open?"

Sage didn't even bother to look. He just grinned at me. "I reckon he wasn't being entirely truthful about that."

"No," I said bitterly. "I reckon he wasn't."

We endured another moment of silence, he watching me, me studying him. I had run into enough brick walls in my life to know when I was confronting another.

Nevertheless, there was one question I wanted answered.

"Have you found the letter yet?" I asked.

Sage lifted his head and one eyebrow went up. "No, ma'am. And before you asked, Ben Evans was searched again."

"Was John Henry?"

"He insisted. He was clean."

"Of course he was. It would have taken a complete fool to return to the scene of the crime with the motive in his possession. I guess you've made a search of the area?"

"My deputy is combing the area now," he said. "I don't think we'll be finding anything, do you?"

I didn't and turned away. "You know as well as I that if Varina Evans wanted this place ransacked, she would only have to say the word."

"I won't deny that, ma'am," he said evenly. "Fact is, Mrs. Evans didn't know a thing about any of this until the wee hours of the morning. She was over at the Findlays'. Ben's wife is laying over there, having a baby. The Findlays sent their boy into town to fetch the doc. He found Lowe at my office, about a half hour after midnight. He didn't know anything about the murder and neither did Mrs. Evans until the doc rode over there to look after Helen."

His gaze slipped down my frame and back up again. "I reckon he would have been in to look after you if he wasn't still at the Findlay place."

I brushed off the implication. "The Evanses have hands in town. One of them might have done this."

"Might have. But you can't arrest a woman for something someone else might have done. In fact, you can't even arrest them for something they might have done themselves, not without evidence, anyway. No matter how convinced you are of their guilt."

"You really think I did this," I whispered. "All of this."

Sage looked around the room, then back at me.

"I think," he drawled, "that you're a mighty determined woman, Miss Goodnight. You want to see someone hang for your uncle's murder. I can't blame you for that."

Ice settled into my bones like an early frost. I drew myself up and, in the best imitation of Grandmother Goodnight, turned my back on the sheriff. Through the office doorway, I could see a small floor safe. The door was open and the contents spilled all over the floor.

"Thank you for coming, Sheriff," I said.

"Pleasure," he murmured and stepped towards the door. "Oh, just one more thing, ma'am."

I waited, deliberately keeping my back to him.

"It might interest you to know that Ben Evans hasn't confessed yet," he said.

That wasn't surprising at all. "Has he denied guilt?"

"Nope. No, the man refuses to talk to anyone, even John Henry and Schuyler, the lawyer, not until he's spoken with his wife. And she, being laid up with the baby and all, isn't likely to come right away. Thought you might find that interesting."

"The only thing I'm interested in is a confession," I said. "Good day."

He ambled out, bidding Jeremiah a good day as he went. Drained, I sagged against the doorway of my uncle's office. I hadn't even had time to tend to my uncle's body and here I was facing another mess. The office had been torn up, the evidence my uncle guarded probably gone, and the sheriff was still determined to pin me for murder. I felt alone. I felt worse than alone – I felt surrounded and besieged.

The sound of Jeremiah picking his way across the floor reminded me that my feelings weren't exactly facts. Jeremiah Danaher might not be an active ally, but neither was he an active enemy. His mother, too. Liam Danaher and his odd behavior was another story for another time.

"Miss Jenny," he said, his face pinched with worry, "you don't think Trigger really had anything to do with this, do you?"

"Do you?"

He shook his head. "No, ma'am. Trigger's a straight shooter. He tells you to your face what he thinks. So does John Henry," he added as an afterthought.

The last thing I wanted in my head was John Henry Evans. "Well, someone broke in here and did this," I said. "And it wasn't me. Tell me, was that safe usually locked?"

"Yes, usually."

"It's open now."

Jeremiah shrugged and shoved his hands into his pockets.

I rested for a moment, wondering if I should have mentioned Uncle Matthew's debt to Matheson to Sage. I decided that I'd have to. They weren't likely to forgive my uncle's debt simply because he'd died.

Thinking of this reminded me of the torn letter in my hand. I turned and gave them to Jeremiah. "Whose mark is on this envelope?" I asked.

He barely glanced at it. "That's for Mrs. Washington."

"So she already approved the ad copy?"

"I guess so. When I delivered the first envelope to her, she said to tell Mr. Goodnight that she'd be by on Wednesday as usual."

"This note says Monday."

"I wouldn't know anything about that," he said.

I read it out loud and asked, "Do you know what he means by *reward?*"

"No, ma'am. Anyway, she never got that note."

"Why not?"

He looked genuinely uncomfortable now, but I insisted: "Tell me, Jeremiah."

"Because he tore it up," he said. "Your uncle. He was in a powerful bad mood on Saturday. I thought he was..."

He trailed off, embarrassed.

To ease his discomfort, I said, "You thought he was drunk."

Jeremiah nodded.

I sighed. "It's very likely he was. He was pretty well past drunk when he arrived at the wedding. But what happened that morning to get him started?"

"He wasn't drunk when he arrived," Jeremiah said. "He gave me a handful of those envelopes and told me to deliver them after lunch. I thought he'd be happy about the Pinkerton letter. I gave it to him first thing and he went right into his office to read it. He was in there a while, so I took out my slate and was practicing my letters when he..." He swallowed hard, and looked at the floor. "He came storming out and found me with the slate and he... well, he took it away and broke it. Said he didn't need another spy in his midst. Then he saw the envelopes in my pocket and he took them and tore them in front of me. Told me to get out and never come back. So I left."

He looked so miserable that I put my hand on his shoulder and gave him a squeeze.

"I'm sorry," I said.

"He was fighting mad when he came out of that office, Miss Goodnight, like someone had just stolen his best horse or something. But I have no idea why."

That bothered me more than anything I'd come across this morning. My uncle was in love with Ben's wife and received a letter from the Pinkerton Agency the night before he died, a letter that sent him into a towering rage, yet hours later, he was acting like he had the high card. There was something missing in this story.

My eyes swept over the floor and the scattered pages upon it. A deck of cards lay like windswept leaves among the rest. One caught my eye and I bent to pick it up. It was the queen of hearts.

"What does it all mean?" Jeremiah asked.

I shrugged. "There must have been something in the letter that upset him."

"He didn't act that way at the party."

"Well, that's the thing about poker players," I murmured, fingering the wear-softened card with the fading hearts and a queen who looked like something out of an Edgar Allen Poe nightmare. "You never know when they're bluffing."

TWENTY-TWO

I left Jeremiah at the office, tidying up and sorting the papers and trash into piles as best he could. He seemed happy for the work. I wrote a sign for the window, announcing that the shop and the paper were closed until further notice. Then I took my satchel with the gun, journal, and the torn card, and went to the undertaker to see to my more immediate family business.

W. Tasker, Undertaker, was on the edge of town in a small, plain wooden box of a building. Several caskets, one unfinished, stood under the porch overhang as advertisements. Unlike the storybook versions, the undertaker himself was a small, round man with an off-putting cheerful disposition. At least, he was cheerful until he realized who I was.

"Yes, ma'am," he said, his attitude sinking to a distant sort of politeness. "Doctor Lowe had the body sent to me late last night. It's right this way." As he led me to the back room, he said, as an afterthought, "I'm sorry for your loss."

We went through the motions of taking care of business. There were plots available on Boot Hill and W. Tasker volunteered his services as preacher at the graveside (he had been ordained strictly for the convenience of his clients). I inquired about shipping the body back home to our family plot, but as they said with my father, the cost was prohibitive and with this heat...

"Of course," the undertaker said, brightening a little, "you can always bury him here and ship him back later."

Something we'd said about my father, too. Transportation cost money, money our proud but poor family could ill afford.

This was third time I'd been asked to decide a matter of this finality. I stood by my uncle's closed casket, the familiar anger and frustration rolling over me like a crushing weight. I couldn't indulge it then, especially not with the impish little undertaker watching me like a wild cat that might lash out at any moment. I was a human curiosity to him, like an object in Barnum's museum: "Step right up, folks, and see the woman of mystery! Did she get away with it? Hurry, hurry..."

I agreed to a temporary burial on Boot Hill with Tasker offering prayers graveside and then I fled the awful place.

That Monday was a particularly beautiful day. The sun was bright, the skies were blue, and a cooling breeze wafted down the streets, carrying the sounds of children's recitation from the schoolhouse. Sarah Lowe was hard at work even as her brother brought another little Evans into the world. I wondered if she regretted not being able to be at Helen's bedside or how she would feel if she were to have Helen's offspring in her class, not that this was likely to happen. Schoolmarms were single, as a rule, and Sarah had made it quite clear that she was not going to be teaching for long.

I turned my steps towards the bank and passed the sheriff's office as I did. John Henry's big black mount was not at the hitching post. He must have gone to check on his sister-in-law, probably after having spent most of the night in the sheriff's office, listening to Sage's theories about the murder and about me, possibly embellishing them with his own ideas.

I shoved that painful thought aside and kept my mind on Helen. What did Ben think of the affair? He had to have known, for the whole town did. Did he know about my uncle's letters to Helen? Had he demanded their return? Did my uncle deny it?

When Ben attacked my uncle at the wedding, he'd pulled a pistol. My uncle was killed with a knife. The only reason I could think for using a knife rather than a pistol was to avoid being heard. But if Ben was trying to be discreet, why run down into the hotel lobby for everyone to see?

This vexing train of thought held me until I got to the bank, where a small sign in the window proclaimed that the banker was out fishing for the day. I blew out a breath of dissatisfaction and turned. As my gaze wandered, my eyes fell upon a poster for Honest Joe Turner.

I wonder what he thinks of this whole mess.

Honest Joe was the direct beneficiary should Ben Evans hang and that might be worth killing for. But why was I thinking about suspects when Ben was so clearly guilty?

I tore my eyes away from the posters and looked around. Legacy streets bustled with activity, men calling out to one another as they rode by on horses and buckboards. Women wandered in and out of shops with baskets. One woman in divided skirts was cinching her saddle while talking with the man from the livery stables. The man nodded in my direction and the woman turned in curiosity. Her expression changed from pleasant banality to curiosity edged in hostility. She said something to the liveryman and he nodded and both turned from me again.

I looked around the street. People glanced away as my gaze fell on them. Others murmured to each other, clearly not looking at me. One woman passing by me on the boardwalk actually lifted her skirts to hurry by faster.

Seems Sage isn't the only one that has me pegged as a murderess.

I remembered his warning about lynch parties.

"...Bold as brass..."

The words floated to me from across the way, as did the disdainful glance the livery man tossed at me. I felt exposed and vulnerable standing there in front of the bank, fearful even. Someone had killed my uncle and ransacked his offices. The sheriff had all but accused me of murder and threatened me with hanging.

I had too much pride to run, so I strode quickly, head up, eyes forward, shoulders back. I was a Goodnight. Goodnights did not run and they did not hide. Besides, I had another piece of business to look into.

* * *

Markum's Hotel was a good deal quieter than it had been last night. The lobby was empty, with no sign of the provocative brunette, and the bar in the side room was dark and still. The only sign that something unusual had occurred was a small bloodstain on the wallpaper on the staircase where someone's fingers had brushed the pattern. I couldn't tell if it was Ben's hands or mine, but I knew whose blood it was.

I rang the bell and waited, trying not to allow my imagination to run away with me.

When Charlie Markum appeared from the back office, I saw at once that he'd been drinking. He was coatless and his rumpled collared shirt was unbuttoned at the neck. When he walked, he staggered, and his eyes were red and dry.

He stopped when he saw me and his eyes narrowed.

"Miss Goodnight," he said. "I..."

He broke off when two women, both dressed in black and obviously from out of town, entered into the lobby from the outside. He gave me a pleading look, as if I were about to cause a scene right there and then, and then stepped forward to attend to the ladies. I will say this, he hid his condition well. When he gave them their room keys and they'd turned away, he practically dragged me into the back office.

The back office was a small room, dominated by a roll-top desk that was open and covered in paperwork. There was a half-drunk bottle of tequila on it and a tin cup, which had left wet rings on top of the papers.

"I don't know what you want, Miss Goodnight," Markum slurred, as he shut the door firmly behind us. "I sent your uncle to Tasker. I trust that'll be the end of it. My hotel has been through enough these past few weeks. I don't need any more trouble."

"I didn't come here to cause trouble," I said. "I've come to collect..."

"Collect!" He snorted derisively.

Startled, I pushed on. "I've come to collect my uncle's things and to see if there were any outstanding accounts."

He looked at me for a long moment. Then he began to laugh. It was a bitter, cold laugh and I, who hadn't expected warm treatment, began to grow alarmed.

"Outstanding accounts?" he said. "Yes, I guess you could say that we have a few *outstanding accounts,* Miss Goodnight, though I'm surprised to find you'd spare the time to attend them. His body's still warm and you come to *collect.*"

I was missing something in the conversation. "I can't promise immediate payment, not until everything is settled, but if you'll let me see the bill..."

He threw himself on his desk chair and looked up at me.

"There isn't a *bill,*" he said. "Everything was put on his *account,* the account that I assume you'll be taking over?"

"Yes, I suppose..."

Now his expression turned cold, hostile. "You're a cool little miss, you are," he drawled. "You've got it all worked out. Now that your uncle is dead, you've got the whole business." He laughed again and the sound bounced off the walls. "And you've come to collect his things..."

He threw back the glass of tequila and began to cough. His shoulders heaved. He turned away from me and pressed his hand into his mouth.

I counted to ten, then I softly went over and stood at his side.

"Are they in his room?" I asked. When he looked up at me with watery eyes, I went on, "My uncle's things. There was a big black Bible among them. Are they still upstairs?"

I hadn't realized how much I dreaded going back into my uncle's murder room until Charlie Markum shook his head 'no'. The relief made me sag.

"No," Markum said mournfully. "It's all gone."

"Gone? Where?"

"Sage has them," he sighed. "All in a box in his office. We went through everything last night. All night, searching, sorting, tearing the whole place apart. But the letter wasn't there. I couldn't find it. There wasn't anything there. Your uncle wasn't stupid, you see. I was, but he wasn't."

Of course it wasn't there. Ben Evans must have taken the letter with him.

Markum reached for the tequila again.

There seemed little reason to stay. I didn't relish another conversation with a drunken man and I sure didn't want to go up to see the scene of the crime again. The only thing worse than that was the idea of visiting the sheriff to pick up my uncle's belongings. After this morning's run-in, I didn't feel like putting up with him again.

I turned to go. Markum, smacking his lips from the mouthful he'd just swallowed, stopped me with this unexpected observation:

"You are younger than I expected," he said. "Look older than your years. I imagine you have lots of stories to tell."

I thought, *"Behold an Israelite indeed, in whom is no guile."*

"I have a few," I said and put my hand on the door.

"Jen-ny Goodnight," he drawled, stopping me again. "The preacher's daughter, devoting her life to the saving of souls. You're like a nun, aren't you? Standing apart from everyone, keeping your skirts free from filth, above the rest."

"Mr. Markum..."

"I heard him once, you know. Your father, I mean. He was lecturing about fire and brimstone and demon rum, or something. I can't remember where, exactly. I moved around a lot, always chasing the rainbow, never quite catching it. But your father was a good preacher, made me really think. I guess if I'd met him when I was younger, he'd have made a saint out of me. As it was, the Lord sent him a little too late."

"It's never too late," I said. "As long as you're living."

He just smiled into his cup. "You *are* his daughter."

Dismissal is a large part of the missionary experience and time teaches you to better recognize those who are willing to listen and change. But even a novice knows never to debate theology with a drunken man.

"I guess I should go now," I said.

"Foolish thing that Evans boy did, running out the front," Markum slurred. "If he was hell-bent on killing the man, he should have come up the back and left the same way."

"I know..."

"Your uncle did pretty well with that paper, didn't he?"

I thought of the dusty piano. "Yes."

"Such a small paper," he said. He picked up an ink covered sheet and tossed it to the other side of the desk. "So many ads. Of course, he was pretty... persuasive." He paused a moment. "I thought it was you, last night. The woman arguing in his room."

All my senses went on alert. I turned around and back to his desk.

"What woman?" I demanded. When he lifted the cup to his lips, I interceded, taking the cup away. "Markum - what are you talking about?"

He sighed and slumped back in his chair.

"I heard a woman in his room Sunday night," he said. "Before Ben arrived. Arguing." His eyes settled on my bruise. "I figured you were settling some business."

"How do you know it wasn't one of your girls?"

"They know better than to argue with a guest."

"But what were they arguing *about*?"

"If I knew *that*, I'd know who she was, wouldn't I?" His gaze turned sly. "I don't suppose it was you?"

"No," I said firmly. "It wasn't me. Did he have any other visitors after that?"

"I don't know. I went downstairs and saw Ben."

"You sent him right up?"

He nodded heavily. "I sent him right up."

"Did he say why he wanted to see my uncle?"

"It was generally understood."

My head was whirling. Off the top of my head, I could think of three women who might have gone to my uncle's room to argue with him: Varina Evans, Helen Evans, and possibly Abigail Washington. But Helen was having labor pains at the Findlay's and Abigail Washington never received the invitation to my uncle's room, so that would seem to rule those two out. As for Varina, I really couldn't see her bloodying her own hands.

"Have you told the sheriff this?" I asked.

Markum shook his head. "No."

That seemed obvious. If he'd done so, wouldn't the sheriff have arrested me right away?

"Why not?" I asked.

He didn't look at me, just traced the bottle with his finger. "I wanted to see where we stood before I did."

I swear, my first instinct was to order him to tell the sheriff about the woman arguing with my uncle in his room. It was evidence in a criminal affair, evidence that could change everything. But if he did, Sage's would release Ben Evans and arrest me. I couldn't afford that. I had to assume that the townspeople would be pleased to sacrifice me in order to restore the balance of power to the Evans family. And if I was in jail, who would care about the identity of the real woman arguing with Uncle Matthew and why? Who would see to it that my uncle's real murderer was caught?

Markum was starting to get sentimental. He looked around the cramped little room, his eyes growing watery.

"I've worked hard for this hotel, Miss Goodnight." He hugged the bottle to his chest, blinking hard as though to stay awake. "I poured sweat, blood, tears, everything I have into this place. I had a vision, I left the old me behind, and I created a beautiful place, a legacy, a name. This hotel will *be* something someday. If I lose it, I have nothing. I am nothing." He was one sharp word away from tears. "Do you know what that's like, Miss Goodnight? To have your identity wrapped up in one role – and to be on the edge of losing it?"

Charlie Markum ran a cheap hotel that serviced men's lowest urges, the anathema of everything my father and I fought against. And yet, in that moment, Markum and I were closer comrades than anyone else in this forsaken town. The realization hurt more than one would have thought.

"I don't want to lose this place," Markum whispered. "I can't lose this place. I'll do anything I can to keep it. Anything."

He looked at me for... I don't know what. Reassurance maybe? I couldn't offer that, for I didn't know what threat he faced. So I gave him what I could.

"I understand," I handed him his cup. "I'd be obliged if you didn't mention that woman to the sheriff just yet." When he looked at me, I said, "I didn't kill my uncle, Mr. Markum. I give you my word."

He grunted, a cross between a laugh and a cry. Already his body was starting to sag, his eyes growing cloudy.

"The word of a Goodnight," he scoffed. "Your word is law around here, Miss Goodnight, but you already knew that. As long as you know what you know, I can't do a thing without your permission."

"Know what I know?" I repeated. "What do I know?"

But he was already passed out and dead to the world. I hesitated, wondering if I should revive him. But he wasn't likely to be any use to me until he'd sobered all the way, and the closeness of the room was starting to get to me. I left him to his tequila and his dreams.

LETTER

(Undated note)

Charlie,
I'll be requiring the use of 207 tonight, as per our agreement.
Put the charges towards your ad account. It may interest you to
know that there was another notice in the St. Louis newspaper a
month ago, but perhaps you already saw that.
Matthew Goodnight

TWENTY-THREE

I emerged from the hotel, blinking in the bright sunlight, my head swarming with questions: Who went to see my uncle last night and why? What did Markum mean by my 'knowing what I knew'? Did it have anything to do with the Pinkerton letter? Perhaps he assumed I'd read it, but what hold would it have over him? It was about Jacob Evans and Ezra Jones. But then, if *that* were true, why was Uncle Matthew so upset after he read it? Could it be that it proved Jacob Evans innocent?

There were other questions, too: who broke into the print shop? Did they find what they were looking for? Why did Uncle Matthew keep Helen's letters and fire Jeremiah for learning to read? What did my uncle mean when he wrote to Abby Washington about a reward? What kind of ad in a small town paper cost $25? That was nearly a month's pay for a ranch hand on a good paying spread. It was surely too much for any small business around here.

I wasn't paying attention and stumbled on a loose board. I caught myself before falling, but not before the satchel swung and hit me heavily on the knee. I felt the spine of the journal through the carpet and suddenly Charlie's words came back to me: "His body's still warm and you come to *collect*."

An idea dawned on me – an awful idea, a truly terrible idea, but one that would make all kinds of damning sense if it were true. I took off running.

Jeremiah was sweeping and humming when I burst into the print shop. My sudden appearance made him jump and he peered behind me, as though expecting a lynch mob. I moved past him to the counter, which was still littered with pamphlets and pencils.

"Jeremiah, what does Mr. Washington do?" I asked breathlessly.

The boy blinked at me, uncomprehending. "The general?"

With a sweep of my arm, I cleared the counter on to the floor. "No, Abigail Washington's husband."

My mess-making didn't bother him. He leaned on his broom and said, "He keeps sheep and farms, like everyone else. Oh, and he does some carpentry. Cabinets and tables and the like."

Washington's Carpentry... I'd studied every newspaper I could get my hands on in the past few weeks, and I couldn't remember seeing anything in the papers for that. Then again, I hadn't been looking at the ads.

I dropped the satchel onto the counter and opened it, withdrawing the journal and the torn envelopes. "Does he do a lot of business in town?"

"Some, I guess. Why?"

"There are some questions that need answering. Have you seen any ledgers or record books that my uncle might have kept?"

"They're in the office," he said, then looked doubtful. "At least, they were. I haven't cleaned there yet."

"I'll check," I said, with energy. "While I'm doing that, get me the last few papers my uncle published."

"Sure thing," he said.

I spent the next hour sorting through the journals and combing through newspapers and the one ledger I was able to find in my uncle's office. I compared the ads printed with the amounts received in the books and there were discrepancies – Markum ran an ad that cost more than Mr. Walsh's ad of the same size, and no matter how far back I went, I could find no ad whatsoever for the Washingtons.

What I found didn't please me in the least.

Jeremiah offered to help with my research, but, unable to read fluently, he couldn't really assist. I'm ashamed to say that I was relieved by this – it was insurance that what I found would stay with me and me alone. It occurred to me that Uncle Matthew had probably thought the same thing.

When I had gone as far as I could go with the ledgers, I turned to my uncle's journals.

The journal was loosely divided between the general news clippings and the Evans investigation. The Evans case was separated from the rest, bound in grimy string and covered in my uncle's fingerprints. There were telegraphs from all over the country, including one claiming to have access to a marriage certificate between Ezra Jones and a woman in town, but Uncle Matthew had written 'false claim' over that one.

The other news clippings were, as I'd mentioned before, just the sort of gossipy, scandal-ridden sort of news that Uncle Matthew would have denounced as sensationalist journalism, articles that my aunts would have publicly condemned and Aunt Chastity would have privately consumed. On some of the pages of the journal itself, my uncle had started scribbling first drafts of articles, usually starting with, "It has come to the attention of this paper that..." and ending in some dishy story. Words and phrases like, "deserter", "show-girl", "ill-repute," "runaway", "reward for information," and "questions unanswered" were rife. Other pages were notes, arranged like mathematical figurations, except that they dealt with words and dates and names, not figures.

The more I looked, the more the pattern became clear.

Finally, when there was no more denying what was plain before me, I sat back in my chair and rubbed my eyes.

"Jeremiah, can you take me to the Washingtons' spread?" I asked.

"Now?"

"Yes. Can we make it before nightfall?"

"It's out of town a ways, but we can make it easy. I can borrow a rig from the livery."

"I can ride." I stood and began to collect up my evidence. After learning what I'd learned, I wasn't about to leave this for someone else to find.

He nodded. "If you don't mind my asking, ma'am, what are you looking for?"

"Answers." I said honestly. "I need to find them sooner rather than later."

It was just a matter of time before Markum went to the sheriff. Once he did, I was lost and the truth along with me.

ARTICLE

March 23rd, 1875
From the *Erie Times Personal Ads*
(Discovered in Matthew Goodnight's personal journal.)

REWARD OFFERED for the safe return of one MATILDA GREENE, of Greene Farms, outside of Erie, Pennsylvania. Matilda comes of a good family, educated, 29 years old, red hair, tall, slender. Suspected kidnapped in March of 1866 by the black man TITUS FREEDMAN. A REWARD is offered for either Matilda's safe return or news that leads to the arrest of Freedman. The Greene family is more interested in news of Matilda than the circumstances of her recovery...

TWENTY-FOUR

The Washingtons lived an hour's ride west of town, on a spread that looked like hundreds of other small starter ranches and farms across the frontier. The main house was a simple affair, small and rough-hewn, doubtlessly built by its occupants. A new lean-to and preparations for another addition spoke of an expanding family.

The barn was larger than the house by far. A milk cow lowed in the pen, her calves munching grass solemnly beside her. Chickens pecked at the beaten front yard and from the other side of the barn, where I could not see, the distinctive snorting of pigs or boar filled the air. In the distance, a few sheep grazed in an enclosed area, a precaution to keep them out of the fields. Corn and grain grew high, their green stalks already showing signs of gold. Living off the land kept the passage of time ever present on your mind.

When Jeremiah and I crested the hill on our borrowed horses, I saw smoke in the chimney of the house and movement in the field, where a team of sturdy plow horses struggled against the drying earth. The kitchen garden grew close to the front door of the house, luxuriously green, well-tended, and boasting blossoms alongside the more practical growth. This was a home, not merely a place of business.

As we approached, a small dark girl appeared in the doorway of the house. Her feet were bare, her braided hair tied with bright pink ribbons that didn't match the blue calico dress she wore. She carried a small square of cloth in one hand and a threaded needle in the other.

Jeremiah waved to her and the girl returned the gesture cheerfully, calling back into the darkness of the house, "Ma! Visitors!"

We'd dismounted by the time Abigail Washington appeared, wiping her hands on her apron. Her expression changed rapidly to wariness when she saw who we were. A second girl appeared, peering around Abigail's skirts, while the first girl ran up to Jeremiah, her face beaming.

"Jeremiah!" she cried. "You're just in time. Ursula had her kittens!"

"Well, now, isn't that fine?" he said, genially. "Esther, do you know Miss Goodnight, here?"

Esther's huge dark eyes turned to me just as her mother said, "Esther! You've work to do."

With a look of promise aimed at Jeremiah, Esther ran lightly back to the house, took her sister's hand, and disappeared into the dark.

Only then did Mrs. Washington come out from the shade of the house to approach us.

"Miss Goodnight, Jeremiah." She kept her arms folded. "It isn't time for another ad renewal, is it?"

It was less an inquiry than a threat. Clearly she didn't want me here and I didn't blame her. I didn't want to be here either.

Jeremiah said, "Miss Goodnight wanted to talk to you about something."

"She did, did she?"

I turned and reached into the saddlebags. The journal was there along with the most damaging of articles and the Evans notes. Until the bank opened and I made arrangements to place these in the safe, I wasn't taking any chances. The paper I was looking for was right on top, a little worse for wear.

"I'm sure you've heard about my uncle, Mrs. Washington," I said, retying the bag.

"I heard he passed away last night."

"He was murdered."

The words sounded stark and aggressive in the open air.

Mrs. Washington shifted uncomfortably. "I don't know what to say to that. I didn't know him. I just did work for him, that's all." Her eyes narrowed in suspicion. "I suppose you have some new terms you want to discuss?"

She sounded almost as belligerent as Charlie Markum and while I understood, I still had to struggle to keep my temper in check.

"What I wanted to discuss," I said, "is this notice that I found among my uncle's things."

Mrs. Washington barely glanced at the headline before she had drawn herself up and was glaring at me as though she'd have gladly cleaved me in two, had the ax been handy.

"You dare to..." she blustered, but I held up a hand.

"In *private*, I think, Mrs. Washington," I said, coolly. "Jeremiah, would you keep an eye on the horses for me?"

"Yes, ma'am," he said, promptly. He was clearly glad to be out of this discussion.

I took the saddlebags and slung them over my shoulder. Then I turned to Abigail Washington and gestured toward the house. "Shall we?"

She glared at me, but we both knew she had no choice. She led me into the darkness of her home.

* * *

The house was a square, with the usual kitchen and living quarters occupying one half. A door led into the back room and at the far side of the building, a wooden ladder rested against the opening of the attic where, presumably, dried foods were stored and the children slept.

The scent of herbs, hay, and bread weighed heavily in the air. Fresh loaves sat cooling on the heavy, well-built wooden table, and a clay pot full of flowers brightened the natural gloom. A basket of laundry stood by, ready for Monday's usual chores. Mrs. Washington, it seemed, liked to stick to the typical schedule. There were a few shelves, one containing a few battered books. A heavy ubiquitous Bible had a place of pride on a shelf all its own, underneath a Currier and Ives print. Bright curtains, neatly stitched, added strokes of color to the palette of wooden walls and dirt floors.

The two little girls were giggling over a Godey's Ladies Book. The little one leaned on Esther, her dark eyes bright with shared secrets and I was reminded of the hours I'd spent with my cousins, doing the same thing.

"Esther, Florence," Abigail said. "Outside if you please. Leave the book here."

Esther hopped up to her feet. "Come on, Florence, let's show Jeremiah the kittens!"

Florence clapped her hands together and let out an ear-piercing squeal to show her excitement. She turned her dark eyes on me and my breath caught, for they were big and bright and almost as black as Little Fox's.

Naturally, Florence took no notice of my shock and, if Abigail saw, doubtless she put her own interpretation on the matter. The two girls were scarcely out the door before Abigail turned on me, arms folded, her face blank and hard.

"Say what you want and be quick about it," she said in a low tone. "I'm a busy woman and I'm sure you've got a list of *clients* that you need to visit."

She didn't offer a seat at the table, so we stood. I adjusted the saddlebags on my shoulder and handed her the little notice.

"I've been going through my uncle's papers..." I began and she snorted.

"You didn't waste any time, did you?"

I plowed on. "Matilda Greene was the daughter of a prosperous farmer. Ten years ago, she disappeared. Her family, especially her brothers, are most anxious for her to come home, so anxious, they've posted a reward for information leading to her whereabouts." I paused and looked at her. "Is any of this sounding familiar, Mrs. Washington?"

She wasn't looking at the article. She was glaring at me.

I tapped the page. "The article gives a very detailed description of the woman and judging by the substantial amount of the reward, it sounds as though family pride has been injured. You see," and here I shuffled my feet in discomfort, "depending on who you ask, Miss Greene either ran off with a black man or was kidnapped."

"Kidnapped," she said bitterly. "I suppose that's the preferred way to explain what happened. After all, a white girl simply couldn't run off with a black man she loved. She has to be kidnapped. No matter how progressive the state, kidnapping is still preferred."

Her eyes, welling with tears, gave her away. She turned from me, clearing her throat.

I felt as though I'd just finished screaming obscenities. I fell silent. Outside, one of the girls started laughing hysterically, as though she were being attacked by a tickler.

When Mrs. Washington turned, she had such malevolence in her gaze that I really thought she was going to strike me.

"You have a lot of nerve, bringing this to my house, using Jeremiah as an escort." She hissed and jerked her head at the door. "Does he know?"

I had to stop myself from taking a step back. "No!" I said, firmly. "I haven't spoken to anyone about this."

"Thanks for small favors." She took a step forward, jabbing the article in her clenched fist like it was a knife. "Look here, Goodnight, I'll tell you what I told your no-good uncle: we don't have any money. We barely own the dirt we're building on. All I have to offer is an exchange: bread and clean clothing in return for... for the ad. It's all I had to offer to him. It's all I have for you and if you had any mercy in your soul..."

I cut her off. "So my uncle *was* blackmailing you."

A beat. Then...

"Yes."

I'd thought I was prepared for the truth. I was wrong. It hit me like a physical blow, so hard I almost staggered. My Uncle Matthew, the prize-winning journalist and pride of the Goodnight clan, had descended to blackmailing his neighbors.

I felt sick, worse than I had when I first arrived. My knees felt weak and I leaned on the table to get a better grip on myself.

I was right. Oh my God, I was right. Oh, Lord, help me, what do I say now?

Abigail was speaking, her fear making her oblivious to my distress.

"He found that notice a year ago," she gestured menacingly with the scrap of paper. "I don't know how he knew it was me they were looking for, I really don't. Maybe the hair, maybe my accent, I don't know. But he knew and I admitted to it before I realized why he was asking. I actually thought he might be sympathetic."

She leaned against the table, her shoulders sagging, her mouth twisted in a terrible grin. "Sympathy! What a laugh. He told me that we'd be safe from my brothers, that he didn't want much. Offered to protect us, throw them off the trail if they ever got wind of where I was. My hero."

I felt breathless, wordless. My hand snaked into my pockets and gripped my mother's beads. Then I found my voice: "Uncle Matthew offered you protection?"

"You don't know my brothers," Abigail said, softly. "They don't want me back. They want Titus. If they ever found him..."

She drew in a breath and went on: "I met Titus before the war. He'd been traded to an abolitionist, who freed him, but he still has the scars on his back where they... Anyway, when the war was over, Titus came back to find me. We could have disappeared in Maine, but Titus wanted to go west. I didn't care where we went, so long as I was with him and as far away as I could be from my brothers. If they ever found us, they'd kill him and no judge in the country would blink before letting them off."

She paused. "Laws out here aren't any better, really. We married in a church back east, but in this state, it doesn't hold. We are simply, as you would say, living in sin. But the people in this town... they haven't asked questions. They've accepted us or at least ignore us. We've carved out a place here. And I mean to stay."

I must have made a noise, for she looked at me sharply.

"My husband is a fine man, Miss Goodnight. But what's more important is he's *my* man and I'll do anything to protect him. Your uncle knew that. He held that notice over me like an executioner's ax." She glared at the notice in her hand. "A *bargain*, he called it. What's a little laundry and a loaf of bread where your family is concerned? Well, he had me there and that was that. Now you know and the cycle continues."

She shoved the notice across the table towards me.

I didn't touch it. I asked, "How long has this been going on?"

Abigail looked at her hands. "Since last June."

"Was that when Ben Evans came home from college?"

"Yes. Reckon it was."

I thought of the beautiful piano in the empty room. "Was my uncle blackmailing anyone else?"

Now the other woman looked at me shrewdly. "I don't know anything about anyone else, Miss Goodnight. As far as I know, I was the only one he had his claws into. If anyone else asks me, I'll say the same thing."

I could respect that.

There was just one more question to ask. I lifted the saddlebags and placed them back on my shoulders. "Just as a matter of interest, where were you this Sunday night?"

The eyes turned hostile again. "I was here, at home, nursing Florence. She had a fever."

Right on cue, Florence's giggling laughter drifted through the chinked walls and flooded the room with reality. Esther, Florence, and the little boy named Jonas: Abigail's children, her children with a freedman. She was right about one thing: the north might boast of more enlightened movements, but no one was entirely comfortable with mixed marriages or their progeny. I only had to look to my own background for confirmation of that.

"Titus was here, of course," Abigail was saying. "But he didn't know – doesn't know – about this. That was part of the deal with your uncle and I prefer it stay that way."

I nodded. "Did my uncle arrange to meet you later this week?"

"No."

"Did he stop by on Saturday, maybe?"

"No." Her eyes narrowed. "Why?"

She could have been lying about that, of course. It would be easily verified if I could get one of the children alone. But I couldn't see why she'd lie at this point.

"I'm glad to see that Florence recovered so quickly. Did you send for Doctor Lowe?"

"No. It was manageable." She leaned forward, her eyes hard. "Miss Goodnight, I didn't kill your uncle and you can't pin it on me. No blackmail goes that far."

That angered me. "If I was looking to *pin* the murder on someone, Mrs. Washington, I would let Ben Evans sit in jail. But I'm not and that should speak for itself."

Abigail didn't flinch. She nodded to the paper on the table. "All right. Shall we get down to business then?"

"There is no business." I slid the noticed back to Abigail. "I don't have any money, Mrs. Washington, or I'd offer to recompense you and your family for services rendered. This is yours and I give you my word of honor that there are no other copies."

When she made no move, no sound, I went on: "My uncle held your family hostage for over a year. There's no fixing that. All I can do is offer release and an apology. I am sorry. These and my silence are all I have to give."

For a moment, all Abigail Washington did was stare. Slowly, she reached out and took the offending page, her eyes wide and confused.

The room was closing in on me. I longed to escape and stood, shifting the saddlebags on my shoulders.

Abigail smoothed the clipping with her work-roughened hands, as though it were a love letter rather than a wanted poster.

"You mean it?" she asked. "This is the end of it?" Fragile hope was plain in her tone – hope and disbelief. She was too old to fully believe in anything or anyone anymore. Except, perhaps, in Titus, the man who'd come back for her.

"Yes," I said. "This is ended."

More silence. Finally, I realized I was waiting for... what, a thank you? An offer of reconciliation? For Mrs. Washington to say, "No harm done"? It was shallow and undeserved. Ashamed, I turned towards the door.

Abigail's voice stopped me. "I ought to thank you," she said. "But I'll hold it yet."

I kept my back to her and my head low. "Right."

"Maybe I was wrong about you, Miss Goodnight. I'd be glad to think so."

I nodded and stepped out the door.

The sun momentarily blinded me. When my vision cleared, I saw Jeremiah, stroking a tiny mewing ball of fur and chatting comfortably with a tall powerful looking black man. The two little girls played at their feet while Jonas, his handsome face creased with mature concentration, unhitched the two workhorses from their harness. The girls were small, but Jonas was of an age where he should have been in the little schoolhouse along with the other children.

Mixed marriages were hard enough on the husband and wife, but their children had it even worse. With the blood of both races in their veins, they belonged to all and to no one. It was their legacy to live as visible reminders that a social line had been crossed. Through no fault or choice of their own, they were doomed to live on the edge of society, ever looking in from the outside and never fully embraced.

I'd had only a taste of such a cross, but it had been enough.

"Such dark features," Grandmother Goodnight had said of my mother. *"Bad enough that Samuel's yoked himself to a papist. Mark my words, there's a savage in the wood pile somewhere and the taint will carry."*

It wasn't the last time that someone would suggest that my dark eyes and hair weren't exactly European, but my differences were slight enough that they could be overlooked. How much worse was it for children like Jonas and his sisters, or Little Fox, the boy who'd been taken away, still clutching my father's old watch?

Little Fox's face filled my mind, bringing with it waves of ever-present guilt. My last memory of him was his distraught face, clinging to his mother even as he reached for me while I stood rooted in place. They'd taken him away. And I'd allowed them to do so.

Where was he now? I didn't know if he were alive, well, dead, or even if his mother was still with him...

Don't go there, Jenny, girl.

"There are others."

Abigail's voice made me jump in surprise. When I turned, she was standing in the shadow of the doorway, her arms folded again. The newspaper was crushed in her grip.

"Your uncle ran 'ads' for others," she said. "I don't know who, exactly, but I reckon Jeremiah knows. Even if he doesn't know, if you get my drift."

I looked across the way at Jeremiah. "You're probably right."

Abigail cleared her throat and said, when I looked at her, "When Ben Evans came home... Things weren't the same for your uncle. He took to drinking, then to gambling. Once a man starts doing those things -" she looked me dead in the eye "- he changes. You know what I mean."

I managed to nod. "Yes. I do."

It was a poor excuse, but I was grateful nonetheless. I think she understood for she nodded and even reached out to clap me on the shoulder. Then, shoving the paper into the pocket of her apron, she strode over towards her family.

Jeremiah handed the kitten back to Esther, shook Titus's hand, and ran lightly over to me. We cinched our saddles and I reattached the saddlebags before swinging back up.

We turned our horses to leave, and as we did, I saw Abigail Washington take her husband's arm. The two little girls laughed and danced around them while Jonas amused himself by playing with the mangy dog that leapt about his feet. It was quite a picture and suddenly I realized that I was watching, not a woman on the run from the consequences of an illicit affair, but a family on the rise. And it was good.

I lifted the reins and turned my horse towards the road.

ARTICLE

November 25, 1863
From the *Albany Sun*
(Discovered in Matthew Goodnight's personal journal.)

DRAFT JUMPERS ARRESTED
Arrests have been made among the immigrant Irish community today. Several young men, all of Irish descent, with no education or prospects, have been accused of DRAFT JUMPING, wherein these men take substitution money for wealthy draftees, then desert and repeat, using a different name. The arresting officer, Sgt. Michael Keenan, noted that draft dodging and jumping is an epidemic among the lower classes.

"Mr. Lincoln's war is being prolonged by these conmen," he said. "It's unpatriotic and treasonable."

Sgt. Keenan was among the many public servants who chose to remain on the job, paying the commutation fees rather than march off to war.

Among the list of arrested parties are John Hurley, Sean O'Brian, Liam O'Neill, Joseph Michael McHugh...

TWENTY-FIVE

We rode for about a half a mile in silence. I rode carelessly, my head on my chest and the reins slack in my hands, my thoughts miles away. I was still trying to match townspeople to the newspaper clippings in my uncle's journal when Jeremiah reined up suddenly.

"That's John Henry's horse," he said.

That drew my attention to a sharp point.

John Henry's big figure was a dark contrast to the reddish brown background. He rode his usual mount, Lane, I think its name was, and since they headed straight towards us, there would be no getting out of meeting him.

I pulled myself up on my horse and lifted my chin. Helen came to mind, but John Henry was riding from the direction of the town, not towards it.

When he reined up next to us, I noted that he looked drained, as though he hadn't slept much. His clothes were in their usual dusty state, though he'd changed his shirt to a dark blue one that suited him. He wore his gun on his side, but I'd learned, since our last encounter, that there were greater things to fear than John Henry's temper. There were, for instance, the nerves that ran like fire ants down my spine every time he looked in my direction.

"Morning," he said, as unmoved as I was discomforted. "You're far from home, Miss Goodnight."

"In more ways than you know, Mr. Evans," I said. "How is Mrs. Evans?"

"Fine," he said and glanced away. "Had a baby girl early this morning."

"John Henry lost his wife in childbirth a while back..."

I wondered how it felt to watch his brother start a family of his own. We don't always choose to stand on the sidelines and I couldn't imagine it set well with a man of John Henry's determined nature. Sarah's appearance was timely – or was it a convenient distraction....?

Jenny Goodnight! You're becoming an old gossip!

"We was just riding back to town," Jeremiah said, as I shook these thoughts out of my head. "Miss Goodnight wanted to talk to Mrs. Washington."

"So I heard." Now John Henry's gaze fastened on me.

"News travels fast," I commented, though I was confused – I hadn't mentioned my trip to anyone.

John Henry solved that mystery. "John at the livery stables doesn't miss much," he said.

I was nettled. What possible construction would this John and his cronies put on our call? What would Sage think? How much truth would be guessed?

The irritation must have shown on my face, because Jeremiah, who was about to say something, looked at the reins in his hands instead.

"The Washingtons are good people." The note of warning in John Henry's voice was unmistakable.

"I'm sure," I said coolly and changed the subject. "Do you live around here, Mr. Evans?"

He gestured toward the hills in the west. "My family owns quite a bit of land that way. But that isn't why I'm out here."

"You calling on the Washingtons, too?" Jeremiah asked.

John Henry had twisted around in his saddle towards his own bags. He shook his head. "Not hardly." He pulled a book, big, black, and all-too-familiar, and guided his horse closer to mine. "I think this belongs to you."

His hand brushed mine as I took my father's Bible from him. It was warm and a little more worn from its ride in John Henry's saddlebags. My eyes immediately and regrettably stung with tears as

I felt the soft leather cover. It was for this that I'd gone to the hotel this morning, this above all else, even above the Pinkerton letter. Just holding it was like gripping my father's hand. I had to stop myself from hugging it.

"Where did you find this?" I asked gruffly.

"Sage found it in your uncle's hotel room," John Henry said. "I, uh, convinced him that it ought to be returned."

"Thank you," I whispered and for a moment, felt safe enough to look up at him. "You rode all the way out here for this?"

The smile touched his blue eyes, creasing his face. "Partially. I also came by to see if you'd be willing to come to the ranch. My mother would like a chat."

All comfort disappeared instantly. I remembered Varina Evan's frozen glare at me the night of the wedding, her queenly carriage, and the unquestioning manner with which people gave way to her. Her son was in jail, accused of a crime everyone would rather I had committed. She would do anything to protect him – had she already done so to protect her dead husband's reputation?

"Why would she want to talk to me?" I asked.

John Henry's high-spirited horse was prancing to one side. Without visible effort, he brought Lane back around to face me.

"Well, now, ma'am," he said. "I can think of one or two things you two might have in common."

His gaze dropped briefly to the bruise on my mouth and his own jaw tensed.

How dare you? How dare you look at me when Sarah...

My irritation made me foolish. "Do you often run errands for your mother?" I asked.

He didn't like that.

"She's a little tied up right now," he said evenly. "Attending to my sister-in-law and all." He looked at the sun and then at me. "I can ride over with you. If you feel up to it, that is."

He must have expected me to pick up on the challenge embedded in his words, for he grinned ever so slightly when I responded.

"I'd be delighted," I said. "I have a few questions for your mother and for Helen, too, if she's up to visitors." I turned to Jeremiah. "You can come if you want. If not, feel free to ride home."

He hesitated. "I promised my ma I'd be back in time for supper."

"You go on home then, Jeremiah," John Henry said, with authority. "I'll escort Miss Goodnight."

The grin was back and I confess, I didn't know quite what to do with it. Jeremiah, looking relieved, turned to ride off when something occurred to me.

"Jeremiah!" I said, swinging my horse around. "Just a quick question. Liam is your mother's brother, right?"

The slight hesitation before he spoke told me the answer.

"He's my father's brother," Jeremiah said finally. "Danaher... you know."

Lying didn't sit well with him and I already knew that Ruth's maiden name was O'Neill. It was common enough, but my uncle had held on to that news clipping and I didn't really believe in coincidences.

"When you next see him," I said, "Please ask him to come and see me. Tell him it's about the terms of my uncle's agreement."

He nodded uncomfortably and rode off.

One down, one on the way, who knows how many more to go.

I swung my horse around to join John Henry where he was waiting a little further down the road. I still held the Bible and, as my own bags were full, I wasn't quite sure what to do with it.

"Here," John Henry plucked it out of my hands and slipped it back into his own bag. "I'll take it from here."

"Thank you."

"Pleasure," he said. Then he lifted his reins and clucked at his horse.

I followed suit and it occurred to me to be glad that Sarah Lowe would be occupied all day at the schoolhouse. *No need for her to know I'm keeping company with John Henry...* I stopped myself before I could finish the thought. Lucky for me, John Henry was watching the passing scenery, not my flushing face.

Time passed in silence. John Henry didn't appear any more inclined to talk than his horse. I had time to wonder what Varina had in mind for me. I did actually want to talk to Varina and Helen. Someone had been arguing with my uncle last night and they were as likely suspects as anyone.

Wonder what John Henry would say if he knew what I was thinking.

I looked over at my escort. He was occupied in thought, his hands loose on the reins and his eyes on the road. He rode as though he'd been born in the saddle, and his sun-burnt skin and calloused hands spoke of hours in the open. He might belong to the most powerful family in the county, but John Henry Evans knew how to work.

He caught me looking at him. I pulled my eyes away and focused on the road ahead. The sun was high in the sky. It was noon or a little past. The rays beat down on my head and though I knew the bonnet I wore was keeping it off, the brim was restricting my view. Without thinking, I pushed it off my head, allowing it to hang down my back.

John Henry's laughter startled me.

"Why, Miss Goodnight!" he exclaimed. "What would those good folk of yours back east think if they could see you now?"

I flushed and said the first thing that came to mind: "My Aunt Alice would be asking me for the pattern for these divided skirts!"

He chuckled. Perhaps he thought I was joking, but then, he didn't know my aunt. Aunt Alice was the first in her neighborhood to make bloomers when they came into brief fashion in the 50s, and she held on to them long after the rage had passed. The graceless, defiant things became something of a family joke: whenever Aunt Alice's husband made a hint of protest against her many committees and social works, she would threaten to wear the bloomers to his next dinner party.

The silence was threatening to come down on us again, so I broke it by asking how far the ranch was.

"We're about halfway there," he said. "It's a nice ride."

"It's a nice day," I agreed.

More silence, then: "The Washingtons are good people," John Henry said. "Timothy Washington is a rock in the community."

It took me a moment to remember that Timothy was the name Titus had assumed after leaving the east.

"He seems like a gentleman," I said.

"He wouldn't hurt a soul," John Henry averred.

"Neither would your brother, I suppose."

"I didn't say that. I said he wouldn't stab a man in the back."

"Why is he staying silent? Why not deny it or talk to his lawyer?"

He pinned me with a look. "If you're so convinced he's guilty, why do you want to question my mother and sister-in-law?" Before I could answer that, he continued: "Sheriff Sage told me someone broke into your shop and trashed it looking for something."

A chill ran down my spine at the remembrance. "Yes."

"Did they find what they were looking for?"

"I've no way of knowing."

We rode for a few more paces before he spoke again.

"If I were a betting man," he said, in a low comfortable rumble, as though we were still discussing the weather or the latest Jules Verne novel, "I would bet that the person who broke into your print shop was the same person who killed your uncle."

He looked at me. The hat shaded his face and I thought, *I wonder if I'll ever get to talk to you when there isn't a crisis dividing us.*

It seemed unlikely. Once I'd cleared up this matter - if I cleared up this matter - I'd be going back to Massachusetts.

"That would make sense," I said.

"What do you think?"

I knew why he was asking. His brother had been in jail when my uncle's shop was broken into. If I agreed, I would be letting his brother off the hook for my uncle's murder and I couldn't do that yet. But John Henry had thought to bring me my father's Bible and Ben was his brother.

"I don't know enough to guess at this point," I finally said.

It was true. The revelations of this morning had rocked my faith in my own analysis of reality. I didn't know enough yet and I couldn't admit anything less to John Henry.

Something flickered across his face before the usual western stoicism settled back in. His eyes searched my face for a long moment and I held his gaze. Whatever he saw there seemed to satisfy him, for he turned back to the road and nudged Lane to go faster. We had an appointment to keep.

TWENTY-SIX

The Evans Ranch was called the Circle E in those days and the Evans house, of which Varina Evans reigned as mistress, was referred to as the Evans Mansion. As the house came into view, about a half mile down a tree-lined road past the over-sized gate, I saw immediately why. The Mansion was an enormous structure that combined the practical needs of a ranch headquarters with the style of a Southern plantation house. Wide and tall, two stories of adobe with a long rambling porch in the front, it loomed over approaching visitors, a visual reminder of who was actually in charge of the county.

Jacob's Kingdom, I found myself thinking.

There was a team and a wagon in front of the house. As we rode up, Trigger Olsen appeared in the doorway with his arms filled with blankets. A smaller man came out after him, carrying a suitcase. Both paused when they saw us approach.

"Afternoon, boss," Trigger said and nodded at me. "Ma'am." He moved to dump his armload into the wagon.

"Afternoon Trigger, Findlay." John Henry swung down from his horse. "Is Mrs. Evans in?"

I followed suit and lashed my reins to the hitching post.

"Just arrived," Trigger said. "She's settling Mrs. Helen in with the little one."

"You missed the doc," the other man said. "He just left for town."

Findlay was more boy than man, a scrawny lad with an open expression and he seemed very pleased to be on the Evans' porch. He looked at me with unconcealed curiosity.

"Strong woman," Trigger commented.

"Must be," John Henry said with an unusual catch in his voice.

"The doctor said she bounced back quicker than he'd ever seen," the boy said eagerly. "But he was glad he got there when he did. It was touch and go at first."

"Yes," John Henry said. "We're grateful, Findlay."

The boy grinned, pleased. "I just wished it hadn't taken me so long to find the doctor last night. When he wasn't home, I had to go through half the town before I found him."

"Well, we're obliged to you and your family," John Henry said again as Trigger smothered a grin. "You be sure to thank your mother for me, tell her we'll be around soon to make our thanks in person." He turned to me and, taking his hat, gestured towards the house. "Miss Goodnight."

I nodded to Findlay and Trigger and stepped before John Henry into the house.

After riding for miles through dry country and spending so much time in my uncle's half-finished house, entering the Evans Mansion was an overwhelming experience. The enormous foyer was decorated in rich wall paper and dark-stained wood. A curving staircase with an ornate banister led to the second floor, passing large windows draped in heavy velvet curtains. The dark wood floor was so highly polished that I feared to walk on it.

John Henry had no such compunction. He strode on through the foyer and gestured for me to follow him. A woman in a long skirt and apron appeared in the hall door. John Henry asked her to inform Mrs. Evans that Miss Goodnight was here, and then he showed me into the sitting room.

It, too, was enormous, a showroom with plush carpeting, ornate candelabras, and heavy furniture. There was a piano in the corner and French doors leading to the outside. It was cool in here, thanks to the heavy curtains that blocked the light. An enormous marble fireplace sat cold and dark flanked by two enormous bookcases, nearly full with books, most new and hardly touched. Settees and chairs were scattered about prettily. With the exception of its exaggerated size, it might have been the sitting room of any well-to-do family back east.

I hesitated in the doorway, feeling displaced and appallingly dirty after my ride. John Henry was as dusty, but this was his domain. He went immediately over to a small table, where a tray of lemonade and glasses sat.

"Come on in, Miss Goodnight," he said, tossing his hat onto a chair. "No airs and graces today."

Once inside, the beautiful piano drew me like a siren and I stood over it, admiring the polished, gleaming wood. I had to stop myself from running my dirty hands over the ivories. A book of music was opened to a page of Schubert's songs. I took it and leafed through it. The book was new, but well used and there was a notation inside the front cover: *Helen: who can turn ivory into gold.*

Helen.

So this was her piano, the second bought just for her in this town. I wondered what kind of pull she must have on men to have twice enticed one to build a palace for her.

John Henry came over, carrying two glasses of lemonade. Despite the fact that he was in his home, his rolling gait was not as relaxed as it might have been. He handed me a glass and raised his own in a toast.

"To life," he said.

I tapped my glass against his and drank. The tangy sweetness felt cool and soothing against my parched throat and I drank greedily. When I lowered the glass, I found his eyes on me. He gestured towards the piano.

"You play?" he asked.

"A little," I said.

"Every woman I know has said that."

"It is generally the truth. At least, it is in my case."

Trigger appeared in the doorway, hat in his hands.

"John Henry," he said. "A word, if you've a minute. It's about the south pasture."

John Henry's jaw tightened.

I said, "I'll be fine here. If you need to go work..."

He hesitated, then strode out after Trigger.

Without John Henry, that great room seemed even larger and I that much smaller. I stood with the empty glass in my hand and a sinking feeling in my stomach. I didn't have long to wait.

Varina Evans entered the room at a stride that spoke of much to do and little time to do it. Her white and gray hair was done up in a crown on her head and her blue eyes were icy. She'd dressed in a casual day-dress, immaculately pressed and stylish as anything I could have gotten up for Sunday. She did not look anything like a woman who'd spent the night helping her daughter-in-law through childbirth.

I immediately felt underdressed and filthy in my dust-coated divided-skirts and riding boots, which I rather think was the point.

Varina halted a few feet from me and clasped her hands in front of her skirts. She stood where the light poured through a space in the curtained French doors, her white hair aglow and her posture as erect as a queen's.

"Miss Goodnight," she said. "Thank you for coming. I trust your ride wasn't too tiring?"

Her Virginian accent was deceptively warm. She'd mastered the knack of making a social nicety sound like a gauntlet being thrown down. Thanks to my aunts back east, I'd long had experience with this sort of thing. Immediately my shoulders went back and my chin went up.

"It was a lovely ride," I said, stepping around the piano towards her. "I was grateful for the invitation. I had some questions for you and Helen. I hope she is doing well after her long night?"

The icy blue eyes narrowed.

"She is exhausted, as you may well imagine. She and the baby are resting comfortably now. I think it'll be some time before she can have visitors." She gestured towards the French doors. "I was about to take a turn in the garden. Maybe you'd like to walk with me?"

At that moment, there was nothing I wanted more than to sit on one of her plush settees and have a long drink of cool water. My eyes had only just finished adjusting to the darker light of the interior and my face was burnt from the sun and the sand-filled wind. But the request wasn't really so much of an invitation as it was an instruction. She opened the French door and waited.

I managed to pass her without touching either her or her dress.

"I find a walk in the gardens to be peaceful and refreshing," Varina said as we walked down the stone-lined path to the west of the house. "I designed them myself and as an Easterner, I think you'll appreciate them, Miss Goodnight."

She showed me through an opening in the shrubbery and I immediately saw what she meant. A square of land had been carved from the enormous, dry landscape and turned into something reminiscent of a house garden. Around the edges were flowers of pink, purple, yellow, and blue, and in each corner, maple trees cast welcome shade. Herbs and vegetables were boxed into rectangles and arranged so that the colors ran through the color wheel. A fountain stood in the middle, trickling water, a wonderful bit of luxury in a land so thirsty.

I stood luxuriating in the scent of herbs and florals. Here was a respite from the enormous sky and the empty lands, the constant reminders that this territory was not where we'd come from. I was reminded of Massachusetts, where hills and trees shortened your view and protected you from the worst of the winter storms. It was the first plot of land that I'd seen since coming here that I could reasonably call 'snug'.

No sooner had I thought this when another realization, strong yet gentle, broke over me. This garden square, enormous as it would have been considered back in my home town, now felt small. I felt as one does upon outgrowing a beloved dress – it was too tight and as much as I wanted to wear it, I no longer could. I wondered if I'd outgrown Massachusetts as well.

I managed a small smile when my placid hostess turned to me.

"It's lovely," I said.

"It was a lot of work," she remarked and moved down the path towards the fountain. "My husband ordered this fountain especially to please me. It took two years to arrive and then another month to route the water and install. He never got to see it here. You are from Massachusetts, aren't you, Miss Goodnight?"

"Yes, I am."

"I'm from Virginia. I grew up on a plantation. Land rich, coin-poor as they say. When my father met Jacob, he told me that my intended was a new kind of man. 'Some men cast a long shadow and the East is too tame for them,' he told me. That was my husband, Miss Goodnight – a man too large for the East."

Her voice was soft. Her hands stroked the fountain basin for a second before she turned.

"Would you follow me?" she asked, too politely. Her eyes gleamed with ill-concealed anger.

"Why, of course, Mrs. Evans."

We passed through a gap in the hedge on the far side of the garden square and found ourselves facing another square, this one fenced by wrought iron and marked not with plants but with gravestones. A family cemetery is a not uncommon sight on a ranch as large as this one, but I was unnerved all the same.

A large granite monument stood in the middle, surrounded by smaller stones. It bore the name EVANS in letters nearly as large as the legend that lay buried underneath. In smaller lettering, I read "Jacob Hector Evans: beloved husband, loving father, town founder. Missed by all who knew him."

The dates bracketing his life were marked, along with Varina's name. Deep purple violets, wilted now from the sun, rested on the ground at the foot of the monument. On the top, a cross of dark stone cast a melancholy shadow across our faces.

I thought, *they will be buried together,* and the thought stung like a whiplash.

We Goodnights had our own spot in the Dandridge cemetery, where centuries of the family were buried alongside each other in a silent family reunion. There was a stone carved with my father and my mother's name, his first wife having been buried with her people out of state. At the time of its carving, no one had known that my mother would revert to her Catholic faith, nor that by doing so, she would be entitled to a Catholic burial in sacred ground. It was only when the priest appeared at our house, dressed in his alien black gown and speaking in his strange accent that we realized: the Roman church wanted to lay claim to their own.

Aunt Alice had tolerated the priest's visits to the house when my mother was alive. When my mother died, Aunt Alice insisted that the question of her burial was not up to the aunts. My father was weeks away from home, but it was summer and the body couldn't wait his arrival. At twelve, I was too young for a question like this, but Aunt Alice insisted: "Should your mother be buried as a Goodnight? Or a Catholic?"

I felt paralyzed by the choice. When my mother reverted to her old faith, the betrayal had wounded me deeply. I felt as though she'd turned not only from my father, but from me as well. Even if I'd wished to, I couldn't have left my father's religion, not while he lived.

My mother's rosary was hidden in my pocket, my father's sisters standing before me, but all I could see was my mother, alone, languishing alone in the dark somewhere. I didn't know any Catholics and the idea of her being buried among strangers terrified me. She may have abandoned me in religion and in death, but I couldn't do the same to her.

"She's a Goodnight," I said. "She should be buried with my father."

I had no way of knowing, of course, that my father would die out in the west, too far and too poor to be transferred back home. My final gesture to my mother had been to deny her heritage, to separate her from her faith in favor of her husband. Ultimately, both had been left stranded.

All these years later, the decision still haunted me, even there in the graveyard with Varina Evans.

I looked at her and thought, *No matter what people like Uncle Matthew say about your husband, you will have the privilege of resting by his side when all is said and done.*

Judging from the way she was glaring at the monument, her face hard, her hands clasped, her body straight as an arrow, Varina wasn't satisfied with this comfort. She was a statue made of living flesh, as animated as stone.

"He loved us." Varina stared at the monument as though she could bore through it to the man buried beneath. "He was a big man. Brash, sometimes rude, even brutal. But he was a good man and I was proud to bear his name and his children."

The wind slid over us, rustling the leaves overhead. My whole body was sore, as though I'd spent the night being beaten with a rod. I wondered if that was how Varina felt while my uncle was still alive. Being at war with ghosts is exhausting, a near-impossible campaign to win, for how can you battle that which has no shape and no voice?

Varina went on: "Your uncle was wrong about my husband. I know it. My boys know it. Half the people in this town know it. He wasn't a coward and he wasn't a thief. He was certainly not a man who'd kill his partner to steal land. He was a force to be reckoned with and if he were alive today, I wouldn't have to be dealing with the likes of you."

She trembled as she spoke. Actually shook, right there in front of me, like the delicate heroine in a cheap novel.

"Why were you so afraid of my uncle?" I asked.

She turned on me with flashing eyes.

"All a man has out here is his name," she said. "The land, the wind, the hardship strips everything else away, but his name remains. When you take that away, what have you got left?"

"Truth, ma'am," I said. "Truth remains."

She looked at me and I thought - I could have sworn - that she was about to ask me Pilate's question.

But she didn't. Instead, she turned and walked two steps to the left and turned again, this time facing a smaller headstone. There was a rose carved into the face of it and the lettering read: "Eliza Jane Evans - beloved wife" and a date. Beneath her name was another, "Frederick - cherished son, gone too soon."

I felt cold all over, for I knew who this was even before Varina said, "This was John Henry's wife. She died in childbirth three years ago."

The silence was awkward now. Varina stood with the wind tugging on her skirt, waiting. I cleared my throat and muttered, "I'm sorry."

"Eliza was good for my son. She wasn't very strong physically, but she was a lady, with a lady's strength and a woman's heart. She was, as you might say, a pearl of great price."

I thought of Sarah Lowe and my throat tightened. Varina, unknowing, went on:

"My sons are good men, strong men, men who have a future in this state. They cannot link themselves with just anyone and they know this." She folded her thin arms. "They are the future leaders of this community, the men who carry on their father's legacy. The woman who stands with them must value that trust. A woman who will stay, a woman whose past is unstained."

Instantly, my mother's white face with her huge brown, pleading eyes was before me, flanked by that of Trailing Rose and Little Fox, those whom I might have loved, had I allowed myself. My betrayal marred their expressions, my heart weighed heavy with the silence of their absence. If I was alone in the world, it was in part because I chose to be. If my past was tarnished, it was because of choices I made.

"Whose past is unstained..."

What a luxury that is.

I reached into my pocket, touched my mother's rosary, and instantly felt calmer.

"Mrs. Evans," I said. "Why did you want to see me today?"

Her lips tightened.

"I want to buy you out, Miss Goodnight," she said.

This was not what I expected. "Buy me out?"

"Yes." She loomed over me, a gray and white threat. "I want the paper and the press, the house and the office, and everything that is in them. I want every scrap of paper your uncle left behind and I will pay you well for them. I want *everything*, Miss Goodnight. Everything."

My thoughts went immediately to the journal in my saddlebags, the saddlebags that I'd so foolishly left on the livery horse. I had to act calm until I could verify that I hadn't been searched.

"My uncle isn't even buried, Mrs. Evans," I said calmly. "I haven't had time to make any decisions yet."

"That's not what I've heard," Varina said. "I heard you intended to go into your uncle's line of... work."

She knows!

With difficulty, I stayed the course. If Varina knew about the blackmail, nothing changed. I still had to do what I had to do and I certainly could not turn the 'business' over to her, however much she thought she could bully me.

"I haven't made up my mind," I said calmly. "Out of curiosity, exactly what do you think my uncle had on your husband, Mrs. Evans?"

Her eyes narrowed.

"That doesn't matter," she said. "I know something of your uncle's activities, Miss Goodnight. I won't let it go any further. I won't allow it."

"I don't see how even an Evans can stop the free press," I said.

"You are very like your uncle, aren't you?" She didn't make it sound like a compliment.

"Where was Helen going Sunday night?" I asked.

Varina's face froze for the briefest moment before she answered with practiced carelessness, "She'd gone for a buggy ride when the labor pains took her."

"She just randomly decided to go for a ride in the middle of the night?"

"Miss Goodnight, I really don't...?"

"Where were you, Mrs. Evans?"

Venomous hate flickered in her eyes. Her fists clenched briefly then released.

"I was at home." She gestured towards the house. "In this house, with the servants, all of whom will vouch for me, should the need arise." She raised her chin. "I trust that won't be necessary."

"I shouldn't think so," I said. Doubtless they would vouch for her – regardless of what the truth actually was.

"So *many* questions," Varina said softly. "Almost as though you had doubts about my son's guilt."

"Do you want to know what I think happened?" I didn't give her a chance to answer, just kept right on going. "My uncle was trying to scare Ben and the rest of you Saturday night. I think he succeeded with Helen and she went to see him. When Ben realized she was gone, he took off after her, but he arrived too late. He panicked and, to protect his wife, made a big show of leaving with bloodied hands." I fixed her with a look. "Ben thinks Helen killed my uncle. That's why he isn't making a plea. He's waiting to talk to her."

Varina was staring at me liked she just discovered something particularly nasty on her shoe. Her voice could have frozen salt-water. "You really think my daughter-in-law took time out of birthing *a baby* to kill your uncle?"

"I think the horror of what she'd done shocked her into labor. I was told that the baby came early."

She laughed, a short, bitter, terrible sound. "You really don't know her at all, do you?"

"It's the only theory I can come up with that lets your son off the hook," I said evenly. "The fact is, Charlie Markum heard a woman arguing with my uncle before the murder happened. It ties in rather neatly, don't you think?"

She was shaking again, her face white with rage.

"No, Miss Goodnight," she hissed. "I *don't* think so at all. Do you know what I think fits better? I think it was *you* that Markum heard arguing with your uncle. Everyone in town knows that he beat you - why shouldn't you take revenge? We know you have a temper. You were barely in town five minutes before you pulled a gun on John Henry. Why shouldn't you save yourself by killing your uncle? Who would blame a little withered thing like yourself?" She thrust her face forward until it was inches from mine. "My son will *not* hang for what you did, Jenny Goodnight."

Her rage was towering now, so potent that I found myself stumbling back defensively.

"You killed Matthew Goodnight," she said in a whisper as powerful as a shout. "You killed him and then gave yourself an alibi."

"I didn't..." I started, but she hadn't finished.

"I'm going to offer you this deal only once. Confess to the sheriff and I'll see to it that you don't hang."

"You *can't* be serious..."

"Confess to the murder, and I'll get you off on a plea of self-defense and make sure that the word gets out that you were a heroic victim. *Then,*" she stopped my second protest with an impatient wave of her hand, "I'll buy your paper and all the research. I'll pay you generously and you'll leave here, Miss Goodnight. You'll go back to Maine or wherever it is you came from, and you will never bother us again. Do I make myself clear?"

The wind whipped about our shoulders, accenting the chill that ran down my spine. Varina Evans stood before me, fists balled, shoulders back, eyes ablaze. I stood my ground, but only barely.

"You must take me for a fool, Mrs. Evans," I said, through a throat as dry as the landscape around us.

Her expression shifted ever so slightly.

"Miss Goodnight, you do *not* want to cross me," she said. "My son will not hang. The only question is whether or not you will. The choice is yours." She took a half step closer to me. "I've seen what Matthew Goodnight has done to this town and to the people in it. The sins of the fathers may be revisited on the sons, but where does it end? Your family has done enough damage to my husband. You will not get your claws into my sons. I'll stop you legally if I can, but I'll stop you in any case. Do I make myself clear?"

In the distance, I heard the sound of drovers, coming in from a long ride, their masculine voices echoing off the hills and mingling with the neighing of their horses. A dog barked and then, through the normal cacophony of a working ranch, I heard the warm rumble of John Henry's laughter.

It was time to go.

I drew myself up and did my best imitation of Grandmother Goodnight: cold, distant, secure in her superiority. "You've made your point, Mrs. Evans. Now, if you'll excuse me, I have a long ride back into town."

Without waiting for her reaction or her permission, I turned and began to stride back towards the house. Her voice, as cold as a December wind, called after me.

"The choice is yours, Miss Goodnight."

I paused and turned.

I only have to close my eyes to see again that tall, thin, wasted looking woman with the fire in her eyes, standing among the gravestones in a land so far away from where she'd come. She stood fierce and determined, holding on so tightly to a cherished memory that she was warping the present and future with it. Like all tragedies, there was something almost noble about her, though I was in no condition to admire her just then.

"I understand you, Mrs. Evans," I said. "More than you can possibly know."

* * *

The saddlebags were still full and apparently untouched. I was cinching my saddle, my fingers trembling with repressed rage, when John Henry appeared.

"I'll ride along with you," he said and he swung up on Lane.

I gave him a sharp look. "I don't need an escort."

He returned the gaze with interest.

"I'll ride along with you," he repeated and there was no arguing with him.

TWENTY-SEVEN

It wasn't until we were out of sight of that dreadful house that Varina's words really began to have an impact on me.

"I've seen what Matthew Goodnight has done to this town and the good people in it..."

I wondered if John Henry knew. My heart squeezed in sudden pain at the thought. Why his opinion should matter more than the woman who'd threatened me only moments ago, I was not yet brave enough to admit to.

How Varina knew about my uncle's blackmailing scheme was anyone's guess. Perhaps one of the victims had confided in her, the peasant seeking recourse from the lady of the manor. Perhaps Uncle Matthew had tried something on her, though I doubted that he, even in the midst of his envy-infused crusade, would have tried something that stupid.

Oh, Lord, help me: this burden is too big...

We rode in silence, John Henry and I. The wind poured around our shoulders, making the grass curtsey and the sand dance. Wind and water have the same strengths and weakness. They do not change things by themselves but rather by the force of their personality, if you will. Water smooths over rocks and levels towns by overflowing its banks. Wind whips the sand and the sand obliterates tracks and the marks of other beings. I've seen whole towns destroyed by both water and wind and I've always found the wind to be the most eerie. Wind doesn't simply shift human evidence – it erases it, sanding down our marks until they are no more. Leave the desert frontier a few years and you'd never know humans had lived there or even passed through. White man or red man, it makes no difference; all signs of them disappear before the almighty sweep of sand-infused air.

It is for this very obliteration that some men come out west. In the East, there is stability: one knows a man by his land, his family, his father, and his father's people. You know where he went to school and which orchards he used to steal apples from. All is known – all is remembered on the great scroll of landscape and memory.

But out here on the frontier, a man has no past. The wind erases it and the river of people comes and goes, taking their memories with them. All that remains is the man himself: reborn, remade in an image that he and his actions alone create. You lose yourself in the winds of the west. You build yourself in them as well.

"The sins of the father are revisited upon the sons..."

Of all the verses in the Bible, this one always struck me as the most unjust. It is also true: action creates reaction as a stone thrown into a pond creates ripples. A man murders a man and his son and daughter bear the burden of being a murderer's offspring. A man is generous and the same is expected of his offspring. But Joseph descended from Jacob the thief and Joseph was righteous. Absalom came from David and was not. How long must a family remain responsible for the actions of another?

Here, the constantly renewing, ever erasing frontier offers sanctuary in anonymity. A man can disappear here. A man can allow the wind and the sand to scrub away his familial faults until all that is left is the bare, soft skin of his own character and personality. Here, you can determine your own legend. Here, you are responsible only for your own actions. Here, the wind and sand and floods have wiped away your past and left you alone to craft a new one. The Promised Land isn't about milk and honey: it's about the freedom to define yourself.

My uncle was not hated because of his venom towards the Evans family. He was reviled because he was reviving the past. He was the east, coming to the west, bearing the ledger book of wrongs and stripping Cinderella of her finery. He was the slave owner with the long-forgotten bill of sale. He threatened not just the Evanses, but every man, woman, and child who'd come here hoping for a clean, fresh start.

I'll have to tell Aunt Alice, I thought and the thought flooded me with a new horror. I tried to pray, but all I could think to pray was, *Oh God, oh God...*

The only reply was the sound of hooves pounding on the dry road and the comforting creak of leather. I reached into my pocket and found the beads. Even they brought only a small measure of comfort.

We'd taken a different road back to town and now reached a bend. John Henry brought his horse to a halt.

"Horses could use a rest," he said and nodded to the west. I turned and saw that there was a narrower path through low bushes. "Your uncle's place is just down that way. Reckon it's yours now. You want to take a look?"

My first reaction was to say no; viewing my uncle's land felt vaguely like accepting stolen goods. However, explaining to John Henry why I lacked curiosity was beyond my exhausted powers of imagination at the moment, so I nodded.

I followed him down the narrow path. The sun was descending, shafts of light gilding the rugged dark pines and bringing out the burnt orange of the landscape. We rode maybe half a mile under the arbor, then the trees gave way and the valley opened up before us. A low, squat building, weather-beaten and in need of work, was situated on the open plain, a barn just behind it. Beyond these, a creek wended its way through a corridor of earth-clutching trees. There were more trees staked out in an irregular pattern on the far side of the house. Cattle lowed from somewhere, and Danaher's nag whinnied in the paddock. It was a sweet piece of land, capable of supporting a small family, and I wondered if that would have suited the lovely Helen, had she not caught the eye of an Evans.

"It's called La Capilla," John Henry said. "Only a couple hundred acres, but a good enough piece of land with water."

When he swung down, I followed suit and held the reins loosely, allowing the horse to graze. John Henry stepped closer to me and began to point out objects of interest.

"There's a well and your uncle made sure to get the water rights on his bit of creek. Good fishing there in the spring, when the run-off happens. To the west, there's more pasture land, some of it good for planting. To the north, someone planted apple trees. A few are still bearing. It's good land, whether you'd want to sell or make a go at it."

The idea of me making a 'go at it' by myself was laughable. When I glanced at him, John Henry was looking off into the distance, his hands on his hips, his jaw tight as though he'd just thought of something that displeased him.

"You know a lot about this place," I said.

He looked at me then and adjusted his hat.

"Well, I oughta." He nodded over my shoulder. "I own the land next to this."

I turned, but a line of scrubby trees obscured my view. "The Evans ranch extends this far?"

"Not the ranch," he corrected. "*My* land." He took a step or two in that direction, pride radiating off of his shoulders. "It's the old Tucker place. Bought it off his widow when she decided to move back east. It's small, just a starter place, like this one. But it's good land and more important..."

"It's yours," I finished.

He looked back over at me and a grin, slow and steady, spread across his face.

"Right," he said, with quiet satisfaction.

I'd known John Henry Evans was a dangerous man from the moment I met him, yet he'd never been quite as dangerous as he was in that moment. That boyish grin, coupled with the quiet pride of ownership, independence, and confident posture, were quite possibly the most threatening thing I'd ever seen in my life. But then, I'd thought so once before, when I agreed to waltz with him.

I turned away and focused on the surrounding landscape, orienting myself. "So, the Circle E ends at the border of my uncle's land and your land is on the other side?"

"Yes, ma'am," he said, stepping back over to me. "The Circle E is the biggest spread in the county. My father didn't do anything by halves."

"Was my uncle here often?"

He shrugged. "I don't know. We didn't get on much, even before the troubles. He'd come here to fish and hunt sometimes, but I don't think he was the ranching type. Liked town life much better, I guess."

"Yes... He did build that house there," I said thoughtfully. "He was raised in the city, you know. Like I was."

He didn't say anything to that. Just squinted off into the distance, studying the lay of the land, the arcing blue sky, and the thin clouds that threatened no one. The sky is huge in this part of the country. It's a constant reminder of your small, insignificant place in the universe.

I cleared my throat. "You said this spread had a name? What was it?"

"La Capilla," he repeated. "Used to be La Pequena Capilla."

"The little..." I started to translate.

"It means the Little Chapel." He gestured again, this time to a clump of bushes I'd not noticed before. Here, a rickety wooden cross rose, forgotten in the shadows. "The fellow who started this ranch was a monk before he decided to be a rancher. Built a little church to baptize his children. It was called Santa Maria Clara."

The name hit me. I clenched the beads until they bit into my hand. "Maria Clara," I whispered.

Of course, it would be called that. I can't outrun it. No matter where I go, Rome follows me. My mother follows me. My guilt follows me...

John Henry was speaking, "That was before statehood, before my father's time. Place was Spanish then. You'll find remnants of their churches all over the place." He looked at me, his eyes squinting against the light. "Are you all right?"

I couldn't help but laugh. "Of course, my uncle *would* have a Roman church on his property."

I sounded bitter, as indeed I was. His expression grew puzzled.

"Are you Catholic?" he asked. He sounded confused, for he'd seen me in the little town church and no Catholic would dare darken that doorway. As indeed, we'd stayed away from my mother's church.

"No. My mother was." I showed him the string of beads with the crucifix, thrust them at him angrily. "These were her beads, her *legacy* to me."

He gazed at them a second before looking back up at me. "I thought your father..."

"My father was a preacher. She converted when she married him and reverted when she got sick. When she died, she left me the beads. Sometimes I think she's trying to convert me from the grave."

"But you won't?" he asked.

I shook my head. "I am my father's daughter. I always have been."

My father, the one who'd wooed a young girl away from her family and faith, who'd left her when she proved too weak for the road. My father, who'd seduced a woman he couldn't possibly marry, refused their son his name, and then let his son be carried off to a reservation. My father, who'd drunk his guilt away and then died, leaving me alone and afraid on the edge of civilization. My father had truly loved me, but I'd learned the hard way that love without character isn't enough.

What I'd said to John Henry was true. I was my father's daughter. When my mother died, I buried her in a Protestant grave. When I met Trailing Rose, I'd refused her the courtesy of her place. When Little Fox had been carried away, I let him go. And when my father died, I'd left him there, in a shoddy grave in the middle of mission land, with no family around him and no stone, abandoned, just as I felt. *"The sins of the father are revisited upon the sons..."* Apparently that verse includes daughters.

"I am my father's daughter," I said again, and there was no disguising the bitterness. I clutched the beads to my chest and closed my eyes against the pain.

I started when John Henry's hand touched my shoulder. When I looked up, he was much too close. His blue eyes, so much warmer than his mother's, gazed into mine with an intimacy I was not prepared for.

"No, Miss Goodnight," he said softly. "You are your own woman. You stand in no man's shadow."

My breath caught.

Somewhere off in the distance, a dog barked, shattering the moment.

John Henry lifted his head and squinted off into the distance. "We'd best get going. We're burning daylight."

Only then did I see that the sun hung low in the sky and the shadows stretched long from the hillside. Even so, it was with great reluctance that I followed his lead and took up the reins to my livery nag. Time is a flexible reality and those past few moments were much too short.

* * *

It was night by the time we arrived in Legacy. My horse was tired, my body was sore, and my head ached for water and rest. John Henry, silent for most of our journey, rode with unflagging energy and capability. I thought he'd leave me at the livery, but he waited while I unsaddled the horse and squared with the curious man in charge. When my business was discharged, he slung my saddlebags over his shoulder and walked beside me on the boardwalk, a silent, lumbering escort.

It had been an extremely long day and my nerves were taut and alive. Varina Evans' words chased around my head and I wished desperately that John Henry would speak, if only to distract me. The beat of our steps on the wooden sidewalk, the jingle of the horse's rigging, the crickets' song, and the gentle, clean light of the moon shafting down on Legacy hinted at a safer, quieter, more loving world than the reality I was currently living. At that moment, however, I wouldn't have changed my immediate circumstances for anything.

My uncle's house came into sight much too soon. Disappointment crashed down on me when John Henry handed me the heavy saddlebags and immediately turned to his horse. He wasn't mounting, however – he was retrieving my father's Bible. His hand brushed mine again, a shock to the system like a plunge into freezing water on a hot day.

Despite everything, the sight of the book and the touch of the worn leather was a comfort. I stroked the cover unconsciously. "Thank you," I said, through the catch in my throat. "This... this was my father's. It means the world to me."

"I heard your father was one hell of a preacher."

I laughed. "He was. Brought many souls to the light."

That much was true. Samuel Goodnight might have been a coward where his family was concerned, but he was a true believer and laborer in the field. It was a complicated puzzle. The curious truth that his strengths were as real as his failings was something that I didn't feel like embracing tonight.

"Bigger than life," John Henry said softly. "My father was the same. He had his faults, but he was one hell of a man."

I nodded, and then I took in a deep breath and forced myself to look him in the eye.

"Do you think your father...? I mean, Ezra Jones and..."

John Henry looked at me so straight that I wanted to run into the house right there. My uncle had done his best to ruin his father's name and here I was questioning it again.

His answer, however, was calm and sure.

"Miss Goodnight, you probably know better than most what humans are capable of, both the good and the bad. The best men can make a mistake. Hell, King David conspired to kill Uriah and Saul was a good man until kingship got the better of him. We all fall. That's a gospel truth: we all fall."

Then, as I was digesting this, he said, with a reassurance that filled the night and made a firm foundation against the sliding scale of good and evil, "The man I knew would never leave his partner to die, Miss Goodnight."

A cloud drew across the moon, bathing me in a relieving darkness. I drew in a shuddering breath and nodded. "I see."

"The trick," he said ruefully, "is how to prove what you know but cannot see."

"Sometimes you just have to go on faith."

The cloud shifted again and moonlight fell on his twisted grin.

"Faith without works is dead, Miss Goodnight," he said. His tenor changed. "I don't suppose you know what was in that letter your uncle was so fired up about?"

"No. I haven't found it yet."

"I'd be obliged if you could keep me informed."

"I can do that," I promised.

John Henry nodded. "I'm grateful," he grunted. "I guess I'd better get going."

He swung up on to his horse. I stepped instinctively after him, barely stopping myself from reaching out to keep him from going.

"John Henry," I called out.

He turned, his face in shadow.

"I don't think your father killed Ezra Jones," I said. "And I don't think your brother killed Uncle Matthew. I'll prove it if I can, but... but I just wanted you to know."

He pushed his hat back and leaned on the pommel of his saddle.

"Is this faith, Miss Goodnight?"

His tone held a note of amusement.

"No," I said, firmly. "You know a tree by its fruit."

John Henry was still for a long, long moment. I couldn't see his face, but I could feel something in the air, a change in the direction of the wind, small but enough to send sailors scrambling to adjust the sails' trim. What's more, I knew John Henry felt it too.

"I'm obliged to you, ma'am," he said, thickly. Then, with a strong, almost vicious kick to his horse's flanks, he fairly fled from my presence.

I never truly understood the concept of 'falling in love'. To be fair, I had never seen it. I am not a romantic by nature. My Aunt Alice and her husband were more business partners than lovers and, though my mother wasted away from loneliness, I had attributed this to weakness of constitution rather than romantic desolation. As for my father, I credited both loneliness and lust to his dalliance and tried my best not to think about either.

But that night, I felt a wave of something I'd never felt before. Loneliness, abandonment, sadness - I was accustomed to all of these. Yet as he moved away, I felt a tug on my soul like I've never felt in my life – as though by going, he was taking part of me with him, a part I could scarcely function without but that was his by right.

I told myself I was being silly. I was too old, seasoned, reasonable and practical to allow myself to believe that two weeks' acquaintance was enough time to establish a claim to grief. I told myself that I was tired, that I was still recovering from my illness, that I was only reacting to the sense of isolation that wrapped me in a blinding cloak of fear. It was a momentary weakness that would soon be forgotten.

Even as I argued, I knew this was a lie. Though my place was in Massachusetts, my heart, or at least a piece of it, would always be here, in Legacy, entrusted to a grim, short-tempered man who would probably never know that he carried it off tucked in his back pocket one dark and lonely summer night. A foolish woman who ought to have known better had given it to him before she knew what she was doing, and there was no undoing what had been done. I was as fated to fall as I had been to bear my mother's black hair and my father's stubborn nature, and fallen I had – I loved John Henry and there was no denying it.

After a long while, I pulled myself together and went into the house. Even when my uncle was alive, the building felt soulless, hollow and empty. Tonight it was even worse. I felt cold loneliness drench my skin as I latched the door behind me. It was so dark in the foyer that I might as well have been blind. I was alone, as I always was.

Only I wasn't alone. I was turning, the saddlebags heavy on my shoulder, hugging the Bible to my chest, tears trickling down my cheeks, when I sensed it – the squeak of a floor board under a leather sole, the scent of smoke from a flame just extinguished, the warm breath of someone standing right behind me.

Then the world crashed down on me and everything went black.

TWENTY-EIGHT

The ground, wet and green, rushed to meet me. My riding crop flew out of my hand as I collapsed into myself like an eight-year-old rag doll. Winthrop nickered and tossed his head as he ran away from me. I wasn't a natural horsewoman, though I would grow to be quite capable. I was a small child and horses were giant, unpredictable things that sensed my uncertainty and took advantage.

Breathless and sore, I pushed myself into a sitting position as Aunt Alice, her face creased with worry, rode up. It was unseasonably hot for May and my head throbbed as though I had landed on it instead of my shoulders.

Aunt Alice's expression changed from worry to annoyance.

"You have to get back up on that horse, Jenny," she said, flicking her own crop. "It's the only way. Get up."

"But I hurt," I whined. "I want to stay here."

Now she was on the ground, standing over me, her face dark with fury.

"You must get up, Jenny," she commanded, but as she spoke, she changed into Uncle Matthew, raging drunk and violent. He stepped closer, bringing the crop up to bear. "Get up."

"I..."

He lost it then, swinging and furious: "Get up, get up, *get up...!*"

I awoke to the sound of my own choking. I couldn't draw a breath through the thickening, hot air. My head buzzed, my ears were filled with a roar, like a thousand bees swarming around a hive. Sweat snaked down my back. Poisonous kerosene and smoke poured into my throat, stopping it. As I gained consciousness, the buzzing in my head modified and became recognizable. I wasn't hearing bees; I was hearing flames.

My eyes shot open. The world was black and red and orange – the flames were everywhere, in the kitchen, the parlor, and the stairs. Over my head, the ceiling glowed eerily. Tongues of flames licked up the sides of the poorly papered hall, chewing through the dry, unfinished wood. As I watched, they thrust towards me with sudden force, making me scramble back. I had to get out. The front door was my only hope.

The saddlebags were gone, but the Bible remained where it had fallen, now inches from the flame. Coughing, my eyes streaming, I snatched it away just in time. Clutching it to my chest, I scrambled for the door, tripping over my divided skirts. I grabbed the door handle just as a piece of the ceiling gave way, showering me with glowing embers. I screamed and beat at the particles that landed on the thin calico. As I did, the front door shuddered – someone was outside.

"I'm here!" I screamed. "I'm..."

Smoke choked off the last few words. I coughed and coughed and my skin prickled with heat. The door shuddered once, twice more, and then gave, hitting me where I lay on the floor.

Hands grabbed at me, pulling me out into the cold night air. I could barely see through smoke-induced tears. They dragged me into the street as others cried for water and buckets. From somewhere beyond my vision, Mrs. Walsh said, "She's on fire!"

More hands grabbed me, rolling me in the sand. The ground was hard and my head hurt all the more for being moved, but I was *alive*.

"Easy, easy," Mrs. Walsh said and the hands released me.

I sat up, coughing up smoke and drinking in the cool night air. When my vision cleared, I saw that my uncle's townhouse was completely engulfed, a funeral pyre for his life and ambitions. The red-orange flames tore into the wood and reached up into the velvet black of the sky, like furious avenging angels, and I wondered if that awful night in Sodom and Gomorrah looked so bleak and so just.

Mrs. Walsh was next to me, throwing a shawl around my shoulders.

"Are you all right?" she asked over the roaring in my ears. "Jenny, are you all right?"

I coughed and choked and nodded. Annie appeared, white faced and anxious, a shawl over her nightgown.

"Annie, get some water," Mrs. Walsh ordered and the girl ran off. "Jenny, is anyone else in the house?"

I looked over at the line of men and women, outlined in the flames, hauling slopping buckets and shouting orders to one another. Some fought the flames directly, others were wetting the neighboring houses. A fire in a dry area like this was as dangerous as in old days of London's great fire. Everyone came to help because everyone knew the risk.

"Jenny?" Mrs. Walsh was still waiting for me. I turned, blinking. "Was anyone else in the house with you?"

"No," I whispered. "I fell – someone..."

"You fell? Down the stairs?"

"Someone hit me..." A fit of coughing overtook me. Mrs. Walsh was turning to Mrs. Danaher, who'd just run up.

"Tom left with the sheriff, too," she explained. "Is Jenny all right?"

"She's fine," Mrs. Walsh said. "She fell, must have knocked something over. Has everyone gone with the posse?"

"Posse?" I wheezed.

"Someone brought word that Matheson was in the area," Mrs. Danaher reported. "He called up the deputies and some of the men to check it out. That was hours ago."

The air was rent with a sound like a shot as something gave way in my uncle's house. Mrs. Danaher ran to join the line. When Annie appeared with a cup, Mrs. Walsh gave me the cup and sent her to pump water for the bucket line.

"Drink slowly, Jenny. Get your bearings. Here." Mrs. Walsh handed me the black Bible, which I'd forgotten about. "You managed to save something at least."

I took the book and contact with it reminded me of something.

"My saddlebags!" I gasped. Everything was in there, including my father's pistol.

Mrs. Walsh prevented me from getting up. "I'm sorry, my dear," she said. "But you're not getting anything out of that house tonight."

She was clearly right. As we watched, the roof of the house collapsed in a shower of sparks and a cacophony of cracking wood and screaming nails. The crowd shouted and surged. Some of the women had taken to beating out outlier flames with wet blankets. Men of all ages shouted and threw water.

I sat with Mrs. Walsh at my side, my head throbbing, the Bible clutched so tightly in my arms that the cover bit into my flesh. My heart was pounding, too, both from the aftermath of shock and from the stark realization that just hit me. When I awoke, the saddlebags had already disappeared. Whoever had knocked me out now had all of my uncle's blackmail material.

As the firefighters battled, the fire seemed to fall into itself, pulling the unfinished house down with it. My hopes of ending this blackmailing scheme collapsed along with it.

TELEGRAM

To: the Sheriff of Legacy
From: the Justice Department

Matheson and gang in area STOP Wanted by Federal agents in robbery STOP Armed and dangerous STOP

TWENTY-NINE

W e fought the fire until nearly two in the morning and even then, we left some embers sparking. I can say 'we' because I pulled myself together enough to help Annie at the pump. The fight was a fierce one. I was afraid that no one would believe me about the stranger starting it, but I was backed by an unexpected party: John Wainwright, of the livery, also caught scent of the kerosene and claimed that the fire was too well spread too fast to be merely an accident.

"How can you tell that?" Mrs. Danaher had demanded.

"I have experience with fires," he said, with a crooked grin that made me wonder if one of the clippings in my uncle's book had been about him.

Now homeless, I went with Mrs. Danaher to her boarding house and took one of the empty rooms. I didn't sleep much. Dreams, dark and intense, kept me from relaxing. I was in the house, being hit by Matheson, then I was out by my father's grave, trying to dig him up. When I finally awoke for good, it was to find myself in yet another cold sweat with Underwood's last words to my uncle fresh on my mind.

"I'm telling you, if we see anyone other than your good self, I can't guarantee the outcome..."

I was relieved to know that sheriff was on his trail.

I awoke when it was very early. The sun was young and its beams weak as water. Mrs. Danaher was already up and ready for the day of course. I went into the kitchen and washed myself in the pail by the door. My skirt and blouse, literally the last outfit I had in the world, was scorched and torn from last night's firefight.

I'm going to be quite a sight when I arrive in Massachusetts.

That was the least of my concerns. Someone had stolen the saddlebags loaded with my uncle's blackmail material and there was no way of knowing what they would do with the information. I couldn't count on these thieves pulling a Robin Hood and returning the clippings to the victims. After all, they'd knocked me out and left me for dead in a burning building. Hardly the actions of the good hearted.

I *had* to fix this. But where could I start?

Mrs. Danaher came out then, brisk with daily tasks. She jerked her head towards the kitchen as she passed me. "There's coffee, salt pork, and biscuits," she said.

"Thank you, ma'am," I said and made my way back inside.

The coffee was hot and the biscuits freshly baked and warm. I didn't feel like eating, but forced myself to anyway. Outside, I heard Mrs. Danaher working the ax and thought, *I wonder where Jeremiah is...*

Jeremiah.

He'd been the unwitting one delivering the blackmail notes. He knew who my uncle had his claws in the deepest. I could start with what he knew.

Mrs. Danaher reentered with a load of wood and I asked eagerly, "Did Jeremiah go with the sheriff this morning?"

"Nope." Mrs. Danaher dropped her armload. "Sent him to Liam's with some supplies yesterday. Reckon he stayed the night."

"Liam's?"

"Your uncle's spread. I should say your spread," she corrected as she reached for the coffee pot. "He always goes there on Tuesday."

"I gotta be sure we meet someplace we both can be comfortable. Like your ranch."

Underwood's voice echoed in my head. My stomach dropped. Suddenly I realized: Matheson hadn't come to raid. He'd come to collect. In all the excitement about the murder and the blackmail scheme, I'd unaccountably screwed up the day of his arrival.

I tried to keep my voice from shaking. "Which direction did the sheriff head off in?"

"South. Someone reported seeing his men by Sand River."

My uncle's spread was north of town, the opposite direction of Sand River. This had to be a diversion. And that meant that Liam and Jeremiah...

I've got to go and warn them!

Mrs. Danaher had already gone back outside. I jumped to my feet, full of nervous energy. I needed hardware and a horse, and I'd been in enough boarding houses to know that no landlord went without protection. Sure enough, in the office, I found three rifles in a glass-cupboard. I slung a Henry rifle over my shoulder, grabbed a box of ammunition, and went outside.

Mrs. Danaher was fussing with the laundry line. Her jaw dropped when she saw me. I shouted as I slipped out into the street, "Matheson's heading for my uncle's spread. Send word to the sheriff!"

I didn't hear her reply. I just took off running toward the livery stables, praying I wasn't too late.

* * *

John wasn't in the livery, so I took a nervous mustang, threw a saddle with a rifle sheath on her, and took off. The town was ominously still as I rode through, the embers of my uncle's house still smoking.

It was clear that my little mustang loved to run. I let her go at the outskirts of town and she launched forward, ears back, hooves flying, her muscles taut and nimble beneath the skin. I lay flat as I could on her back and prayed, "Don't let me be too late. Don't let me be too late."

We ate ground. There were no signs that the posse had been this way, no sounds of gun play, nothing but the pounding of hooves in the dust and my own heart beating a tattoo of dread. When we rounded the last bend in the road and saw the brush that indicated the entrance, I reined the mustang to a halt. She was breathing heavily, yet still danced her disappointment that the race was over so soon. I slipped off her and stood in the middle of the road, listening.

The wind rustled the dry branches and kicked up dust to sting our eyes. A fly buzzed around the mustang's warm flanks. She nickered and pulled at the reins. Still I listened.

Then it came: the sound of a pop, like a champagne cork, but with an ominous echo. A man's shout followed hard after. Both came from the direction of my uncle's house.

I hopped back on to the mustang, pulled the rifle out of the sheath, and kicked her into motion. She sprang forward and we thundered into the narrow path.

About halfway down the path, it occurred to me that I was, for all intents and purposes, running head long into a shoot-out. I slowed the mustang to a walk. As we drew near, we heard more shots and someone bellowed, "We ain't leaving 'til you pay us what you owe, Goodnight!"

Apparently, they were unaware that Uncle Matthew was dead.

I stopped the mustang before the brush gave way and slipped silently to the ground. She was a well-trained horse, for when I dropped the reins, she remained where she was, ears pricked forward as she began to search the ground for edible greens. I crept forward, and sensed, for the first time, the nickering of other horses a short distance from me, the squeaking sound of leather, and masculine throat clearing. The brush ended and, holding the rifle in my increasingly slippery hands, I peered around the obstruction.

Twelve men were spread out around the clearing surrounding the house. Some were on their horses, others on the ground. One man was sitting, swearing viciously as he sought to staunch the blood that trickled down his sleeve. All were dusty and dressed in sun-faded finery, and heavily armed. They watched the house, keeping the few trees that dotted the open space between them and the shuttered windows. The smoke chugging out of the chimney, along with the wounded man, spoke of a siege.

One man, cradling a shotgun, his red beard mottled with dirt and dust, turned to spit a stream of tobacco into the sand. His eyes scanned the clearing and the bushes beyond it. For a heart-stopping moment, I thought he had spotted me. But his small eyes, sunk deep into his weather-beaten face, moved over my position without stopping.

I saw Underwood, looking greasier than ever, his long blond hair trailing out in a dirty braid over his vest. He was rubbing his unshaven face and standing by a medium-sized man on a big brown stallion. The man on the stallion had a jagged scar on his cheek and, judging by the deferential manner with which the other men treated him, I guessed that he was the much-sought Red Eye Matheson.

Matheson bent over to listen to Underwood's whispered advice. I scanned the area, looking for somewhere to put myself. I knew too much about men like these to believe that they'd go peaceably when I explained the situation to them.

Matheson snarled, "I thought you said he was willing, Underwood."

Underwood shrugged. "He was."

A shot rang out, accompanied by a puff of smoke from one of the gaps in the shutters. The Matheson gang stirred and swore. Two of them pulled their own guns and fired back. My mustang snorted and I grabbed her reins, quieting her.

Matheson straightened in his saddle and shouted in a voice that was peculiarly high-pitched; "You're surrounded, Goodnight! Just pay me my money and we'll all go home!"

The only one who seemed unperturbed was Underwood, who stood with his arms folded, squinting in the sunlight.

"No figuring people," he drawled.

As the gang settled back into their positions, I spotted a flanking position which would put me where I could support the men in the cabin. To get there required me to run a short distance in the open toward a collection of brush, a risky proposition, but not quite as dangerous if the gunmen were otherwise occupied.

So I waited and, sure enough, the occupants of the cabin fired once more. As the gunmen pulled their weapons to return fire, I started forward. I didn't get very far. An arm snaked around my waist and lifted me from the ground. A hand covered my mouth, choking off my scream. My attacker drew me backwards and down as the gunshots rang out.

I fought until I heard John Henry's whisper: "Quiet, Jenny!"

When I relaxed, he released me. As the clearing quieted, I turned to John Henry. He was armed, not only with his pistol, but with a rifle of his own. He nodded to the left, where I saw movement in the bushes. I wondered who he'd brought with him.

John Henry pulled me closer to whisper in my ear: "What're you *doing* here?" he demanded.

"I could ask you the same," I hissed. "Why aren't you with the sheriff's posse?"

"Trigger and I heard a commotion and came to see what was what. You shouldn't be here."

"Jeremiah's in the cabin," I said.

John Henry's eyes narrowed and he craned his neck to see through the brush. I looked, too, and didn't like what I saw. There were twelve armed men, one more wounded, and all of them reputed to be vicious. We were three and had no idea how much ammo the cabin dwellers had.

"Where's the sheriff?" John Henry asked.

"He's gone to Sand River with a posse. They thought Matheson was headed that way."

John Henry muttered something. Another shot rang out, followed by a stream of curse words. Then Matheson's high-pitched voice filled the air.

"Goodnight! I want to talk to you!"

The brush on the other side of John Henry rustled. I jumped, but it was only Trigger Olsen, returning with a grim expression on his face. He shook his head when John Henry gave him an inquiring look. "This seems to be all there is. No pickets, no lookouts."

Matheson was saying, "All I want is what you owe me, Goodnight. Nothing more, nothing less. We can all live today."

"Is he looking for you?" Trigger whispered to me.

"My uncle – gambling debts," I explained.

"Jeremiah and Liam are inside," John Henry said. "Sage is at Sand River."

"Shit," was Trigger's assessment.

"I'll give you five minutes before I burn the place down, Goodnight," Matheson declared. He turned to Underwood. "Dammit, Underwood, I thought you said you handled him."

"Guess I shouldn't have let it set so long," Underwood said with an oily smoothness that sent shivers down my spine. "We got time. Sand River is a helluva ride from here."

Matheson said, "I ain't waiting too much longer." In a booming voice, he shouted, "Four minutes, Goodnight!" and pulled a flask out of his pocket.

John Henry tapped my rifle. "You know how to use that?" he asked.

My expression of disgust answered the question. He turned to Trigger.

"Take that flank and wait for me."

Trigger set off through the brush. John Henry turned and nodded behind me.

"Can you get to that gap in the brush without being spotted?" he asked.

He was indicating the spot I'd already picked out. I nodded, my mouth dry.

"Get there, stay out of sight," he ordered. "Let them leave if they want, but don't let them come back in. I'm going to go further around and let them think they're surrounded. We'll frighten them, and then give them an out. Got it?"

I rubbed my sweaty hand on my skirt. "Got it." I started to get up, when his hand caught my arm and stopped me.

"Jenny," he said softly. "Be careful."

No point in letting him know that my insides felt like jelly and the thought of having to shoot a man was making me break out in a cold sweat. I just nodded.

We crouched at the edge of the tree line, waiting for the moment to run. Across the plain, the gunmen moved about restlessly, rifles held carelessly in their arms, wiping their noses with their sleeve, dirt and sweat running down their faces in rivulets. They tried to look casual, but nervous movements and frequent glances towards the cabin gave them away.

Finally, a shutter door cracked open. As one, the bandits turned towards the cabin. John Henry and I ran across the open space, the sun beating on our heads and the very air crackling with tension. I hit the dirt and rolled into the opening made by the bushes, and John Henry disappeared into the brush, moving as silently as a native.

My heart was pounding so hard it was making my chest rattle with the pressure. I could have sworn we'd been spotted, but though Underwood was looking around with a suspicious frown on his face, no one else was moving. We'd done it.

Through the still air, Liam's voice, thin with the distance, filtered through. I couldn't make out the words, but whatever he said caused

Matheson to pull the hat off his head and slapped it against his thigh.

"You lie!" he roared. "I ain't leaving until I get what's owed to me, Goodnight, one way or the other! Now, you've got three minutes..."

"Two," Underwood corrected gently.

"Two minutes," Matheson went on, "before I send in my boys. Two minutes, you hear?"

I didn't hear Liam's response, but I did hear the chattering sound of a bird on the far side of the clearing where Trigger had gone. Underwood heard it, too, and lifted his head in that direction. When an answer came from the other side, Underwood whipped around as though expecting an ambush.

"What's the matter with you, Underwood?" Matheson groused, dropping his hat back on his head.

"Something..." he muttered, his eyes darting from one direction to the other. "Something..."

Fire erupted from the house again and this time, the bullets made the gunmen swear and their horses scream. One of the gunmen lost his seat as his horse bucked in panic. Two puffs of smoke revealed that there was more than one occupant in the house with a gun. When the firing died down, the echoes of the shots seemed to ring even louder across the plain.

Matheson swore viciously.

"That done it," he said, and then shouted for the benefit of the house dwellers: "That done it, Goodnight!" To Underwood again, he said, "Take them out."

Underwood's features sharpened into wolf-like ferocity. He turned to the others and made a motion with his arm. A war-whoop went up, wild and vicious. Jubilantly, they pulled their weapons, and heeled their horses. One man lit a torch.

Just when all hell seemed about to break loose, more shots rang out, only these were closer and from opposite sides of the opening. John Henry and Trigger had better aim than those in the house. The man with the red beard cried out and dropped his gun, blood blossoming on his hand. Another man jerked and fell from his saddle. Underwood lost his hat and one more man shouted as one of his reins were snapped in two.

The firing stopped. The horses danced and men swore, their easy confidence shattered.

"What the...?!" Matheson shouted, jerking his beast around wildly. He turned all the way around and stopped, his mouth opening. Soon all his men were staring in the same direction.

I had to lean forward to see what they were staring at.

John Henry strode across the open-space, his still smoldering rifle held low and ready. His gait was steady and unhurried, his head erect and his shoulders back. His presence loomed even larger than Matheson's. He was so exposed that I wanted to scream, *Go back, go* back*!*

He kept walking, of course, so I brought the rifle to bear on Matheson and adjusted my hand hold for a better grip. There was some solace in knowing that I was a pretty good shot. I just prayed I'd be quick enough.

John Henry walked until he reached a large stack of cut wood that stood in the clearing near the brush line. There he stopped, placed his foot on one of the loose logs, and leaned forward, his rifle at the ready, looking for all the world as though he'd just come by for a friendly chat.

"All right, boys," he said easily. "You've had your fun for the day. Now why don't you just get on out of here before things start getting messy?"

Matheson's dark-tanned face turned a tone deeper.

"Who the *hell* are you?" he asked.

"The name is Evans. John Henry Evans. And if you're looking for Goodnight, he's dead."

Matheson tossed a look at Underwood, who shrugged. "Dead?"

"Died Sunday night," John Henry said. "Someone slit his throat."

Matheson snorted. "Why should I believe you?"

John Henry shrugged. "Reckon you don't have to. But I do have you surrounded and out-gunned. If you believe nothing else, I suggest you take that to heart."

The men began to grumble, looking about. Even Matheson's face went a shade lighter. An enemy you cannot see is always more frightening than the one you can see.

"Goodnight owes me money," Matheson said. "This is a private affair. And 'sides," he nodded towards the house. "Someone's been shooting at us and I don't intend to take that lying down."

Sweat curled down the sides of my dress. The tension was unbearable. Technically, we had Matheson surrounded, but he had more men, was more mobile, and had considerably less to lose. We might get him in the end, but at what cost?

John Henry nodded slowly, his blue eyes glittering under the shadow of his hat.

"You do what you need to do, Matheson," he said and adjusted the rifle so that its aim was a little more true. "We'll do the same."

"This ain't your affair, Evans."

"I'm making it my affair."

Matheson opened his mouth, but it was Underwood who spoke. "How many men did you say you had with you, Evans?"

John Henry said, "I didn't."

"Maybe it's just you, then?" Underwood suggested, taking a step out, away from Matheson. He was squaring off to John Henry, yet carefully keeping his hands clear from his pistol and he sounded so smug I had to restrain myself from turning the gun on him then and there.

John Henry's eyes glittered.

"I wouldn't bet on that," he said.

That's when the man with the red beard, whom I'd forgotten about, pulled the second pistol from his belt with his left hand and fired at John Henry.

All hell broke loose. John Henry fell backwards. Underwood dove, Matheson's horse threw him and the others took off, riding in a wide circle towards the house. I was firing and Trigger must have been, too, for the clearing was a wall of sound and fury. Pandemonium reigned. I could barely see anything through the smoke that stung my eyes. I fired and tried to locate Underwood and John Henry. I saw Matheson getting to his feet and turned the rifle on him. He staggered, grabbing at his leg. The men on foot were now scrambling towards the pathway, dodging my mustang, who came out kicking and bucking. I let them go and focused my attention on the riders, who were making one last ditch-attempt to get at the house. I fired, others fired, and a few fell. My mustang bucked into my view and I stumbled out of my hiding spot, fumbling to reload as I did so.

The air was thick with the sharp tangy scent of burnt gun powder and the slick, sour-sweet smell of sweat and fear. The riders swept back to where Matheson was pulling himself back to his feet, shouting for a horse. Trigger rose from his crouching position to get a better aim. The door to the cabin opened and someone began firing from behind it. Gun smoke covered everything.

I slipped a round into the chamber and looked towards the woodpile. John Henry was rising up, his rifle in both hands, and fire in his eyes. He looked angry and his hat was gone, but otherwise, he was whole. He brought his rifle to bear on the red-bearded man, who was advancing on Trigger. The rifle barked and the red bearded man and his horse went down in a tangle of arms and legs and terrified pain.

I turned to see Matheson, hauling himself up onto a horse. I was bringing my rifle around on him when I heard the mustang scream from behind me.

I turned again. Underwood had mounted the little mare and was racing towards John Henry, whose attention was on the men sweeping past the cabin in one last gesture of defiance. I saw a pistol in Underwood's hand and fired without a second thought.

In my haste, I didn't have a good grip on the rifle. The recoil caught me hard in the shoulder, making me stagger, but my aim was true. Underwood rose in his saddle, turned, and fell as the mustang went charging into a startled John Henry. He turned, saw me, and his hand shot forward in warning. It was too late.

Something slammed into my chest, knocking me backwards and off my feet. I hit the ground, pain exploding in my back, neck, and chest. My already wounded head resounded with pain, so blinding, so overwhelming, I couldn't see or hear or feel anything else. The world was a blank space filled with pain.

I've been shot. I've been shot!

My ears roared. John Henry was over me, mouthing words I couldn't hear, then he was gone again. I rode crimson waves of pain, unable to catch my breath – each movement of my lungs was like trying to swim through mud. I closed my eyes and concentrated on breathing and choked on the dust. The wracking movement caused even more pain, but this time, the pain had the effect of clearing my head.

I could hear again: men shouting, horses neighing, hooves pounding on the packed dirt. John Henry shouted and Jeremiah called my name. I opened my eyes and there he was, running across the clearing, a smoking rifle in one hand, and his eyes wide and frightened. His long legs cut through the space like a racehorse and he dropped to his knees beside me.

"Miss Goodnight," he shouted as though from far away. "Are you all right?"

I tried to push myself upright, but my side was throbbing and I was dizzy. I reached for my fallen rifle and looked around. Underwood lay stretched out in the dirt, his crumpled body still. Trigger had slung himself up on to a horse and was heeling it after Matheson while John Henry forced three others, including the wounded red-bearded man, to sit Indian-style in a circle. Liam pushed a fourth man across the clearing with a double-barreled shotgun.

Jeremiah hovered. "You're bleeding," he said.

Blood soaked my dress just under my collarbone. I could feel the bullet lodged in there, oddly enough, but though I was cognizant enough to recognize my wounds, I couldn't quite comprehend them. It seemed a distant notion. I reached to touch it and John Henry's hand covered my own.

"Don't, Jenny."

He'd left Liam to watch over the prisoners and now crouched down beside me, cradling my head and shoulders in his arms. He examined the wound, gently tugging at the sticky calico. My heart was calming now and the pain had receded to a centralized throbbing that intensified when John Henry pressed it gingerly. I squeaked and he stopped.

"Bullet's still in there," he said through tight lips. "Jeremiah, find something to stop this bleeding."

"And get me some rope!" Liam hollered.

Jeremiah obediently ran off and John Henry put his hand on my cheek.

"Are you all right?" he asked.

It was difficult to nod, but I managed it. He looked even more grim.

"We've got to get you to the doc," he said. His eyes dropped back to my shoulder and traveled downward. My sleeve was a mess of burns and blood. When he saw the burn holes, he frowned and I remembered that he didn't know about the house fire.

Trigger came riding back, leading a saddled horse, his lean face grim.

"John Henry," he said. "You'd better come."

"Let them go," he snapped.

"They're heading for the Circle E."

John Henry looked at Trigger, then at me. I was shivering now and managed to keep my teeth from rattling as I said, "You better go stop them."

Still he hesitated. Jeremiah came loping back with rope and a stack of rags. Liam caught John Henry's glance.

"You go on, John Henry," he said and cast a baleful look on his four bedraggled prisoners. "We've got it covered. Jeremiah, the rope."

John Henry took the cleanest rag from Jeremiah and pressed it onto my wound. I moaned, but he held it there and said, "You've got to stanch the blood. Keep this here, just like this."

I winced and put my hand where indicated. He stood and looked down at me for a second. Then he said, "Jeremiah – as soon as you're done with them, get her to Lowe."

Jeremiah looked up from where he was trussing the red-bearded man with surprising ease and finesse. "Yes, sir."

Trigger said, "John Henry – Matheson."

John Henry turned then and threw himself up on to the horse.

"We'll be back," he said to Liam and then once more to Jeremiah, "Get her to Lowe."

With that, they were gone.

ARTICLE

June 1874
From the *Louisiana Weekly*
(Discovered in Matthew Goodnight's personal journal.)

MYSTERIOUS DEATH CONFOUNDS

The death of wealthy James Cunningham has confounded authorities. Although he initially appeared to die of natural causes, foul play is suspected.

Mr. Cunningham was under the care of a man who called himself Dr. Frank Davidson and Dr. Davidson's wife, both of whom disappeared shortly after Mr. Cunningham passed away. Mr. James Cunningham's son, Earle, called for an investigation when it was discovered that valuable items had disappeared. Further investigation revealed that Mr. Davidson never completed his medical studies at Yale and, further, has been peddling medicines up and done the coast with his wife, Nell.

Although murder has not been proven yet, the Davidsons are wanted for questions. A full description is listed below...

THIRTY

O nce Jeremiah and Liam were reasonably assured that the gunmen couldn't escape, they patched up my wound to the best of their ability. We managed to stanch the blood, and although the bullet hadn't appeared to penetrate anything vital, it was deep. Even Liam, who'd volunteered to pull it out himself, hesitated when he saw how deep it was.

"John Henry's right," he said. "This is a job for Lowe."

So they trussed up the wound, Jeremiah hitched up a wagon, and we left Liam standing guard over the four gunmen. The man with the red beard complained that they were bleeding, too.

"We'll send Lowe," Jeremiah promised.

"Don't hurry," Liam said with vicious glee.

Jeremiah drove as fast as he could to Lowe's. The sun was climbing into the sky, searing the air with heat, and the jarring of the wagon wheels on the road made me worry that it was drawing the bullet deeper into my chest. I leaned on Jeremiah and fell in and out of consciousness.

The Lowes lived in Doc Brown's old place, which, fortunately, was closer to us than the town. When we pulled up to the house, the chimney was smoking. To my surprise, Sarah stepped out of the doorway, apron-less and statuesque. She frowned when she saw the dust and blood covered bandage and came down to meet the wagon.

"What happened?"

I was getting somewhat woozy at this point and didn't pay attention to the clamor of conversation. Jeremiah helped hand me down and Sarah took me by my good arm. Her grip was tight. Up close, she was even prettier, though older than I had thought. The scent of rosewater clung to her. The world seemed to shudder when I stood and I wondered how on earth I was going to make it into the house.

I didn't have to try. Someone swept me off my feet and Lowe's deep, accented voice said, "Sarah, prepare my tools."

"Yes, of course."

Lowe carried me inside, through a tiny front room crowded with furniture and into a back room that was an office and a surgery. It was a plain room with built-in cabinetry, two sets of large windows, a roll top desk, and a high wooden bed that he laid me on.

"Now, you just lie there quiet, Miss Goodnight, and we'll have a look at you," he said in his soothing way. But his movements were jerky and quick and his eyes glinted uneasily. His fingers probed the wound, irritating it.

"Who shot you?" he asked.

I coughed. "I don't know."

"Bullet still in there?" he asked. When I nodded, he turned away from me. "Well, then, we'll just have to get it out."

I closed my eyes. Sweat beaded at my forehead and my mouth was dry. Doctor Lowe fussed with something in the cabinets and I heard the clinking of glass. From outside, the rattle of wood and the slap of reins announced Jeremiah's departure even before Sarah entered the room.

"It's all right," I heard her say. "I sent Jeremiah to his mother's. She'll attend the wounded men at Liam's while you work here."

"That was good." Lowe sounded impressed. "Very good."

"I thought so," she replied. "What about her?"

"Miss Goodnight's in bad shape. We'll need to act fast."

Instinctively, I reached into my pocket for my mother's beads, trying to calm my pounding heart. My fingers touched nothing but cotton. The beads were gone.

My heart sunk. I felt deserted and it was all I could do not to cry. A silly reaction to missing beads.

They took no notice of my movements.

Sarah said, "I just can't believe it."

"I know, I know. We're going to need to tie her down."

Tie me down?

My eyes popped open. Sarah was moving across the room towards the roll top desk while Doctor Lowe bent over his drug making. I opened my mouth to ask... I didn't know what to ask, so I closed my mouth again.

Then Sarah opened the desk.

It was cluttered with paper, but these weren't a doctor's usual paraphernalia. They were newspaper clippings, clippings that I knew almost by heart now, papers that bore Uncle Matthew's familiar notations. A leather journal lay open under the pile and when my gaze slipped downward, I saw saddlebags underneath the desk.

My saddlebags.

Terror shot through me like a lightning bolt. I must have gasped, because suddenly Doctor Lowe was on top of me, one hand gagging my mouth, the other pinning my neck to the bed.

"Nell!" he snapped. "The door!"

She ran out. Doctor Lowe leaned on me, his body weight pinning me into the bed, almost suffocating me. I writhed and he pressed on my neck until I choked. He eased up then, only a little, and snarled, "You keep still, you little..."

Sarah came back in.

"He's gone," she said.

"Get the rope, Nell," he growled.

I fought, screaming into his hand and throwing my body one way and then the other. He held me in place, but lost his temper and slapped me hard across the face. I was dazed for a moment and I heard Sarah say, "Not yet, Frank!" as she ran back into the room.

They tied me down to the bed. The ropes bit into my flesh as they knotted them tight. Sarah, especially, seemed to take great pleasure in making me cry out under Lowe's muffling hand. Only when I was tied so I couldn't move an inch did the doctor release my neck. His grip on my mouth tightened and he twisted my head so I was looking him in the eye.

"You won't scream," he ordered.

Terrified, I nodded. When he removed his hand, I gasped at the intake of clean air.

"We don't have much time, Frank," Sarah said.

Frank. Nell.

Who *were* these people?

"Right." Lowe, or rather Frank, picked up something from the cabinet and went around the other side of the table, closer to where my bandage was. I tensed as he touched me, but he only began to gently lay the bandaging back on my wound. "Miss Goodnight, we need your help..."

"Who are you?" I gasped. "Who *are* you?"

"That's not important right now," he said. Then with a swift motion, one hand covered my mouth and the other pressed flat on my wound. He pushed.

There was an explosion of pain. His hand pushed into my shoulder, into my flesh until I thought the bones would crack under the pressure. I screamed and writhed uselessly. I could feel the bullet, too, and the tears running down my face.

He released both the wound and my mouth at the same time and I gasped.

"Where is it, Miss Goodnight?" he demanded in a low voice.

"W-what?" I gasped.

"You know what," he snarled and pressed on the wound again. I couldn't hold back the scream. Sarah cried, "Frank!" and his hand slapped down on my mouth again.

He released me and asked again, "Where is it, Miss Goodnight?"

"I don't know what you want!" I sobbed. "I don't *know!*"

"The *letter,*" he hissed. "The letter from the Pinkerton Agency. Where is it?"

"I-I don't know," I whispered and whimpered when he placed his hand on the wound. "I don't know, someone took it, someone ransacked the print shop..."

Now Sarah leaned over me.

"It wasn't there," she said. She grabbed my chin and turned my head to face her. "I tore that place apart Sunday and it wasn't there, Jenny. It wasn't in the envelope that I took from him Sunday night and it wasn't in the house or the saddlebags. So *where is it?*"

"I just wished it hadn't taken me so long to find the doctor last night. When he wasn't home, I had to go through half the town before I found him."

Suddenly, I understood the significance of what the Findlay boy had said. The night Helen had her baby, he'd gone to Doctor Lowe's house first and found it empty. But he shouldn't have, because Nell, the woman I'd known as Sarah, was supposed to be home.

I blinked up at her through watering eyes, unable to speak. Her grip tightened on my chin, her beautiful eyes glittering. "Where is it, Goodnight?"

"If I were a betting man," John Henry had said, *"I would bet that the person who broke into your print shop was the same person who killed your uncle."*

"You killed my uncle," I whispered, dazed. "You. You killed him and you ... hit me."

Her grip tightened. "I'll do worse than that if you don't tell us about the letter."

"I don't know-"

I didn't have time to finish before her hand covered my mouth and again, Dr. Lowe leaned on the bullet wound. I was drowning in a world of pain, a burning, throbbing sensation that made me feel as though I were going to break.

"Where is it? Where is that letter?"

I writhed and cried and they paid no heed at all. Finally, when I felt as though I was going to break, Lowe let up and said, "Where, Goodnight?"

I was breathing too heavily to answer, so he tapped the spot and asked, "Tell us."

"I-I..." I was trying to think, but my mind was clouded with pain and confusion. I didn't know where the letter was, but if I said that again...

"Give me the knife," Sarah said.

Lowe handed her the scalpel. She grabbed my chin and twisted my head again, laying the scalpel against my cheek.

"You'll tell me," she said. "Because you and I both know it's possible to survive a scalping."

The knife blade danced up to my hairline. Her beautiful eyes were like stone, her expression ice and steel. Lowe swore and his fingers pressed into my skin, igniting the pain once more, but this time, if I writhed, the scalpel would go into my skin.

There was no getting out of this. I couldn't free myself from the ropes and even if I could, I was trapped. All I could do was buy time. My body sagged in defeat. Lowe saw this and gestured to Sarah. She dropped the knife to my throat and held it there.

"Where?" she demanded.

"It's... it's..." I sought a plausible excuse, fighting my fear to keep my wits. "It's in the safe in the print shop."

"You *lie!*" she hissed, pressing, and I'm ashamed to say I whimpered in response. "I *searched* that print shop, it wasn't there!"

"It wasn't there then," I cried. "It was in the journal. The letter was too dangerous to carry around, so I put it in the safe yesterday." The knife remained where it was. "You have to believe me, it's there!"

Lowe leaned in now. "You read the letter?" he asked. "Did you tell anyone about it?"

His hand ground into the bullet wound.

"No!" I cried out. "No, I didn't, I didn't..."

He wouldn't stop, he just wouldn't stop. I forgot about the knife and twisted and turned, trying to get away even while knowing it was futile. Sarah stepped back, tapping the scalpel thoughtfully to her lips, watching as I writhed and pleaded, until finally she asked again, "Where is it?"

"In the *safe!*" I sobbed, as the ropes dug into my skin and my shoulder was alive with fire. "The safe, the safe!"

"Combination?"

"It's unlocked. It's always unlocked, oh, stop, oh, please, just stop..."

He let go suddenly. My body went slack at the sudden release. I bit my lip to muffle the sobs.

"You'd better go see," he said, leaned on the table.

She gestured to me with the scalpel. "What about her? If she read the let-,"

He interrupted, "She'll wait until you get back. Go quickly. Try not to let anyone see you."

She didn't leave right away. Instead, she took the scalpel and traced it lightly down my cheek and across my throat.

"I saw you with John Henry last night," she said. "You should know better than to trespass..."

The knife pressed and Lowe snapped, "Not yet! We need that letter first."

Frustrated anger crossed her pretty face, but she relented. She turned to Lowe. "Wait for me. I want to be here when it's done."

She handed him the scalpel, tossed me a baleful look, and strode out. Lowe followed her. I was left alone with a throbbing shoulder, bleeding wrists, and the sure knowledge that I wouldn't be allowed to live long, even if I had told the truth about that letter.

THIRTY-ONE

I must have blacked out for bit, for when I awoke, Lowe had returned. He was bent over his mixing equipment, occupied and worried. He paid me no attention and I had time to think.

That the Lowes were going to kill me was obvious – they had to, now that I knew the truth. Escape seemed impossible. I'd been well tied and between my head injury from last night and the blood-loss from today, I was as weak as a kitten. I closed my eyes and let my thoughts wash over me.

"What I have here is the end of the Evans legacy. I'm going to ruin you, John Henry Evans. Better still, I'm going to let you ruin yourself."

That's what my uncle had said the night of the wedding, when he'd waved that empty envelope in front of the Evans boys and the entire town. He'd spoken about ruining the Evans family, about ruining John Henry. But he hadn't said how.

The letter hadn't been about the Ezra Jones scandal at all: it was about the Lowes.

They'd changed their names. It must have been for some reason...

Already I was running through the lists of clippings: the immigrant deserter, the runaway who'd married the black man, the husband and wife con-team, the man who'd run off with a dance-hall girl, the woman who'd killed the man who'd beaten her... There were at least a half dozen more, but none of the articles had anything to do with a brother and sister team.

Abraham and Sarah. Abraham and Sarah.

Those names had to have been chosen for a reason. Abraham and Sarah were the patriarch and matriarch of Israel, the direct ancestors of Jesus. Of course, they didn't start that way. Abraham had been Abram, Sarah had been Sarai and both struggled with their faith. Before they'd become aged parents to Isaac, they'd wandered through the desert, visiting other courts and lands, using their wits and even lies to...

That's when it hit me: the answer to my question lay in the names my captors had chosen.

I remembered the frozen look on Lowe's face when Sarah arrived at the wedding party on John Henry's arm. I thought of the way he'd draped his own arm around her in the church, and how he'd waited to walk her home that night when John Henry and I had come upon them, the annoyance that had washed over him. Jealousy was perhaps a better word, for Abraham and Sarah were not brother and sister. They were Frank and Nell, husband and wife.

Lowe turned then, playing with the scalpel. He saw me staring and grinned at me.

"Well, now, Miss Goodnight, you look as though you've seen a ghost."

"You're Davidson," I whispered, horrified. "Frank Davidson, the man who... who..."

"Now, now, now," he said soothingly. "There's no point in you worrying, Miss Goodnight. The situation's out of your hands. Why don't you just lay back and relax?"

"You killed a man back east," I exclaimed. "You and your wife... You're trying to get your hands on the Evans fortune, by pretending Sarah is your sister and marrying her to John Henry."

He shrugged. "Reckon that's about the size of it. Just out of curiosity, how did you figure it?"

"Abraham and Sarah also pretended to be brother and sister."

He chuckled. "Should have known better than to cross a missionary woman. Folks around here were all too willing to accept us at face value. Even your uncle was taken at first. Only Doc Brown knew and he was too willing to help a pal out."

"Brown covered for you?" I asked.

"I knew Doc Brown from back when I was in school. I told him we were running away from creditors," Lowe said. "We weren't going to stay long, mind, just get back on our feet again. Then John Henry took a shine to Nell. Brown wouldn't have stood for bigamy, of course, but when he got sick..."

"You let him die."

"He was an old man already. Anyway, he went peaceable enough and Nell started working on John Henry and everything was gravy. Until your uncle started poking around."

Lowe left the medical counter and went over to the roll top desk. Standing over the journal, he began to finger the clippings. "Your uncle didn't take too kindly to being thrown over for an Evans. By the time we got here, he was already a drinker and a gambler. One night, he was stumbling drunk and caught Nell and I..."

He paused and smirked at me. "Well, you can imagine. Anyway, he soon had a pretty good handle on who we were. He didn't know about the Doc and I told him the man in Louisiana was an accident, not intentional. He wanted to hurt the Evans family, so he chose not to ask too many questions."

"You were okay with letting your wife marry another man?"

"Do you have any idea how much the Evanses are worth? Most ranchers are land-rich and coin-poor, but not them. They have the devil's own luck when it comes to making money and they've gotten a little too comfortable. They are *ripe,* Miss Goodnight. They are *ripe.*"

His grin slipped. "But then you arrived. You and your pistol and your fine starry-eyed virtues. Because of you, Goodnight remembered he had a conscience. Just your telegraph was enough to send him running to the Pinkertons." His hands balled into fists. "He started asking about Doc Brown, and the man in Louisiana. Suddenly, my background began to matter. You really upset a lot of things around here, Miss Goodnight."

It was all I could do not to shrink into the bed. "So the Pinkerton letter wasn't about the Evans family past: it was about you."

"A two-bit hustler your uncle could work with. But when he realized that the Louisiana job was more... complicated, he didn't like that. He told Nell that he couldn't marry even an Evans to known murderers. He was going to expose us, but as a courtesy, he offered us a twenty-four-hour head start." Lowe grinned again. "He didn't know my wife very well. Nell only needed about twenty-four seconds to solve the problem."

"So they'd proven that it was murder in Louisiana?"

That alerted him. His head tilted in curiosity. "If you'd read the letter as you said, you'd already know that answer." He stepped forward. "Did you read that letter, Miss Goodnight? You led me to believe you had."

My mouth opened and shut and no sound came out.

Lowe took another step forward. "If you lied about reading the letter," he mused, "I wonder what else you might have lied about."

The moment stretched to the breaking point.

Finally, he shrugged. "We'll know soon enough." He turned back to the desk. "If you haven't said your prayers yet today, Miss Goodnight, I suggest you attend to it. Mrs. Davidson will be back soon enough."

* * *

I did pray. I prayed feverishly and when I ran out of words, I found myself praying the rote ones my mother had tried to teach me as a child. Until that moment, I'd had no idea how much her teachings had stuck with me. She'd taught me the Rosary, as I had said, but in her native French, not English. The Rosary is not something daughters of preachers are supposed to know, but when you've run out of road, you use whatever comes to mind. When I got stuck on the Creed, I moved on to the *Notre Pere* and the *Salut Marie*. I prayed and prayed and my hand ached for my mother's beads.

I prayed the prayers until I lost count and lost time. No plan came to mind, no rescue presented itself. But as I worked the prayers, one after another, the French smooth on my tongue, I became aware of a strange sense of calm, of presence, of being. I don't know what to call it. I don't remember thinking that all would be well, for there was no possibility of that – it was more the sense that I was where I was for a reason. And that I wasn't alone.

This feeling fled the minute I heard Sarah's boots on the rough planks of the front porch. Lowe had taken to working on his ledger in a weird sort of businesslike calm before the kill. She burst in furious and red-faced.

"It was empty!" she raged. "*Empty!*"

Lowe's face went white. "You didn't find it?"

"No, I *didn't find it.* I searched the office and the safe, twice, and *nothing!*" She turned and bore down on me, eyes flashing, her whole body shaking with fury. "It wasn't there, Frank, it wasn't there!"

She punched my wound, sending an explosion of pain through my system. I writhed, biting my lip until it bled to keep from crying. She hit me again and I couldn't see for the pain. When my eyes cleared, I saw she'd moved over to stand by Lowe, who was rubbing his chin, processing this new information.

"I'll work on her again," Lowe muttered.

"There's no time for that," Sarah snapped. "The sheriff's come back. He'll be around here, asking questions, and anyway I'm beginning to think she doesn't know a thing about the letter."

"She never read it," Lowe offered. "Maybe it doesn't exist."

"It exists. Goodnight couldn't lie to save his life." She turned to the counter where the surgical tools lay gleaming in tidy rows. "We don't have time to play around any longer. The sheriff will come and this needs to be finished before he gets here." She picked up the scalpel. "It has to look like an accident."

Oh God...!

Lowe answered calmly. "It will. I prepared a potion. Give that to her first and then we'll do the surgery." He turned a grin towards me. "I'd like to say you won't feel a thing, Miss Goodnight, but I wouldn't want to lie to you."

Sarah took up the vial. "Let's get this done then."

Pure panic took over. I began to scream and thrash, the rope cutting deeper into my flesh. They moved quickly. Lowe pinned me down as before, his big hand on my chin. His eyes glinted as he held my head still in the vice-like grip.

Oh, Maman, oh God, oh please...!

Sarah loomed over me, the cup in her hand. Her face was like ice, her cold fury barely contained as she forced my mouth open.

"Don't make this difficult, Goodnight," she muttered.

I wrenched my head out of their grip and let loose one last scream. It echoed off the walls. Hardly had it began when Lowe slapped my bleeding wound once again and the wall of pain cut off my air supply. They had my head again, Lowe gripping my chin while Sarah forced my mouth open. The cup tipped and I could see the liquid sloshing at the rim.

"Do it, Nell!" Lowe said, his teeth gritting tight.

Jesus, Mother Mary, help me! Mother, mother, please, Maman, please....!!

There was an explosion then. Liquid sloshed over my face. Lowe froze as a booming voice filled the room.

"What the hell is going on here?"

I opened my eyes. John Henry stood by the wreckage of the door he'd just kicked in, his face black with fury, his eyes jumping from Sarah to Lowe, to me. Behind him, the ever-present Trigger slipped into the room, dusty, weary, and wary. John Henry stepped forward and I saw my mother's rosary beads dangling in one of his hands.

Maman!

"What," John Henry repeated, "*are you doing?*"

That was the first time I ever saw Dr. Lowe afraid.

Sarah whipped around and flew at John Henry. He swatted her aside, pushing her towards Trigger as he bore down on Doctor Lowe. There was a struggle, but not for long.

I barely saw any of it. Waves of exhaustion and darkness washed over me. My wound throbbed and the world, which was pain and black, began to spin and recede. I remember nothing after that, except for a feeling of comfort that I'd not felt since a day, long ago, when I was twelve and in a small, cramped back room...

TELEGRAM

From: Sheriff Sage of Legacy
To: The authorities in Rockingham County

Caught the Davidsons, posing as a doctor and his sister in Legacy STOP Nell has confessed to murder of Legacy citizen STOP Am waiting for the arrival of the judge to determine jurisdiction STOP Regards ETC Sage

THIRTY-TWO

I have vague memories of voices, of hands on my shoulders and chest, of excruciating, exploding pain, of voices telling me to be still while I pleaded for mercy. Fiery hot needles prodded me. No matter how I thrashed and begged, they wouldn't stop.

Then my mother was there, laying her hand on my forehead, her gentle face flush with health. "*Ah, ma Genevieve, c'est bon, tu es ma Genevieve...*"

"Lay *still,* Jenny," another, deeper voice commanded.

I trusted that voice.

I sank deep into a dreamless void.

* * *

I awoke abruptly, once again in a stranger's bed in an unfamiliar room. It was cool and dark. I lay under clean sheets in a nightgown that was not my own. At first, my memory was as clean and blank as the ceiling above me. It was only when I tried to roll over and the heavy bandage on my shoulder shifted painfully that it all came flooding back.

Doctor Lowe - Sarah - John Henry-!

I sat up with a gasp. Immediately dizziness overwhelmed me and the pain from my wound caused me to cry out.

"I wouldn't do that if I were you."

Varina Evans rose from the shadows in the corner, her skirts rustling crisply, not a hair out of place. I stared at her as she advanced on me, her sharp eyes analyzing my movements. She might have been an angel of mercy, except that her expression was stone cold.

"What happened?" I asked, wincing. "Where am I?"

She lowered herself on the bed and, placing her hands on my shoulders in the only places where it would not hurt, lowered me back down on the pillow. "You're in at the Danaher's boarding house, recovering."

"The Lowes...!"

"...are in jail, waiting for the judge," she finished coolly. Already her nimble fingers were checking the area around the wound. When she lifted the bandage, I gasped at the sudden cool touch of air. "I managed to get the bullet out, but the Lowes did a thorough job. If John Henry hadn't shown up when he did, they would have killed you. You've been out for several days and lost a lot of blood."

"Is John Henry...?"

Her ice blue eyes turned fierce. "He's fine."

I breathed a sigh of relief and closed my eyes. "Thank you, God!"

Her fingers went on working silently. I could sense her dislike of me drenching everything like a fine mist and I wondered why it was she that was nursing me. I was too weary and grateful to care.

I whispered, "They killed my uncle, you know."

Tears stung my eyes.

Varina's voice was cool. "I know. They made a full confession to the sheriff, thanks to a little influence from John Henry." She tugged the bandage back into place. "I guess that this was the second time that woman tried to kill you. She was searching your house when she saw you outside with John Henry. Apparently, she hit you over the head, set the fire, and left you for dead. You have more lives than a cat, Miss Goodnight."

"Where are the documents?" I asked feebly. "My uncle's journals?"

"Jeremiah brought them here," she said and nodded to the side.

I turned and saw my saddlebags in a jumble in the corner, my father's Bible on top of them. When I gestured, Varina reached over, took the Bible, and handed it to me. I lay back against the pillows, the heavy book on my stomach. I felt reassured. This was my last tangible connection to my beloved father, a strong man, a flawed man who'd made mistakes, but who had loved me greatly. Despite all his failings and shortcomings, he'd given me a foundation and taught me to recognize the strengths that made me who I was now: a woman who'd come far and who had miles still to travel if she were going to make up for the mistakes we'd both made.

Varina settled into the chair next to my bed, adjusting her skirts as she settled.

"Jeremiah wouldn't let anyone touch them, said they were important," she commented. When I met her narrow-eyed gaze, she said, "Will you be carrying on the family business?"

I wondered if she knew the extent of the blackmail or the gambling debts that went with them. She knew about the Lowes – did she know that Uncle Matthew was involved and encouraging them? How much blackmail would they have extorted from the Evans, once they'd married Sarah to John Henry? Did Varina know how much she'd been spared?

If only I had that letter, I thought. Then it dawned on me: there was one place that I had not searched.

I opened the Bible and flipped through it, looking for loose pages. None fell out, not even when I flipped it over and shook it over my chest. Varina watched me, clearly unimpressed. My wound was throbbing with the effort and I was beginning to lose faith. But then, as I fingered the back cover, I realized that the paper binding was pulling away. Something had been inserted in between the leather and the paper. More to the point, it had recently been reglued.

I tugged gently at the gap and pulled out the folded paper that was hidden in there. When I opened it, the letterhead told me all that I needed to know.

Varina was watching, her expression sharp and wary.

"The Pinkerton letter wasn't about your husband," I said. "It was about the Davidsons. Uncle Matthew wanted to ruin John Henry by allowing him to marry a married woman. But then he learned that they weren't just cons, but murderers. That's why he was drunk at the wedding, Mrs. Evans. He had to make a choice. In the end, he did. He called Sarah into the hotel room and told her to clear out, that he couldn't go through with it after all. That's why Sarah killed him, Mrs. Evans. Because my uncle was about to go to you."

There was some comfort in knowing that, in the end, Uncle Matthew had recovered himself. His sense of justice had come too late, perhaps, but he had died for it. That had to count for something. It did with me and for now, that would have to do.

I handed her the letter. "I'd appreciate it if you'd give the sheriff this. It'll strengthen his case."

She took the letter and held it without unfolding it, her face a mask that I couldn't decipher. I fell back into the pillow, sleep crashing over me again.

"I don't know if your husband killed Ezra Jones," I said, closing my eyes. "If it's any consolation, my uncle didn't know either."

"It doesn't matter," Varina said firmly. "*I* knew my husband. And I knew what he was capable of."

I thought I understood. There are some relationships too complicated for outsiders to fully understand and there are things that we can *know* without having proof. My father, my mother, Trailing Rose... these were not for me to understand, any more than I could know the truth about Ezra Jones. Some mysteries remain unsolved. Varina knew her husband and for the moment, that would have to be enough.

"I'm not going into my uncle's business," I said. "I'm burning his papers and clearing all debts. You might get the word out to any concerned parties."

Her eyes glittered. "I will."

"Thank you." A thought struck me then, an afterthought. "What happened to Matheson?"

"He's dead," she said calmly.

She didn't explain what happened and I didn't ask. I thought of Underwood and wondered if I ought to feel guilty. Later, perhaps, I would, but for the moment, all I could remember was his gun trained on John Henry's back, his voice threatening my uncle, his smile when he called for the killing of Liam and Jeremiah.

Yes, perhaps tomorrow guilt would come. Right now, relief was too strong.

Varina was standing over me, her fingers curled protectively around the letter. I wanted to sleep. I turned my face away and closed my eyes, but she cleared her throat to speak.

"It appears," she said, tucking the letter into her waistband, "that you've saved both my sons from danger. One from being hanged and one from disgrace. I'm in your debt."

Her expression left me in no doubt of her distaste. Varina was too proud to enjoy being in debt, even one of honor and especially to the likes of me. I was a Goodnight and in this town, that name would probably carry a negative connotation for a long time yet. Every family has a legacy, you might say. Yet even so, I was not alone. The people in this town had gone out of their way to look after me, even knowing my uncle as they did. That had to count for something, too.

"You took a bullet out of me," I said and she waved that off.

"If there's anything I can do..." she offered.

It was on my tongue to say that there was no debt, that we were clear. I was still holding my father's Bible and an idea came to me, a family matter so personal it was painful. As much as I hated to ask for a favor, it would square the deal with Varina and set to rest something that had been bothering me ever since I left the mission.

"You might..." I said and paused to gather my courage. "I had to leave my father's body at the mission. My family doesn't have enough money to transport him back to Massachusetts where my mother is buried and... Well, I'd like..."

I trailed off, embarrassed.

Varina was still for a moment. Then she said, "I'll see what we can do." When I opened my mouth, she silenced me with a wave of her hand. "It's a small enough gesture. We'll make the arrangements before you leave."

It was clear what Varina Evans meant, of course. The sooner I left, the better.

I shut my mouth again and nodded.

She looked at her hands. "It might interest you to know that my son, Ben, has decided to drop out of the race." When she saw my look of surprise, she said, "He is a father now. And he is young. There's time enough for politics, I think."

Yes, I thought. When the dust from this debacle had settled and the Ezra Jones controversy faded back to nothing, then would the ambitious mother revive her son's dream again. But for now, disaster had only just been averted. It was time to heal. My uncle's desire to run Ben Evans from the race had been realized, but there was no glory in it. Only Honest Joe Turner benefited.

I said nothing of these thoughts to Varina. I just nodded and let her tuck me in with brisk, efficient movements. Her every move served to remind me of the fact that we were not friends. In fact, we were barely acquaintances. Then she touched my forehead for fever and, looking into my already heavy eyes, ordered me to sleep. I obeyed before she'd even left the room.

* * *

John Henry came the next day. Annie was in my room, fussing over me and telling me all the news, up to the exciting fact that Jeremiah was actually reading his first book. She went into blushing silence when John Henry appeared in the doorway, wearing a new pale blue shirt and looking as slick and clean as if he'd just had a scrub up moments before. Thankfully, Annie had just helped me to brush and braid my hair, so while I still looked a mess, at least my hair wasn't as wild as it had been.

I hadn't been expecting visitors and seeing him was both a relief and something like pain. After all, his mother had practically told me to leave town and probably made her opinion known to her family. And yet here he was, grinning at me from the doorway.

"Morning, ma'am," he said. "You're looking a mite better than the last time I saw you."

Words escaped me.

Annie, grinning slyly, cleared out of the room, taking my picked-at breakfast with her. We were alone before I was quite ready for it.

John Henry stepped into the room, his boots heavy on the wooden slabs. He left the door open, as was proper, and approached my bed with his hat in his hands.

I finally found speech. "I have to thank you..." I began.

He interrupted, shaking his head and reaching into his shirt pocket. "Thank your mother."

He took my hand, setting my nerves on fire with his touch, and pressed the cool, familiar beads into my palm. I closed my fingers around them protectively and closed my eyes as emotion surged up from deep within.

"You found them," I whispered.

He closed his fingers over mine, possessively. "Found them in the dirt where you'd fallen. Thought you might have need of them. Lucky I found them, too."

"Yes," I whispered. "Lucky."

For a moment, my hand rested secure in his. Then he released it and sat back in the chair.

For a few seconds we sat in silence, I playing with my rosary, he toying with his hat, neither one of us wanting to speak over the huge presence that sat in the room with us.

Finally, he said, "They say you lost a lot of blood."

"Your mother did a fine job stitching me up."

"She's good at that," he agreed, then smirked. "Ben and I gave her plenty of practice."

I smiled, too.

Another moment of silence, then he said, "I reckon you'll be running things now? The paper. The ranch..."

I shook my head and kept my eyes on my rosary. "I'm shutting down the paper and I'll... I'll be leaving once I finish up a few affairs." When he looked at me sharply, I said, "My aunt has offered me a place back east. I guess I'll go there."

"Back *east?*" He sounded disgusted.

"It's where I grew up," I said, then found myself admitting, "I'm not looking forward to it. I don't know what I'll do. There's not a lot of work for someone like me."

Immediately, I wished I hadn't spoken. I sounded so pathetic. I searched for other words, something to offset the tone, but my mind had dried up and I was wordless.

"You could teach at the school here in town," he said, grinning. "I hear the schoolmarm got herself in a bad way."

"Oh, John Henry!"

He grinned again, then grew serious.

"Fact is, the town could use a woman like you in the schoolhouse. Upright, honest, kind, able to teach boys like Jeremiah." His voice dropped a tone. "A damn shame if you left."

My face flamed. I looked at the rosary in my hand.

He reached out and took my chin in his hand. "Fact is, ma'am, *I'd* hate to see you go. I feel as though we've just started."

I didn't even realize I was crying until tears, streaming down my face.

"You barely know me," I whispered. "Your mother hates me."

"My mother doesn't know you like I know you," he said quietly. "I've seen you under fire. I liked what I saw." He tucked a lock of hair behind my ear. "At least give me a chance to prove to you that there might be a reason to stay, Jenny."

"Genevieve." He looked at me and I said, "My real name is Genevieve."

A slow smile, the kind that can stop your heart and make the whole world glow, spread across his face.

"Genevieve," he said and my name was like honey on his lips. "Genevieve. I like that." He was toying with my hair now. The gently possessive touch was addictive. "Stay, Genevieve."

Oh, how I wanted to say yes. My heart drummed in my ears. My whole being ached to be in his arms, my very soul cried out to say yes. Even my name, once hated and buried, took on a new resonance when he said it. But my business was not finished yet. I couldn't promise to stay until I put to rest one important matter.

Looking back, I know now that I needed to say no. My whole life I'd been chasing after powerful men, hoping to be useful, living in their shadow, a kite tossed about in their storm. I needed my own identity first. My father had left his legacy. It was time I started building my own. And I needed to set my story straight before I joined John Henry's.

I ought to have simply said no and left it at that. It would have been easier. But I couldn't, not when he was stroking my hair and making me feel wanted, needed almost. So I told him the truth and I told it plain and I braced myself for the withdrawal.

"I can't stay until..." I drew in a deep breath and confessed, "My father had a son by a native woman. They were my family, in every way except in the law, and they were sent to a reservation. And I... I let them go. I need to find them. He's my brother and she's... I let them go once. I have to find them now."

The silence that followed was quite possibly the longest in my life. I waited for the hammer to fall, waited for him to get up and leave. All the same, I never wanted anything so much as his reassurance that there would be something, someone waiting for me when I got back. It was an unreasonable thing to expect, yet I was dying for it all the same.

Finally, he spoke.

"You'll ride out to the reservation?" he asked.

I nodded. "Yes."

"Ask them to come home with you?"

"If that's what they wish, yes. I have the ranch. We can make that work."

His eyes studied my face. "And if they don't want to go with you?"

This possibility had occurred to me. After all, why should they come? I'd already shown my faithlessness, my ability to abandon my own. I needed to make things right, but they were under no obligation to relieve my guilt by allowing me to help them.

My voice was surprisingly sure when I answered. "They're free to do as they please. But they need to know that I'd welcome them, that they're family. I need to tell them that because... because I wasn't able to before."

It was a terrible thing to admit, even to myself. I'd learned so much since I'd come to Legacy and among them was that sometimes good people fall. But the thing I remembered most clearly was the look on Abigail Washington's face as she stood by her husband that day at the ranch. Things weren't as simple as I'd once thought they were and life was better because of the complexities. All that remained was my acceptance of these realities – and better still was the embracement of these.

If only John Henry Evans could be made to understand this.

I watched his face, analyzing and memorizing each line and scar. His eyes were dark and his expression unreadable and, oh, how I loved him.

"And once you do tell them?" he asked.

I placed my hand over his.

"I can make promises then," I said.

It seemed an eternity before John Henry nodded, a weighty acceptance. "All right," he said and pulled my hand down into his. "I'll ride along with you."

"I can't ask you to..."

"Genevieve." He leaned in closer. "I'll ride along with you." His gaze softened as he looked into my eyes.

I closed my eyes against the sudden, sharp contracting of my heart. I thought of how he'd found me on the dance floor the night before my uncle's death. He'd found me again on the road and then outside the ranch on that terrible day. Even though there was no claim and no debt, John Henry had been there before I knew I needed him. Then that last time, when I was at my most vulnerable and lost, he'd appeared, carrying my rosary. It was just as though my mother, my always-faithful, long suffering, abandoned mother, had sent for him.

Oh, Maman, I thought. *Merci, Maman, merci. Je t'aime.*

Warmth filled me and the thought came, as though from elsewhere: *You won't ride alone.*

It was almost more happiness than I could bear.

"I'd like that, John Henry Evans," I whispered. "I'd like that a lot."

LETTER

Dear Aunt Alice,

I am sorry I've taken so long to write. Much has happened since Uncle Matthew's passing, which I related in my previous letter, and there's a great deal that I need to tell you. Chief among these things is that I've made arrangements to send my father back east to be buried with my mother. I now truly believe that this is what she would have wanted. I feel as though a burden, long carried, has finally been rolled off my back.

I won't be coming back to Massachusetts. I am going to find my father's second family and once I do, I will be finalizing my plans from there. But here is where I belong. I have discovered the place where my weaknesses are challenged and my strengths best used. I cannot go back to who I was or where I had been. The future is calling me forward and I must answer the call.

I'll write more when I'm able.

Your affectionate niece,

Genevieve

ABOUT THE AUTHOR

Killarney Traynor is a New England-born novelist, director, actress, history buff, and martial artist. She has published five books, including two co-written with her sister.

Killarney works with Narrow Street Films as a writer, director, and producer. She's written and directed two feature films, *Michael Lawrence* and *The Dinner Party*, as well as a several short films. She is also a co-host on the weekly TV show, *The Early Late Night Live Show.*

When she isn't writing, she can usually be found rummaging through used bookstores, scouring the internet for little-known Sci-Fi shows, getting lost in Boston, traveling, or searching for the perfect cup of tea.

Find out more at www.KillarneyTraynor.com.

MYSTERIES NEXT-DOOR

MYSTERY, ADVENTURE, ROMANCE - ALL IN THE GRANITE STATE

SUMMER SHADOWS

All Julia wanted was a peaceful summer to bond with her new family.
Moving next door to a haunted house complicates things. Set in Franklin, NH.

NECESSARY EVIL

Maddie Warwick is about to lose everything. And the only one who can help
her is the last man she can trust. Set in Chester, NH.

MICHAEL LAWRENCE - THE SEASON OF DARKNESS

His daughter's in a coma, his marriage is on the rocks. Can this detective
keep it together long enough to stop a killer? Set in Portsmouth, NH.

THE
ENCOUNTER
SERIES

(written with Margaret Traynor)

Lovers of the Twilight Zone, take note – this series is for you…

TALE HALF TOLD

1971: Snowbound in a haunted house, four friends battle, not only to save their
lives… but their sanity.

UNIVERSAL THREAT

1985: A relaxing hiking trip turns into a struggle for survival when three
teenagers come across a downed alien ship.

Made in the USA
Middletown, DE
07 August 2020